Panic and the Inner Monkey

Mark Hendy

Published by Lyvit Publishing, Cornwall

www.lyvit.com

ISBN 978-0-9926029-1-8

No Part of this book may be reproduced in any way, including, but not limited to, electronic or mechanical copying, photocopying, recording or by any information storage or retrieval system now known or hereafter invented, without prior consent from the publisher.

This book is sold subject to the condition that it shall not, by way of trade or otherwise, be lent, re-sold, hired out or otherwise circulated without the publisher's prior consent in any form of binding or cover other than that in which it is published and without a similar condition including this condition being imposed on the subsequent purchaser.

All Material © 2013 Mark Hendy

For Alex

This book has been 9 years in the making.

In my early twenties, I developed anxiety and started to reel from the effects of panic attacks. Whether or not it can be said that I was ever diagnosed with OCD is debatable, but without order, the chaos in my head was, and still is - something that I need to address.

I am an intensely private person, and therefore when attempting to relive some of my experiences, I have felt more comfortable in transferring them to a new character and setting – hence, the panic monkey. Absurdly, the characterisation of what I consider to be – at times, my driving force, is critical. Perversely, it is only by distancing myself from the topic, that I can be truly honest.

At 21, after my world began to fall apart at the seams, I attempted to get some of these ideas down on paper, but quickly scrapped it. I can only put this done to youthful impatience, and perhaps a disbelief in myself, my "skills" as a writer, and perhaps more importantly – the state of mind that I found myself in. Memories can be twisted – for better or worse.

The mind is a powerful tool – we are all a walking result of the sum of our experiences. Our hopes and fears we take with us on our journey – we are all children and we are all blagging. The dawning realisation that perhaps no one is really driving this thing, and that we are all ultimately alone should be addressed, but not to provoke melancholy. The world is a ridiculous place, people are fragile.

We are living on a knife-edge and the cosy surroundings and sometimes puerile relationships that we grow hold us together like glue. So much of life is being held together by a thread and most folk don't let that thread simply be. You either toy with it, watching it fray, or you strengthen it. Life is a game. An overused phrase – but fitting. Those that play by the rules often succeed – those that rebel in some way may also succeed, but everyone pays a price...some more than others.

I have no answer – and I'm not so arrogant as to suggest that what I have written will make anyone feel any better about their lives. I'm not sure that this is even an objective.

If the planning stages of the work took years, the actual process – albeit a messy period of my life, was a short affair. If you choose to read this, I hope you will take something from it.

I need to get on with the rest of my life now.

Chapter One

Hello.

My name is George and I live in Norfolk. I've never really been good with introductions; it's a failing. I never know how to introduce myself or if there's ever really a need. I see folk at work sink into what seems to be a flawless introduction, and a subsequent relationship flourishes over time as I look on with amazement and awe. By the time I have made a decision that this new person fits into this category and have trawled through my mind to try and relinquish a frame of reference for this human, it is often too late and I find myself mumbling my name and offering my hand.

If I have time to be around this person before an introduction has been made, things are better as I can work out my plan of attack and size up what needs to be said and how best to say it. It's not a concern anyway, someone at my first place of work told me that it doesn't matter how you appear on the first meeting; you could be having an off day, they could be having an off day. The most important thing is how the second meeting goes, for that can either dispel whatever it was that went wrong the first time, or it will reaffirm the positive nature of that initial conversation. So first impressions don't count. Well that's not strictly true; the things that matter are on the outside to begin with. We all make judgments and we don't live in an ideal world so put on a tie, make an effort. Be something you're not, it's easier in the long run.

I'm thirty-four; immediately you now have an idea of the place I'm in because you can think about where you are in your life. I didn't think I'd be here in my mid thirties, age was never a concern until I hit twenty five and began to compare where I was with my peers, and even at this early stage, I had crippling thoughts of whether I was in the right place, on the right road. When you're young, the only thing on your mind is where you're going and the moment you're in... for the lucky. The world can be a daunting place but it's pretty exciting. There's a whole load of firsts to get out of the way and there's a ticking clock that you must beat, you've gotta beat your peers and even if you have your head screwed on enough to know that this is bullshit, you have a mechanism inside that has a burning desire to beat yourself. There can only be two things in the mind of a fifteen year old; I need to get laid soon, or I don't need to prove anything, when it happens it happens. Either way, it's an issue.

You're a child and then suddenly you have an exciting list of rites of passage that lay in front of you. Many are self-destructive but most are exciting. When you're young, you want to be older because age dictates freedom, a freedom of choice that opens up all the doors to the adult world and can turn any dreams you have into a reality. Jesus, I'm almost getting excited about being young again. And that's the thing, there's so much scope - you can be anything you want and you have the delicious excuse of youth for anything that goes wrong; and it will. But it's okay.

I've been in this job for ten years now, I don't really know how that happened. Yeah, how *did* I get here? I'm not in a relationship although the opportunities have been there. I kid myself that I seek perfection and that at that time, it just wasn't right. I quite like my own company and find difficulty in engaging in meaningful relationships. It's me, not you *is* usually true in my case and I have no embarrassment or awkwardness (and I should) in using this hellish phrase to discard what could be a lovely future. I've grown up with stability and I don't any know divorcees. Perhaps I do, but I'm choosing to ignore them so I can back up my point. My point being that things have to be perfect. I know nothing's perfect and you should work at a relationship but *goddamnit*, things should be perfect, things could be...

I got this job through an agency after spending three years in and out of positions that slowly eroded my soul. Okay, that's a bit dramatic but I had no idea what I wanted to do and found that as much as I tried, I tired of any new exciting opportunity that came my way. Those days were a struggle, not only financially but also mentally as I would clamber onto a whirlwind of worries and doubt, wondering where I would be at this time the following year. Thankfully, many of my friends were in the same boat so I could easily group myself into what I saw as a collective problem, blaming anything from the inadequacies of my secondary school, to the state of the nation as a whole.

When I was twenty-four, I took it upon myself to go to a careers advice centre in town. As I walked in, I was tingling with fresh faced excitement as my eyes glazed over the box files with exciting job titles, shiny new *Macs* that craved to be touched, and busy wide eyed young people tapping away and researching companies and courses. The same place existed five years ago in a different office down the road, and it used to be grimy. There were no computers and when you entered, you were greeted with what looked like a refugee school table (the wooden ones with the ink well). I came out of there, as I guess many kids did feeling pretty down beat about my future. But this.....*this* excreted progress. I knew that there was the distinct possibility that this was style over substance in the most grotesque way, but my cynicism and natural inclination to pick holes was blown away with the atmosphere.

I approached the young lady at the desk with bouncy charm. "Hiya, I was wondering whether I could see somebody today, talk through my options?"

"Hmmm, we're quite busy at the moment." She flicked through her diary, deliberately shielding it from my view, "When were you thinking of?"

"Well as soon as possible really, perhaps I could make an appointment now?"

"Yeah, that's not really how it works you see."

"Oh okay, how does it work?"

I immediately realise that my comment may have riled her. She starts to explain things I don't really want to hear about; the process of booking an appointment and that it's a very busy time of year and that I can't just walk in for advice. After ten seconds, I switch off and start nodding sagely. I kind of know the gist of what she's saying but instead of focusing, I begin to wonder how she got this job. Not because she is useless, she seems to be very good at the whole booking an appointment thing, and later she may even find me my ideal path. But I wonder how anyone got their job and whether they are doing what they want. I make a scenario in my head that she went to the careers office and just stopped at the door, thinking, 'This is it. I'm home.' But of course, that's not what happened at all, she's just doing her job, trying to get an appointment for me and probably thinking about knocking off in a bit, or what she'll have for lunch.

"I'll see if Sarah is free if you'd like to see somebody today. She's with someone at the moment but if you'd like to take a seat over there, she may be able to squeeze you in."

"Fantastic, thank you very much."

As she mentioned her colleague's name, she glanced over to a small office over her left shoulder and so I got up and had a quick look at the layout of the office that I would be entering shortly. It's always best for me to do this so I can prepare myself fully. One of the walls to the office makes up a part of this office, the other one is half glass (the top half), and half board. I can just make out a young girl's head and shoulders, she seems to be dressed for business – black and stern looking. She looks like she takes her job very seriously. She is facing a young lad with a beanie on who is nervously playing with a pencil. He momentarily looks down at his lap to a piece of paper that she must be referring to in between her bouts of advice.

The only thing I can deduce from the setup is that the chair the guy is on has its back to the door and so I know my first course of action when I enter is to turn it around so its back is against the wall. This is something I **have** to do. As I peruse the leaflets and brochures on local courses, I wonder what pearls of wisdom this woman can give me. I have a degree, I have work history. If I'm honest, I have no particular aspirations or desires to do anything. I then wonder what the hell I'm going to say to her. It becomes my turn and I enter the advice chamber. The conversation rocks back and forth with ease but I don't mean any of it. If I told her what I really thought, where I want to be and what's going on in my life, I've no doubt she'd send me away with a referral for analysis. But I'm used to bullshitting and I do it well - that's my skill. I amuse myself by sending her up alleyways and watching her tap on her database in an attempt to match my interests.

"It would appear that you have a strong disliking for work in categories A, C and D, you have no strong feeling either way for category E and you have a slight interest in Category B."

"Okay, is that good?" Sheepishly, I'm expecting a sarcastic answer. She chuckles, perhaps nervously...

"Well it depends on what you want to do; it appears you like order and routine."

"I guess so, yeah..."

"Yes......" There's a horrific pause as she studies the paperwork, "Is there any particular field you are interested in?" I work out which system she is using as I recognise the questions from my school days. This is a good thing as I know this is designed with school leavers in mind and I've gone through it umpteen times in *General Studies* as a youngster. It's pretty rubbish to be fair.

I wrap up the meeting promptly, she gives me a few brochures on improving my computer skills at the local college and I'm on my way. What more did I expect? They're playing *The Smiths* in the reception though and that's all I need.

I've done personality tests for work placements in the past and the business equivalents are startlingly accurate. There's usually a time limit on the completion causing you to give honest answers (*Damnit.*) That's no fun. I'm always quite pleased with the results even though they often contradict themselves; perhaps that's what pleases me about them. The last one I did was three years ago, it was emailed to me by *Brightford Associates*; I had half heartedly applied for a position with them doing pretty much what I'm doing now, but in a different environment. I have no idea why I applied as the money was no different. Well, fractionally better but not worth the upheaval of having to go through all of those new introductions.

So what do I do? Well does it really matter? I know what my job description says, and I know what I do each day. I also know what I'm expected to do, what I should be doing, what I have done, and what other people think I do. None of it tallies. I got this job as a junior, undertaking menial tasks. The temporary nature became permanent very quickly and after Julian Hicks became ill, they asked me to work in his office for a bit, sorting out old paperwork. Julian never came back and in the meantime, I had made myself invaluable working in other departments, creating webs and procedures only I knew how to untangle and redirect. I am an administration monkey. But I am *King of the Administration Monkeys* and my colleagues aren't too sure whether I am invaluable or not. They know very little about me and that's just how I like it. If any of them really knew what I got up to, there'd be uproar; turmoil? But who's to say if any of us really knew what any one got up to, there'd be chaos. As long as nobody knows what each other is doing, or what wage we pull, then everything's fine.

We're not public sector but we're a big enough company for this building to be a sub sector (of a sub sector) of a branch - as long as we're ticking along, no questions are asked. Every now and again, I'm called in for an appraisal by Charles, who I get on with. I feel he fears that he will be made redundant by next week, every week and I don't exactly feed off of this fear, but I never mention his job or ask after him or his welfare because, not only am I genuinely not interested, but it's not my concern. His concern is how I'm doing, and how's he's doing and whether he's going to get fired. My concern is to maintain his concern.

So my work is generally bullshit. I relish the day-to-day tasks, the filing and the order frees up my mind to think about other things. I also like the way in which I have allowed myself to structure the day and I pretty much know what I'll be doing in each segment. It's got to the point where I can say an exact time:

Eleven Thirty Seven - *Checking the tapes have been finished, think about lunch, prepare stats for after lunch.*

Things happen out of the blue every day and things occur that I am not prepared for, but because I know I have a system and I know my stapler is always slightly to the left of my back up paperclips in my drawer, I know things are going to be fine.

I smoke at work, I've started to smoke profusely and it annoys me. I don't smoke when I get home or at weekends anymore and it baffles me why the week is such a source of frustration that I reach for the fags. We didn't used to have a smoking room and this was fine with me, as I would shuffle downstairs and puff outside. This kept things nice and ordered and also I could work out the times other people I liked had their fags and we'd become synchronized. Sometimes, I forgot about the times when these people would have their fix and would leave my desk only to see them on the landing merrily breezing down for a puff. I'd like to think that this happened too often to be mere coincidence and took pleasure in believing we had some weird connection. I never told them this; that would just be weird.

We now have a smoking room and it has created a big divide in the company. I don't know why this concerns me exactly for I don't empathise with either party. There are five people at work I like. Three, I really get on with but barely see and two I have become familiar with like family. We would never socialise outside of work but I feel comfortable in their company, comfortable enough to be able to be quiet in their company. Pretty much everyone else I have no time for.

This is not deliberate but years of small talk and listening to their idle stories has left me numb. I used to join in and attempt to be bawdy or at the very least, pretend to find *them* bawdy but the inevitable awkwardness that both parties felt led me to believe that we're all better off without it.

Because of all of this, I have no idea how I am viewed within the company. Well, I suppose I do, but I don't like to think about it. I know Fiona Thompson hates me, and that's okay; I hate her too. Maybe more than she hates me, I do hope so. My friends at work and those who are directly affected by my decisions know me to be pretty much how I am. I have had one to one conversations with most of them and so they know my interests, my sense of humour, and David can recognise my thoughts on a subject from a mere look and, *apparently*, can read me like a book. I can take the piss out of three people at work; two of them are people I like and the other one I just do to relieve the boredom and because it's so easy. I don't search for him and I am certainly no bully but he brings it on himself by continually trying to engage me in the most banal of conversations. I feel I'm justified in doing this when he'll make some unforgivable comment that makes me quiver that such thought processes can exist. I can't think of an example so maybe he's not that bad.

I don't like seeing Fiona Thompson outside of work, nor do I like seeing any of my colleagues out of context. All of my friends are from childhood or friends of friends, or from temporary assignments before I undertook this job. There's something unsettling for me about driving through town on a Saturday and seeing colleagues pushing buggies or buying bread. That's not what they do, they work, and then they go into suspended animation, or in Fiona's case - some form of vacuum, and then they return on Monday morning having not bothered me or entered my private sphere. They may have news of drunken antics on the Friday evening, or shock news of Big Brother or some paedophile and/or immigrant they have read about in *The Daily Mail*, they may have cakes (now I'm interested), but generally it's the same old shit from the same old faces. I begin to hate myself more than I hate them for thinking that I am on a higher plain than them. Because I don't, you know, I really don't. If anything, I am insanely jealous.

Home time comes when I've finished work. I'm no longer wishing the day away like I used to do in my twenties. I complain about work and I moan about the fact that I have to get up if I've had a particularly enjoyable evening the night before. I always think that a particularly good evening should be followed by a late morning and a general loaf before getting on with the next day. I complain as I say, but I have responsibilities to the company and to myself which I have every intention of fulfilling. Not only does achieving things fill me with some amount of pride, but I am at the point where I am able to set my own goals at work, and achieve them. This of course is through my own vicious refusal to comply with - no, that's what I want you to think. This is because I have ducked and meandered around prying eyes at work and created such a complex web of intricate lies and complicated procedures that no one knows what I do. So when I do work, I only have myself to answer to. Myself, and the odd validation report and appraisal with Charles.

I sometimes find home time difficult. It used to signify freedom, it used to be a relief but now it is just a change in environment. I no longer look forward to the end of the day like an impatient child waiting for the school bell; the internal *hooray* that sparks off the recklessness of evening isn't there anymore. I convince myself that this is an age thing and that it's perfectly natural but see other people at work that convince me otherwise. I am (still) constantly asked like clockwork what I'm going to be doing this evening and I am finding it increasingly difficult to come up with a plausible line. I hate going away and I tire of my social obligations but at least I can tell my colleagues about them and they can nod sagely and pretend to care, and I can feel normal for a little while.

My flat needs a desperate overhaul. I am told that it's fine and that if anything, for the area I'm in and the...I usually switch off at that point because it's usually about property prices, inflation and tax which I try not to think about. I try not to think about a lot of things and they are the things that if I did make an attempt to think about, maybe I could improve my situation. But I don't know if I really think this, or I have just been informed of this so many times that I am beginning to believe it.

I do believe it.

I took the brave step (in my eyes) to move out from living with friends four years ago. Most steps I deem to be brave and most I dismiss as being insignificant. I've lived with girlfriends, friends, family, acquaintances, colleagues, and idiots. I've liked living with all of them. I liked the support and I liked the company. But I also enjoyed disliking them; little quirks that got on my nerves, and points of view that clashed with my own kept me sane and less self-absorbed. I think I've become (more) self-obsessed since moving out on my own. I think other people think this; how do I ask my friends if this is the case? Surely the question itself would only come from the lips of a man with only himself on his mind?

I zoom home as per usual. There's nothing pressing at home and the drive could actually be rather jolly if I put some *Sigur Ros* on, slowed down a bit and took some of the scenery in. But it's 6pm for fuck's sake, everyone just wants to get home. Everyone is in a hurry and everyone has a shit load to do before they begin Groundhog Day tomorrow. I could be different, but the sheer weight of numbers of people that are in the same boat crushes my thinking and I join in, I actually rather like it. As I put my pedal to the floor and screech to a halt at the lights on Tamworth Junction, I secretly like it. I pretend that I need to get home to do this and this *and this* and that, I'm in a hurry! I like having things I *have* to do.

    I get back to find a text from Tom stating that he's coming round. I don't switch my mobile on at work anymore as I like to have a boundary. I like to switch it on the minute I get home so as to signify the start of my evening and/or weekend. It keeps everything in order and in its right place. If people need me at work, they can ring me at work, or email me. But only my work email. I have no idea when Tom is going to get here and usually this lack of knowledge would grate, but it doesn't matter with Tom. He could let himself in and a watch a film whilst I'm in the bath and I have no knowledge of it, and it would be fine. Obviously that would be a bit weird, but you get my point.

The flat is fantastically clean.

"Jesus, the flat looks like a show home."

"I'll take that as a compliment, Tom."

"You shouldn't, it wasn't intended as one."

I snigger, relishing in normality after another stifling bout of polite small talk at work.

"Tea?"

"Always........." He looks around the flat for something to amuse himself with whilst I make the tea. He naturally opts for the remote control, "Let's see what shit is on at this time."

"I hope you're not fucking up my flat with your general messy demeanour."

"Is that tea ready yet?"

I bring it in and find him gazing beyond one of the many shopping channels. "What's up then man?"

"I'm just thinking about buying a magi-table for the bargain price of £39.99. You?"

"I'm thinking about quitting work." I half joke.

"You're always thinking about quitting work. So am I, we should quit work together and do something."

"Yeah, that's a great idea Tom. Or we could just do this for the next ten years and become increasingly jaded and bored."

"I'm up for that."

"You're not thinking about quitting are you? You've got a great job."

"It pays alright but it's shit. Do you know what I do?"

I have no idea what he does.

"Yeah." Sheepishly, I look vacant.

"Ha! You have no idea what I do, do you? Do you even know me?"

"Do you want me to answer that?"

"Not really, I want to go to the pub instead."

I groan. Not because I don't want a drink or I don't want to have a pint with Tom but because I just can't be bothered. Unfortunately, he knows this and he knows I know this, so now I can't be bothered to argue because it's just wasting time that could be spent in the pub. I'll enjoy myself when I get there. I just need to work out who is likely to be there and where we're going to sit.

I sometimes wonder what the hell I'd talk about with Tom if we were both satisfied with our lives and our jobs. We'd find something to complain about I'm sure. I've known him for twenty years and aside from taking the piss out of each other, ourselves and belittling everyone we see, when the time comes to have a proper conversation, it usually has the basis of disillusion or dissatisfaction. Ten years ago, it was money and peers. Chiefly the lack of the former and the fact that the latter may have more of the former than us. Now it's our status, our jealousy of those friends that appear to have achieved that golden ticket of a family and fulfilling career. The fact that they may be as unhappy as we claim to be doesn't come into the equation because this is about *us* goddamnit.

Tom is a kindred spirit. The closer I get to my friends, the further away I feel from the rest of the world. It's as if I'm building a house in the middle of a city and as each year goes by, I board up more windows, make the structure more secure and generally improve the security so no one else can get in or penetrate my little world. To those that attempt to, no matter how fragrantly, I no longer feel the need to make excuses why I don't want them in, and I pull down the shutters with great force. I don't think I like other people very much.

We get back from the pub and Tom is wasted. I can't get wasted anymore, nor do I feel the need to. I can't remember the last time I was drunk. I'd like to say that it's because I like being in control but the truth is that I just can't be bothered anymore. The times I have been drunk, the people I don't like become bearable, but I wake up feeling ill. It took me a long time to realise that I didn't need to make this bearable, because I didn't need to go. Tom says that all of this is bullshit and that I should just go out more often and get pissed. I do, and I have a good time.

Everyone at work gets drunk. Sometimes whilst at work. Business Lunches with prospective clients are laced with pints and often go on for hours. I have nothing against them, the people who partake in them or the events themselves. I'm just glad I'm not a part of them, thankful really. I am jealous and a little angry that I can't enjoy them. I am not angry that I am not invited because my job does not warrant them, and if I did go, I would be out of my depth. Bring me the prospective client and sit him down in front of me and I can work my magic; that's not how it works though and for that I'm also thankful. Everyone seems to know their place and in which particular zone they excel and yet I know I am the only one who feels bad for not excelling in an alien zone. I think I am the only one who thinks about it. I *think*.

The person who is directly above the person directly above me, David Seargent, has left. He no longer works here and for that I am not thankful. I didn't really like the guy and don't think we exchanged words for the six years we were aware of each other. A polite nod in the corridor often occurred but I don't think he knew who I was. I make it my business to know who everyone is, as knowing the personnel make up gives me strength, at least I think it does, so it does. David Seargent went for a lot of business lunches, I think he had a lot of people to impress, or at least keep on side.

    He must have been on a good salary; I have tried to work out the scale and where he came from and he must have been pulling thirty five thousand at least. Maybe that wasn't actually that good considering the work he did and the hours he put in. Hell, he may have been mortgaged up to the hilt and have a massive family and a wife with ridiculous demands, he might have been on the breadline for all I know. I knew nothing about the man except one thing which I don't think anybody else knew.

He left very quickly under strange circumstances. Not really strange to me but then again, I find normality pretty fucked up. He quietly gave his notice in to head office and no one learnt of this until his last day when a rumour got out that he had won the lottery. He had, but a modest amount at twenty thousand. The only reason I know this is because he told me in the cigarette room on his last day. I have no idea why he told me as it would appear he told nobody else; yeah, I could kid myself that he trusted me but it was probably more the case that he knew I wouldn't want to talk about it to anyone else. He probably knew I couldn't be bothered. His real reason for leaving was that he was canny with his cash, and had spent years investing and dealing and could now afford to retire. He was young.

I remember seeing him in town a year later. *This* was okay as he had left and so the file that I had placed him in (in my mind) was open and I had no expectations of where he should be or how either of us should act if we met. I wondered if he had the same filing system in his mind because he looked genuinely happy to see me. I was sort of happy to see him too. It turned out that he had started his own business, ironically but somewhat logically doing what he had been doing for my company. He had spent a year trying to retire beforehand but got bored.

"Everyone struggles, George," he lamented, "but if you take away that struggle, things can get quite boring."

"Yeah well I'd like to see what it's like struggling on a six figure salary." I can get away with saying that, he knows it's not directed at him but it is pointing in his general direction.

"Even the guy on a fat wage needs to push himself. Otherwise he'd just sit around smoking weed all day."

"Ah! Now I know what you've been doing all this time!" I wisecrack.

"Heh, you know what I mean, you of all people must know..."

I don't know what he means by this but I do agree with his point. "I know what you mean - you have to go through the bad times to appreciate the good."

"I knew you knew."

"I know."

"So you're climbing the ladder?"

"Hmmm..." I don't know what to say now, I'm trying so hard not to speak in clichés, "I'm not sure I like the view though."

Damnit.

I wonder when he's going to ask about work, about his colleagues but I realise that he doesn't really care and that he's not the kind of person who will pretend to care unless it will progress him. There's a fine line between honesty and bastard and I think he rides it well.

"Well, look after yourself Sir." I hope he realises Sir is a term of affection.

"Yeah, it was nice to see you George."

And that was that, I'll never see him again. And if I do see him in town, or if he sees me, we're clearly going to blank one another and we both know that it's the right thing to do. Because that was our only conversation, it had been stored up for that moment and now it was spent. I leave his company on a definite high though. Partly because he said it was nice to see me and as saying that would not progress him, he must have meant it, but mainly because that meeting freed up some room in my mind for some other awkward conversation I'll have to have with somebody else in the near future.

Unless of course he was being nice to me because he wants me to report favourably back to the company that he's doing so well since he left, like a different person. In that case, what a bastard.

Tom falls asleep on the sofa and I potter around the flat, levelling things up and making sure everything is in its right place. I almost forget that it is Friday and I don't have work tomorrow. I stay up as late as I can even though all I really want to do is go to bed. The television becomes more inane and puerile the nearer Saturday morning gets, and it's just what I need.

Sleep is approaching and I am dreading it. In my teens and twenties (early), sleep was never an issue. I revelled in the process and would look forward to night time. I don't remember having naps or ever really feeling tired during the day, and I didn't used to touch coffee. At university and to a certain extent at college, I would have difficulty waking up but only because it would signify the end of a glorious refreshing slumber that I was reluctant to break, and my body unwilling to come round from. Now though it's very different and every night, there is a dreadful sense of foreboding doom as I prepare myself mentally for a disturbed night, drifting in and out of passive bad thoughts and the odd night panic. I always manage somehow to drift off but beforehand what seems like an eternity passes as I change the position of my eager frame from foetal to corpse, to drowning corpse and back again. I don't worry about exercise as I have convinced myself that this nightly involuntary workout is all I need.

Here are some ***interesting*** facts about sleep:

1. We need 8 hours. This apparently is a fact from a national foundation and it's in print, on websites and there's been plenty of research into it, so it is the truth. It makes us more alert, less prone to fucking up, and it dramatically improves our immune system. So what's that? Average job starts at 9.00 am, some 9.30 am, need to get up at 8.00 am at the very latest so I need to be in bed by half eleven at the latest. Right, sorted.

2. There are two types of sleep; REM (Rapid Eye Movement) and Non REM. The definition of REM sleep hurts my brain but in a nutshell, it's more prevalent in the final third of the sleep cycle and is usually where all the weird dreams occur. I lose sleep worrying about the definitions of electroencephalograph and sympathetic. Non REM accounts for about 80 percent of our sleep patterns and contains different sections, delta waves, sleep spindles. Jesus, do I really need to be thinking about this? Knowledge is Power. Knowledge is Power.

3. Mediterranean cultures have a *siesta,* Britons have a nap nap.

4. Margaret Thatcher didn't sleep much, and look at *her.*

I need a regular routine in the evening. I need to not be stressed, I need to eat well and exercise regularly and I need to sleep.

I never worry about the bigger picture and sometimes it gets me into trouble. I've never had a five year plan and I don't know where I'll be this time next year. I have no dependants on which I need to worry, and this worries me. The times I have had a partner, a pet or I've had the pleasure of looking after something for somebody or been responsible for something that will directly affect someone else's well-being, I have just got on with it. Because that's all you can do. Alongside the nagging monotony of being tied down, interspersed with momentary pockets of pride and self worth, the time we indulge ourselves to feel put out or put upon is dispersed by the responsibility itself.

I love my family and they love me, that is all anyone needs to know. I look upon my parents and my friends' parents, and at any parents with the exception of rubbish parents, with awe and massive respect. When I was younger, there was a bubbling sense of resentment for everything and unfortunately, my parents were included. I don't think I want to talk about that anymore actually. This is one of the things that I must keep simple, because it is.

So begins my internal monologue as I attempt to enter sleep. I feel as if I'm waiting at sleep's door, rocking aimlessly from foot to foot, flicking cigarette ash involuntarily onto my new trainers, and tutting as I wait impatiently to be let in. And to amuse myself whilst I wait, I think about anything and everything. Thoughts come in twos and threes and I have to queue them up in my mind to be dealt with after I've gone through what is fast becoming a very long list. This is becoming a task. But it's okay because at the end of every task, there's a break. Maybe I could get some sleep in the break.

What *will* I think about tonight? Maybe I'll get so tired that the things I'm thinking about will merge with my dreams and my sub conscious will take over the night shift for a bit. Yes, I'll wake up having provided my brain with the adequate documentation, my brain will search the database/archive and I'll awake refreshed and contented. Fooling myself is something I've become an expert at. Alongside raising my guard and analysing what you meant by that comment...because you meant *something*.

I am worried.

I am worried about how other people view me and whether they are right and they know more than me. I am worried that everyone knows something I do not, and I have a vacant thirst for absorbing that knowledge. I buy books on subjects I think I should be interested in and research subjects that I think will enlighten me. I read infrequently and make lists of those authors I should read, and access companies who will tell me other authors who I might also like. These companies are presuming that I actually read those books. Some I have.

I worry that I spend too much time worrying and that that time could be spent on more productive healthy activities. I worry that I'm not able to enjoy the activities that do I partake in, and that one day I will run out of things to do. I update my CV constantly and pay more attention to the hobbies and interests section than my career. This worries me.

When I was younger, I took a holiday in Northern France, to the town of Lille. It was after my college courses ended and before I took it upon myself to go to university. Many of my contemporaries took a year out and went travelling and I worried about this. I don't particularly like travel. The old adage is right that it is better to travel than to arrive, and I still get a perverse thrill from riding on a train. You can't do anything on a train, there are no expectations and there's plenty of time to lose yourself. Strangely, it is the times I am trapped on a train; aligned, alone with my own thoughts that I am at my most concise and relaxed. *Stress free.* I can mp3 my way to London and lose myself in a book or enter a silly world I invent in my head. I try to work out where other people are going, who are they are going to see and how much money they have. Where they get their clothes, whether I could be their friend. It always comes back to *me,* in the end.

I didn't want to go to Australia for a year. I had little money and no aspiration to seek out new ventures or meet new people. I worried about why this was the case. Everyone who went seemed to have a thousand fantastic stories and had tales of exciting people and drunken antics and I enjoyed hearing about them. I felt connections as they told me of their fears, their days and how they pushed the envelope and how now they are a better, more rounded person. I am jealous that they are a better person. I want them to have had a shit time and it was a mistake so I can justify to myself that it was the right thing to do (not go to Sydney). The fact that I just don't want to go and the fact that I know I wouldn't enjoy it is not good enough. I am told that I do not know if I will enjoy something until I try it. That sounds so plausible and in line with the way in which I think that it causes a malfunction in my brain, and I worry. I can almost hear the connections in my head fizzing as I try to find the right words to tell them to stop talking as my brain hurts from all this fucking *good news.*

So Lille. What a lovely place. It really is, it's a student town and when I went, it had a great atmosphere. Everyone seemed to get on and the old relished the young as they made the town a vibrant bustling place. I had a feeling there was a mutual respect between the inhabitants and the architecture, and the cafes and rambling cosmopolitan nature of the place made me feel comfortable and secure. I made an effort to speak the language and was appreciated for it. My naïve attempts at banter in newsagents and shops were seen as cute and willing and I enjoyed the fact that I was enjoying this. At home, I'd rather go without crisps or a newspaper, or fags if it means having to engage in some weird awkward social exchange in a British shop.

I enjoyed myself, for a bit. I quickly ran out of money and things I wanted to do. The first week was spent in a small hotel, which I had arranged and pre-booked months in advance. I was very proud of myself for doing this. It wasn't cheap but I had figured I wanted to stay in a nice place in the centre of town as I got settled in to my holiday. I had the notion that this was going to be an adventure and that I would meet lots of interesting people and we'd talk about our aspirations and dreams and share new and daunting experiences which would at first be outside of our comfort zone, but would become a story to tell to the fools back home. Hell, our comfort zone would then be stretched and we'd be able to walk our home streets with big stretchy comfort zones.

But it wasn't like that. *At all.* All of the cool interesting people were in the hostels with rucksacks. They had guides and went on excursions. They liked other people, they were *like* other people. But they weren't; they were mavericks - individuals who were discovering themselves and pushing boundaries. Actually, looking back, I think a great number of them were just tired, skint kids with manky rucksacks from *Millets* spending all of their Mum and Dad's cash. They might have put in a stint at the local factory before they went, and fair play to them, but……..well, *whatever*.

I had booked myself into a nice hotel for a week and that was it, that's as far as my mind had taken things. It was an open-ended holiday with insufficient funds to continue. The first five days were spent in blissful refusal to accept what would happen the week after. I enjoyed munching on a baguette on a wall by a library with a tiny scarf and a copy of a French CD I had just bought from the market. I was exactly how I wanted to appear to myself in my head, and it was great.

I had booked breakfast and bed. It wasn't bed and breakfast (I'll have you know). What do they call it, half board? No, that's lunch as well. I had the option of lunch (I think) but I hadn't paid for it so it would just show up on my bill if I did decide to venture down to the restaurant. I didn't. That would have been awful. I'd wander downstairs to the reception and idly glance through the brochures of things to do in the town and catch a glimpse of the place and it was full of families tucking into some great looking food. How out of place would I have looked there? People would have pitied me, I wouldn't have fitted in. Yet I feel like I fit in more here than a ghastly hostel.

I tried breakfast once (I paid for it goddamnit). I got up early enough on the first day to get down at the first sitting and munched on some French toast with cinnamon (which was disgusting). The coffee was nice though. As I was the only one there, I felt good. The waiters may have thought that I had lots to do that day and was meeting my friends later on and I was my own person. Look at me, eating breakfast alone in a French hotel as if it's the most natural thing to do in the world. It certainly felt authentic.

The day quickly came that my money ran out and I went into an enormous panic. The hotel, quite rightfully and dutifully informed me that my time with them had come to an end. They didn't even ask me if I wanted to stay on, they must have presumed that I was some kind of fully functioning adult who wouldn't get into a stupid situation like this. I had a return ticket to get from London back to Norfolk, and I had a ticket that got me on that fast train thing directly to London. But that was it; I had no other funds and no credit card. I'm not *that* stupid, have you seen the interest rates?

I don't want to talk about what happened next.

It was at this point that I realised how fragile everything is. Everyone is just walking around, benefiting from whatever organisational skills they have and what forward planning they have put in place. They have small compartments in their pockets where they keep cards where they can access money that they have earned. They could lose this compartment frighteningly easily and then they must access their back up plan and have numbers in their heads with which they can sort out the problem. They must have people they can rely on if something bad happens and they must be secure in the knowledge that these people will help. Perhaps they spend their whole lives working on relationships to make sure this happens. But there's no written document. There's no signature. Shit, I need to rely on myself. I can't tell who I should be ringing, or if I should be ringing anyone. Where's the fucking phone?

The holiday was a lesson that I didn't learn until years later. My back up plan was to hoist the problem on those that *have* to look after me, and that was something that I was deeply ashamed of. I worry how I allowed myself to get into this, and I worry more that it may happen again some day, but this time when there is no one at the other end of the phone. I worry about the phone running out of battery power and the car breaking down. I worry that not only will no kind stranger stop and assist me but also that some one *will* and that my story of how I got into this predicament won't be funny or humane or sad, but annoying. I worry that I will have to try and enter their world momentarily and talk about their interests because I don't have any, and the ones that I have are weird or out of context. I worry why I can't lie more convincingly and have to be so fucking honest with everyone and I worry that it's now been thirty minutes since I tried to sleep and I'm nowhere near completing my list of worries.

I am fascinated

I am fascinated with other people and what they get up to and why they do the things they do. I am fascinated with the fact that no one seems to talk about being fascinated about things.

I am fascinated with television.

Perhaps most telling of all, I am fascinated with myself. I can be interested in how others think and show a willing concern for their welfare. Hell, I *do* care for their welfare. But nobody really knows what goes on in someone else's mind. Everybody lies and everybody puts on a front. The successful people just have more of a front than others and they have constructed a belief system; likes and dislikes that they keep to and feel comfortable with. They've branded themselves and take this brand wherever they go. Acquaintances talk with them, and about them to other acquaintances and their experiences define their brand further until they reach a point at which they are truly secure and content. They push themselves further and things happen. Or so it seems. Some people seem to have had this since birth and others never seem to acquire it. For some it comes easy and for others it takes effort.

I am fascinated with my arrogance that I presume I know what everyone else is thinking.

Chapter Two

(I am also irritated and annoyed; but isn't everyone?)

I wake up. I've managed to sleep somehow, even though my lack of clarity suggests that I haven't. I'm still massively tired and need coffee. But it's still the weekend and so it doesn't matter.

I like to watch TV in bed of a weekend. It's my routine now and it's somewhat of a treat and I feel very decadent. I like the idea of having freshly squeezed orange juice, coffee in a *Boden* cafetiere and crispy warm croissants with jam on a tray with the Sunday papers. I've always craved for this lifestyle but the reality is usually an instant coffee and the TV guide in front of *Saturday Kitchen*, playing on my mobile and feeling groggy. I don't live in a cosy drama, and there's no one watching, so I can be my own kind of decadent and not feel bad about it. Although I do. I wonder if those people with perfectly formed trays of fresh organic breakfast really exist. I then wonder what's so fucking difficult about getting a croissant and juice from the kitchen and enjoying it and why I prefer to dream about it instead.

I'm going to a fayre today. It was advertised in the local rag and my friend Mary has offered to take me. Mary is a friend of the family, not really my friend but she is like a distant aunt to me. I like being in her company even though I am rarely myself with her, and she knows it. I like the decorum that exists between us and the quiet respect we have for one another. I couldn't spend a long time with her, nor would she want me to, but a morning at a fayre is perfect. I don't have to think of an excuse not to go and perhaps that's the real reason I am looking forward to going.

When I say fayre, it's an *alternative* fayre, promoting natural health remedies with tents and stalls selling ideas. I'd like to buy a few ideas I think, or at least window shop. Maybe I could trade some of my ideas in for better ones. If it were a fair, I would have immediately thought of a suitable excuse because I fucking hate fairs. The noise baffles me and the incessant eagerness of young faces annoys me.

Tom appears to have left. I didn't hear him leave. I don't even like croissants.

I pick up the fayre leaflet that Mary left at the flat.

The Natural Way, the Norfolk fair trade fayre. Established 2002: the Alternative Therapy and Natural Products Fayre.

FIRE WALKING!

I won't be doing that but I want to see other people do it. I want to see it go wrong. I don't want anyone to get hurt but I'd like to see someone psyche themselves up and chant mantras and edge towards the fire, as supporters look on with amazement, only for them to put their toe near the fire, yelp "Oooh! That's a bit hot!" and cower back to their shoes. I'd then like the partner of the person attempting the walk to go mad, and threaten to sue the fayre.

Unless *I* try it and that unfortunately happens to me, in which case I want no one to see it and everything to dissolve with dignity. Or I succeed and do the walk, and it is life changing. I'm okay with others succeeding walking on fire but I can live without it. Good for them.

CRYSTALS AND OTHER STUFF!

Yeah, the leaflet is telling me a lot of stuff about *things* and what I can expect and I begin to just browse the pictures, mainly the ones of people walking on fire. Maybe I should walk on fire. At least then I would have a fresh anecdote that I could bring up at a suitable time and it would provoke a reaction from those that I told it to. I could lie and say I did it anyway (but I won't).

It's just a day out really. I shouldn't think of it in such simple terms though because Mary obviously thinks I could truly benefit from some of the stalls there. And doubtless I could.... I mean - *I will*. I've started to use lavender oil on my pillow in an attempt to induce sleep and I tried one of my sister's herbal remedies last week. It all helps, but I can't help but think that no amount of positive energy or alternative therapy in any form is going to go any way in helping to alleviate my worries, for they'll still exist no matter how much tea tree oil I ingest (*you should never ingest tea tree oil*).

It takes me a long time to get ready. I'm meeting her there and I have a list of things I need to do when I return to the flat and it's annoying me that I haven't finalised it. At the moment, it's not really a list; just a random set of words sprawled on the back of *The Culture* - last week's culture.

I'm glad I'm meeting her there. I have a get out clause that enables me not to have to use it. The fact that I have my own transport and I know she has hers means that I can leave whenever I want to, go wherever I want and have to do something awfully pressing. I probably won't, but I am entering into a social situation with a massive security blanket and I love it.

I go to the fayre, it's alright. I spend most of the time meandering through crowds and picking up strange looking potions, trying to decipher the ingredients and whether they would look good on my shelf of amazing looking potions. I don't have such a shelf yet, but *MFI* is just down the road from the grounds of the fayre and I'm sure I could get one. Then I could erect it next weekend and I'd have something else to say to the work force when I return on the Monday. "Oh, just some DIY." How impressive and normal is that? I went fire walking one weekend, and the next, I'm 'just doing some DIY'. This is great.

Mary picks up some wind chimes, and I persevere with trying not to belittle her purchase. I hate wind chimes. I hate dream catchers and I don't care much for books that tell me to love myself and search for my inner child. There is a stall that is rife with this fodder and we seem to be hanging around this one for the most amount of time. She sporadically passes me books that she feels I will be interested in, or will help me. I'm never honest with her and she knows very little about me apart from what my family and the complex set of fused acquaintances and friends that fuse us together have told her.

Things I know about Mary:

A. She's 38.
B. She's looking for love. She's been looking for love for ten years and she is constantly being set up on dates with inappropriate men. I feel sorry for her, but there's probably no need.
C. She works at a *Howell and Sons*, which I've never been to, but I believe it sells ready made curtains, bathmats, all that kind of stuff. If ever I need any of that stuff, I think I will go there.
D. She has a massive heart.
E. She drives a Renault Clio.

That's it - those are the facts. I know nothing of her background nor do I ever really get an insight into her set of rules, her ethos that she lives her life by. Most of our conversations are based around my family and what we did last time we met. They never go off on a tangent, and they never really progress into anything else. I normally meet her with a mutual safety guard, someone who knows us both equally and who can channel the chat into the right dimension. I like people like that. They act as a director for the conversation, and sometimes even as an editor, making everything flow. This newfound responsibility of having to freestyle the exchange I am finding a tad unsettling but heck, I may even learn some stuff about Mary and we can start hanging out more.

That's not going to happen.

I buy some Haematite and some Echinacea. I already have both and find them to work for me. Echinacea is the herbal remedy that temporarily boosts your immune system and Haematite is my stone of choice. I once entered a shop in Oxford to kill some time as I waited for the train and was immediately drawn to this big block of clean shiny, well it looked like metal to me. It's a kind of dark grey graphite colour and I can imagine a very expensive kitchen top being made up of a similar looking thing. It looks powerful and sexy and strong. I think I've seen the *BMW **M3*** in that colour, and that looks great too.

I didn't used to know much about crystals or precious stones, but many members of my family like them and I think the alternative healing market has grown substantially since the millennium. Everyone wants to better themselves and people (are beginning to) distrust *Glaxo* and the *NHS*. You are able to tailor make your own alternative health and regardless of whether it is effective, the feeling of well-being you may get from the process is as good as if it really has a positive effect. I think about this a lot and have concluded that it doesn't really matter, who cares if it's a placebo if it works? I can fool my brain even when I've tipped my brain off that what I am about to tell it may be bollocks, and that it shouldn't listen. I **wink wink** at my brain to ignore this warning, and it does.

Mary told me that this was an important thing, the fact that I became immediately transfixed on this little block of black stone. People tend to gravitate towards the stone that has the properties and healing 'powers' (POWERS!) that they require in their life. I nod politely and feel the need to play my interest down. I am actually interested in her comment and want to know more but leave it there. I'm not used to genuinely being interested and the usual response of over exaggerated questioning feels redundant and my brain switches off. I think this may have appeared rude, but I hoped she thought I wanted to find out the properties myself. Hell, it's quite a private thing. Anyway, maybe she knows the properties of this stone and now thinks she knows me better. Shit, she has got the upper hand here.

I have a book on stones. I *knew* it would come in handy. The book has plenty of information on the history of the stone, the identification and the lustre; it's metallic to splendent, folks. I skip this information and look for the description of me. I'm rather excited; it's like reading my stars but with an added portion of credibility and possible truth. I have it in my mind that astrology is mumbo, and jumbo, and that stones are of magnificent wondrous natural significance. Maybe this is my ethos; I can feel my head buzzing as a bit of the person who I am is defined a little clearer.

Haematite:

Haematite has a metallic lustre. It helps us to realise that all ideas of our limitations are of our own making. It aids in sorting out the mind, bringing in new and original thoughts that you may have previously not allowed yourself to give serious consideration to. It is the stone of the pioneering spirit, allowing us to take risks while having the presence of mind to understand them.
   "The Anti-Stress Stone" Haematite reflects back negative energies to the sender (so you don't end up taking them on yourself). Haematite dissolves the issues when one meets with confrontation. Haematite helps balance the chakras.

Genius. I feel a little weird. I should feel spooked that this has happened, amazed that Mary was right. Whatever, I should be feeling a mixture of strange positivity, the feeling those people in Sheffield must have felt last year when a group of graduates threw vast amounts of money over a bridge as some sort of statement, and let's face it, to get exposure for *something*. The amazement that this is happening, the confusion as to why this is happening. The luck, or fate that they should be walking under the bridge as this momentous occasion took place. The natural inclination to follow the stuffy English awkwardness and ignore this crazy stunt somewhat embarrassed, **gone** in an instant as they grab manically as if there lives depended on it, or at least so they could act out their own Crystal Maze fantasy.

I don't feel that though. I feel dumb struck, as I am unable to consider my cynicism as being appropriate.

I love declaring I am a cynic because it distances me from the wide eyed hope I've seen others bare, only to be shattered as it becomes clear they are disillusioned. Perhaps the pleasure I get from being miserable will always outdo the pleasure I may get from pleasure itself.

I don't think about what happened any more. I just buy lots of Haematite. There's a force at work here that is clearly acting in my favour.

It's been a nice morning. Mary suggests we could get lunch and we do. We both get a jacket potato on the hoof, I trust implicitly the food stalls here; most are them are serving organic food and a lot is vegetarian. The burgers aren't just burgers, they have mozzarella and sun dried tomatoes instead of cheddar and ketchup. It's basically the same, and I'm really not sure it's going to do us any better. I'm not even sure I prefer the taste but it certainly makes me feel better about myself. We don't have them though because there's no queue at the spud stand, and I feel a little sorry for the guy standing there, amusing himself by rearranging tubs of toppings and looking confusingly at the burger queues. I wonder if he's thinking "Damn, I knew burgers was the way to go.", whether he's relieved that he can chill out, although by the look of him, I don't think he's enjoying doing nothing.

We walk towards him and I'm glad that I no longer have to think about what he's thinking because now I know. The food calms my fuzzy tummy right down. I reach for potato or pasta at every nearest opportunity because I crave the slow release carbs. I like the idea the food is working for me hours after I have eaten. Tiny little worker carbs in my tummy releasing energy rays into my blood stream.

Meanwhile.........

Nothing is happening elsewhere so I can't be honest. I tell Mary that I better get back because I have to give Tom a lift to the station. She doesn't ask where he's going thankfully and we exchange pleasantries about how the nice the morning was (it was), and how we should go round to my brother's house and have a meal sometime. I say that that's a great idea (it *is*), and we zoom off in opposite directions, neither of us having anything more pressing than the other to get on with.

I have to give a presentation at work. This is ridiculous and unnecessary. I look after the stats for this section of the company and have to collate information from other departments and produce graphs and give an insight into their meaning. It used to be my job purely to get this information and pass it on to someone at Personnel who would do this for me - either Julie Graham or Ted. I don't know Ted's surname. This was not in their job description and landed in their laps much as it has now landed in my lap. It doesn't take long to do and is a welcome break sometimes. It means having to identify trends and suggest solutions and appears to be an excuse for paperwork and more procedures.

I have the information already, *all ready*. This used to take a long time and when the task was first given to me, it was as daunting as anything else I have ever been daunted by. The person who used to do it did it well, but seemed to go round the houses, taking an inordinate amount of time, visiting each office and asking formally to see the manager or whoever was deemed to be in charge that day for sheets of paper, faxes and reports. The first time I went with her to see how this was done, I panicked at the scope of what I would be doing.

Now, I send out a group email every month asking for five attachments with an email, stating the codes needed and providing a link to a previous attachment they have already provided to jog their memory. I then ask the same people to fax over a paper copy of the pre approved sheets and the *D 17s*, and again tell them where these are (I moved them when I started this job as they weren't in the right place). I say it's pressing, and send a copy of the emails to the people above the people who are above them, but not to their direct superiors. This is so they worry that their boss's boss (some kind of super boss) will know that this was asked of them on this date and I have the proof. They *will* comply. Their boss's boss will read the email and have no idea what these words mean, nor do they need to. They are just aware that someone lower down has asked someone else to do something, that it appears they are *supposed* to do, and they know it relates to stats and marketing as they deal with the businesses that deal with us.

And all this is done with one click of a mouse. That's two hours saved. *For me.* I wouldn't be surprised if it ate up a great amount of my colleague's time searching for these files and using the fax machine even though it's like clockwork, it's the same every month. They do seem to be rather foolish. I sometimes wonder whether they will complain to their manager about what I do but I've been doing it for so long now, I can't see it happening.

I've done that, I've clicked the mouse. But I haven't looked at the information, put them into any graphs or worked out the nature of my presentation yet. As long as I use *PowerPoint* and use key words and everyone thinks that we have progressed since last month, and I can identify ways in which this may have happened, everyone is happy. We never improve, but I make sure it looks as if we have. I'm still not sure why I do this. I don't lie, but I spin an awful lot. And I always put on a good *PowerPoint* slide show; I'm known for it. I usually buy doughnuts as well. Doughnuts make everything better.

I haven't done it yet - I need to do it.

Oh yeah. Another thing I have to *do* is be a part of a birthday celebration for Rebecca Vicker - a girl who works in accounts. I don't know how it happened but it is down to me to get her a card big enough to fit everyone in the company in. She has six people she works with but she deals with everyone in every office to some degree. Even though I have never emailed her, and only spoken to her once or twice, I nod politely if I see her in the corridor. I passed her in the car once and politely lifted my hand and made a funny face. My name was copied in to an email that loosely referred to her. So I have to sign it. **Happy Birthday Bitch!** I want to put. I wonder what I *will* put.

I say I don't know how it happened but I do; I was at reception and Sally was talking to someone who worked in Accounts and mentioned that someone better get a card. There were four people there who know her very well, or at least, perhaps involuntarily are a direct part of her world, and they chose to ignore the comment. The reception, for two minutes and thirty-seven seconds was filled with the most incredibly awkward air; an atmosphere that was making my head spin. And so I broke the spell and said I was going into town on the Monday and could pick something up. I *think* they thanked me. Stopping talking was thanks enough. Thanks.

That's tomorrow now. I have to do that tomorrow. Today I have to write this presentation. I still haven't sorted that list out from the jumbled words that are on the back of *The Sunday Times* supplement. A text has just come in from Mary. She has a date for a meal with my brother and his girlfriend. She's made arrangements; can I make it? Or more: Why can't I not make it??? I need to do a shop. My washing too, that needs to be done. And the ironing. And then I've got to think about some stuff before tomorrow so I don't think about the stuff when I'm at work and have to do the presentation. Shit! Then I have to *do* the presentation. And I don't want to do any of it. Perhaps ever again.

Sunday evening is a terrible evening. Even at the best of times I hate Sunday evenings as the threat of a new week starts looming as early as lunchtime. Constant reminders declare their presence from two pm onwards, and I'm unable to relax or unwind even if I have fully prepared for the day ahead and what it could possibly bring. Sunday television doesn't help; I shouldn't watch but I always switch it on at some point and instantly regret it. I get sucked into a routine of worry and monotony, panic and foreboding doom. I like to have things I have to do when I haven't got them and then when the things become things I *have* to do because I haven't done them because I need to relax, I get so bogged down in their importance and vital nature that I fear the consequences of these things not been fulfilled. Every journey starts with a first step, yet the journey of fulfilling these mundane tasks is crippling and one I don't want to take. So I choose not to take it, and my mind crashes with gloomy expectation and reminds me of my holiday in Lille.

NEW >> How about next Thurs for meal with your bro? Let me know if that's ok.

Hmmmm......

<< I'll give u txt tomorrow, might be working on presentation
SEND

NEW >> Okay, no problem. Take Care. X

I go to bed having achieved nothing that is on my list, primarily because I don't have a fucking list because that was going to be number one on the list of things to do but it never happened because I didn't have a list as a guide. I manage to allow this to happen as I decide that I don't need lists and that other people probably don't use lists apart from a shopping list and by going to bed in such an unusually disorganised manner is actually a step forward. It is progress if anything, and I am becoming more of a normal person because normal people just go to bed on a Sunday evening. I know I am trying to fool my brain and initially it is sceptical about this and asks me to think about Lille again. I inform my brain that it is foolish and I know what I'm doing.

Strangely, I sleep. I sleep heavy and I sleep hard. The only thought, well the last thought I remember having is simply *'I'll deal with everything in the morning.'* Because it's not a time constraint. Everything that was going to be on the list can be achieved in a very small amount of time and I can get back on track and everything will (probably) be fine. I listen to the radio on my clock alarm as I doze off, I put it on thirty minute snooze and relish in the fact that I can half listen to the talk and not have to think about interrupting my encroaching sleep with a frantic grabbing in the dark in a vain attempt to hit the right button to switch the thing off. What if I hit the wrong button and never wake up? Well, maybe that wouldn't be so bad….

I like listening to the radio and it's something I vow to do more often when I can give it my full attention. I listen to radio shows on the net when I have the inclination and listen more to stories and news reports than I ever used to. I like the fact that I can control the output on the Internet and decide what and when and how I am going to listen. I can also pause, fast-forward and rewind shows, make notes of new music I need to download and shows that may interest me in the future. It is also a bit of a bugbear though as it requires utilising my brain and making a decision about what I want to do. I have the same problem with DVDs in the lounge. I am perversely proud of my extensive collection of films and music shows and comedies and documentaries I have painstakingly collected over the years. I enjoy sitting on the sofa, watching shit television momentarily glancing at my DVD files, all in pristine cases, divided into genres, sub genres and dates. I could watch anything I want (at any time) and nobody's going to stop me.

They add to the person that I am, and I take delight in other people looking at them. We *could* watch one. I am the same with CDs and enjoy the flooding memories of where and when I bought the CD and play a song back in my head that instantly transports me back to a conversation, a journey or a thought. I buy and download more music now than I ever have done before. I have money now, the net, and a wider circle of friends. I have a greater knowledge of where I can find out about new trends and releases. This has led to a constant flow of incoming music. This means that collation has increased, enjoyment has remained static, but really getting to know an album or building up a relationship with a song has declined. We are in a decline. I believe this is why I hold songs that I fell in love with in my teens and twenties with such high regard.

The first album I bought was on tape (I wanted it on vinyl but didn't have a player and refused to share my Dad's). It was *Ocean Rain* by *Echo and the Bunnymen.* I shudder to think what would happen if that album had been released now; maybe I'd download it and forget about it, or it would be just another purchase from *Amazon* that never really got played. Maybe I'd play it a few times and then it would slide under my consciousness as I bought something else. When I was a teenager, an album was a big purchase that I took weeks over, sometimes months. I'd hear about the fact that the band were recording and writing and I'd pencil in the possible date. I'd wait patiently for the radio to give me a glimpse of what was to come and it never came. I'd stay up late, I'd watch *The Tube.* I'd ask my friends if they'd heard it...*WHAT'S IT LIKE*? I'd put the money aside and hear a snippet of a song whilst out in town, and I'd start to bubble with anticipation.

And then I'd get the album and I'd play it over and over again. I'd pick out my favourite tracks and I'd sit patiently through the ones that preceded them, sometimes getting impatient and fast forwarding the tape, sporadically changing fingers to play, *is it there yet*? Friends would come round and I'd play them a song and we'd have a chat about what Richard Fowler said at lunch break; what an idiot, I can't *believe* he said that. And that - alongside a handful of other albums, would soundtrack the next six months of my life. The songs would become a part of my world and be as significant as photographs for documenting my childhood, my formative years. Now I click and file, click and file, click and file. We live in a click and file age; it's great huh? I probably would still have discovered *The Killing Moon* in this age. I have confidence in myself of *that.*

I wake up and I am fine. I know that this is the calm before the storm and I know that there is nothing I can do the stop the storm from coming. I wonder how I'll weather it and whether I am going to collapse under its colossal weight. I am now thinking about procrastination and the only way out of this is to buy myself some time. I have succeeded in buying some time with Mary and my brother, and nothing bad came from that. I remember the significance of the feeling that washed over me when I opened the first text from Mary, and the polar opposite emotion I felt when she said that it was no problem that I had made an excuse. Because she knew it was an excuse. Most significantly, I remember the **x,** and that means everything is fine.

I put '*Vauxhall and I*' on as it has soothed me in the past. I forget momentarily about the lyrical state and think about switching it off.

"There's gonna be some trouble..."

I don't switch it off and I go to make myself breakfast. I am going to be significantly late this morning. I never make breakfast for myself. I usually hurriedly switch the kettle on, have a shower, dress and then gulp down two cups of very strong coffee in front of the Breakfast news. I used to get annoyed at other peoples thirst for news, and used to suggest that they watch something else. Something entertaining. Now though I feel compelled to watch and read and absorb at every given opportunity; stuff is occurring everywhere, all the time. Some of it is shocking and significant, some of it can be used for conversation. It's becoming a vital part of my day and of my life.

Today is different as today I have a distinct clarity that I must take my time and start to procrastinate. There are so many things that I need to avoid, I better get busy putting things off. I have decided that I am going to pretend to be ill, even though I do feel wretched and it's therefore not entirely a lie. I feel ill through my thoughts (though), and this is not a valid illness. If I am sick at work through my thoughts and nerves about nothing in particular, it can become valid in the eyes of my colleagues because I am **physically** ill. I may even get some sympathy and some time off. I am *going* to get some time off.

I make breakfast last as long as possible, stirring my *Weetabix* until it becomes uniformly sugary, and slowly sipping my coffee, like I imagine you're supposed to do.

I make a list. Oh so *now* I make a list.

1. I need to inform everyone who needs to be informed that there will be no presentation. This is because there was a problem with my email, and because I am ill. I will not go into specifics about the problem

but I will state clearly that all information was not collated. No one will check my computer, why would they?
2. I need to be ill, and everyone know I am ill, and it not be weird, and I need to last almost the whole day and leave at 4, having tidied up any loose ends in the office. I'm such a trooper, 'He's such a trooper - he came in looking terrible and almost lasted the day.'
3. I need to have an idea of why I am ill so people can tell other people and it not be weird.
4. I need to get that card, and decide what to write.
5. I need to make a list.
6. I need to do all my household chores, and more.
7. I need to work out what to do next.
8. I need to speak to someone................probably.

I get in my car and drive to work, as fast and frantic as I ever do, glancing down at my list that I scrawled on a post it note and now placed on the passenger seat, directed so I can see key words if I chose to look down when the lights turn red.

It looks like this:

<u>INFORM</u>
<u>GET OUT</u>
<u>ILL?</u>
CARD
(LIST)
(CHORES)
(NEXT?)
(SPEAK)

The bold words are those that I have to do now and think about now, if they are also underlined it dictates that they are pressing and they need further thinking before I get to work. Those not in bold are less important, and if they are within a bracket, I don't really need to concern myself with them until I get home and get out of this day.

At Tamworth, I make a decision to go to see Charles as soon as I get in and tell him about the problems with my email. I intend to just put my head round the door, not really enter into his domain. I will explain that my email is down and that I have I.T on the case but the presentation has been put back until all the relevant information has been collated. The key words here being - *the presentation has been put back*; it's been done. He is within his rights to ask why I hadn't looked at this problem before, as I should have started the report last week and so the only way in which this would be a problem *now* would be if I hadn't started the report and left it to the last minute.

However Charles knows me and he knows me to be meticulous. I *have* been for the last five years at least, and this report makes up a very small part of my workload. It's not hugely important and everyone worries about it because they think the person directly above them thinks it is important. He will have asked the question of why this has happened in his head and immediately dismiss (I hope) the possibility that it is anything but someone else's fault. I know this, and he knows that I may know this, but even though we both know what each other knows about the others persons knowledge, it's still okay because the bottom line is: I wouldn't ever put myself in the position that I have just put myself in because that would be nuts. Is this my grown up Lille I ask myself?

I do exactly what I intended to do and Charles nods. God, is it that simple? It clearly is. He asks if I'm okay, which allows me to get the **ILL?** item ticked off. He doesn't look like he's busy so I enter just a tad so the door is fully open, I'm just about in his office but I have my hand on the doorknob, as if to signify that I am busy and things are pressing. Obviously the first thing I did this morning was liaise with I.T to sort this email problem out, and I clearly need to check on progress and then find out if it is actually I.T, or the that the other departments have fucked up and given me the wrong data. All of this I am communicating to Charles without speaking.

"You don't look so good George."

"Yeah, I don't feel the best. Had to be today as well, I'm snowed under upstairs. I'll have a coffee, I'll be fine."

"Alright."

"Oh, whilst I'm here, do you want anything from town today? I've got to go and get a card for Rebecca. Thought I'd take an early lunch at have a look around town."

He looks quizzically at the window as if he is going to be reminded of a tuna baguette by looking at the trees. "No, no I don't think so. Do we need to get a cake or something? Rebecca...Remind me where she works?"

"She's training I think."

I know he doesn't know whether I mean she works in training, or she *is* training and this amuses me.

"Okay, well better get some cakes or something. Maybe not *a* cake, just do your thing at the cake shop, and get some fucking rest mate."

"Yeah, I might try and book an appointment with the doc - I was being sick all night."

"Well good luck with that, you can only get a same day thing with the local quack. You're with *Hodges* aren't you?"

"Oh God, I don't know, anyway I'll catch you later. There's a new temp starting today and I need to brief her on...stuff."

I laugh, quite genuinely and sound tired and despondent. Charles laughs with me and can see that I am tired and despondent and is probably laughing at the idea of me having to guide a temp through what I do. There's no temp coming, there probably will be soon and I will probably have to guide them through what I do.

I feel slightly better now that I am working through my list. I just need to get the card and then leave and I can pick up the pieces at home. I sit at my desk and seriously think about the possibility of locking my door and going to sleep. I wonder how long it would take for anyone to notice, or if I just did this every morning until lunch, how long it would take for the company to feel it. It would start having an effect on a few people, and then clients would wonder why my answer machine was always on. I am talented enough to be able to last three weeks I think. I laugh to myself at the challenge and then dismiss it as childish and start work.

I have chosen the out of town shopping place, *out of town* as the place to get the card and the cakes. I am safe here as I will not bump into anyone from work. I don't really know what other people do for lunch at work. Everyone does their own thing. The managers don't appear to eat, I think one or two business lunches each fortnight seems to suffice. I know they all smoke and I know they all drink coffee - espressos and plenty of them. They should be buzzing, maybe they are.

We have a canteen and I often venture upstairs if they're serving scampi. I never eat in though, I am able to walk straight to the lift and go to my office with a hot steaming plate of scampi and chips, and scoff it down in relative privacy. People know I do this, and my boss does it too so I don't care what they think because they are thinking it about him too, so it doesn't matter. One day, I'll get in the lift with my scampi and it will be full, and I will feel terrible. Or it will be great, and I'll offer round chips like some savoury *Willy Wonka* and we'll joke and laugh and meet for a drink later. They'll tell their friends and my name will go round the company as that man who takes scampi in the lift. That would be quite nice.

But that day hasn't come and it probably never will because I can usually hear, or at least sense if the lift is full. And even if it was and I hadn't sensed it, there's another lift right next to that one and I'd look sheepish and wait for the next one. Or I'd just walk. I walk around the company a lot come to think of it. I can get away with walking around the company with a handful of letters and a pile of reports for hours. I pop in and out of departments asking for advice and making other people feel good. I know which people to ask and which to leave alone. I often ask someone who I know would like to help about something I need no help in doing. Equally, I will avoid approaching someone who I desperately need clarification on a matter and end up muddling through it myself. I'm often right, and this pleases me. When I am wrong, I don't cover up my mistakes because there's no one to pick me up on it within the company. The mistake shoots out into the ether and I get an email or fax correcting my error. I thank them for picking me up on this discrepancy and subtly blame someone else – If I *need* to. But I rarely do, because outside companies are always making mistakes. In fact, much of my time is spent clarifying things for *them.* Ha. The ridiculousness of everything shoots me in the face and I break out into a smile.

I arrive at the supermarket, tired. I'm so tired. I sit for a minute in the car listening to local radio and I reach for a cigarette. I don't want it, and my body may even try to reject it, but it will give me four minutes to try and work a few things out. I forget what I'm attempting to work out and just stare at my post it note. I wonder what exactly I'm supposed to do with the last two words and begin to fret. I decide not to worry or think until I have finished my cigarette and begin to worry about the fact that the cigarette has an end and when it gets three quarters down, I only have a quarter left with no worry. I also hate filling the car with tobacco smoke as I own a lovely car that I want to be like it's just come out of the showroom, forever.

I finish the fag and clumsily open my door, reaching for the post it note, which I put into my jacket top pocket. I pat my left pocket - keys and phone. My right - wallet, fags, chewies. My lighter, where's my lighter. I decide I don't need my lighter as I will not be smoking in the supermarket. In which case, I will not need my cigarettes. I pull them out of my right pocket and my chewies fall out. I bend down to pick them up and feel a little bit sick.

I enter the shop. The lights appear to be buzzing overhead and there's a fat security guard looking right at me. I quickly look away which immediately gives him cause to be suspicious. I go straight to the sandwich section and spend a good five minutes perusing the selection. I look at the special section - feel the magic sandwiches, or something. They claim to be different and better. I think I want one of them, but then look over at the normal ones, for normal people. They look pretty good too. As I stand and look blankly at the packages, people bustle around me, some stop dead in front of me as if I don't exist and do what I am doing, but *right* in front of me.

Others are poised on the periphery, waiting to pounce as they spy their sarnie of choice. Hands fly in and out of my view and cheese and onion, egg salad, and prawn mayonnaise fly in all directions. I stand here for as long as I can without it looking weird and now and again, I pick up a sandwich and pretend to read the packet. I'm not even thinking about anything anymore.

The task at hand or my post it note, or work, or even where I am. I've got a nagging pain in my head that hasn't yet developed into an *ache.* I spy some orange juice and reach out for that. Amongst all the fizz and boring water, it seems like a friend. It's tiny, and it's expensive.

I don't buy a sandwich, maybe I'll get something from the canteen. Maybe I will have left around three and I'll get something at home. I'm not hungry anyway. I practically jog to the card section. Everyone's in a rush so I may as well be too. I kind of am; I want this experience to end so that's as good as any reason to be in a hurry.

I get to the aisle and there's nobody else there, which is fantastic. The good news washes over me like when you get into a hot bath, or someone tells you that they appreciate you. It's the same aisle as the culture and it's a pretty nice aisle. Books and CDs and DVDs surround me. They're all what we're expected to buy, and people do, and the sales dictate success and so they stock up with more of it.

I glance the culture and pick up a few things I was unaware were released. By the time I get to the cards, I feel as if I have been in this supermarket for about half an hour even though my phone assures me it has not even been seven minutes; it's been six. A man turns the corner at the other end of the aisle and begins to walk toward me. I immediately and startlingly have a bad feeling and my guts turn, and complain. Something isn't right and I know that something bad is about to happen.

The sense of fear becomes greater and I look around to see if anyone else can sense it. Another man enters from the other side with his wife and kid. I presume it's his wife and kid. I quickly look back at the original man, and back to the family. There's nothing I can do to stop what is about to happen but I refuse to accept that and I wonder if there's anything I can do.

The man gets closer and lifts his hand above his head and in slow motion I take two small steps backward. My face begins to go numb and my heart speeds up to an alarming rate. I can hear shouting behind me and I prepare myself for something I could never prepare myself for.

Chapter Three

I bend down and crouch on the floor and grab the nearest thing I can decipher that's on my eye level. I think I may just pull this off and not spark any alarm with anyone.

Three years ago, I went from the top floor to the ground with Susan Pilchard at work. Yes, that was really her name. Two floors went by and uncharacteristically more people entered until we had a full lift. This in itself posed a problem for me, not a serious one but I didn't know where to look or how to act. Everyone who got in was from the same department and their chat flowed effortlessly. Susan was with me, she was a PA from personnel and I liaised with her often. I liked her and I think she liked me. I met her on the top floor as we were both doing something in the training room. Doubtless what she was doing was far more important than what I was doing. I have no reason for going to training so I may have just been wasting time.

But we ended up getting the lift down to the ground floor and were going to have a ciggie together, and I was looking forward to it. We both felt awkward in the lift and her slender frame appeared to be being crushed by the ferocity of the large characters that had entered our world. She came and went very quickly and I think I miss her. The lift broke down in between level three and two and she had a panic attack. I held her hand and pretended nothing was happening as she fell into an abyss of fear. I turned to her and calmly told her it was fine and the rest of the lift agreed. They started making stupid jokes to try and distract her, one gave her a hug and I could see that everything they were doing was making her worse, a lot worse. She gripped onto my hand with all her might and I kept silent, gently nodding to her that it was fine, because it was. This went on for ten minutes and I knew how she felt, God I was with her every step of the way. I zoned in on her and tried to help her but I knew that nothing could, maybe my hand was the best I could offer. The jokes and banter kept coming from the crowd around me and I felt angry and alone, but unlike Susan, I travelled inward, as she howled and hollered as we waited for the Fire Brigade to come. And they did, and we were saved (hooray!) and I helped her fill out an accident report and then went to the canteen and got her a massive sticky bun and a sugary tea. It was over, and it was a story, and it provoked massive sympathy and she knew that lifts that break down make her panic.

I am a fraud.

I am almost on the floor of this supermarket and I know that there is no frame of reference for other people who pass me by as to why I am on the floor. I am panicking for Britain yet you wouldn't know it. All of my energies are concentrated into making this appear as normal as possible and I'm internalising every weird physical symptom and mad reaction which makes it worse and I want to die.

I am aware of every inch of my body and my left foot has started tapping like a drum. The guy who lifted his hand has put it down and he is thinking about coming towards me, or maybe he isn't. I think I'm looking normal. The family aren't paying attention so I must be. I wonder what would happen if I whispered 'Help me...' to the next person who came along. It would be awful. Maybe even more awful than this.

My heart is now beating so fast I actually fear I *will* die. It begins to pound so that I can feel it all over my body. Strangely, my ears take the brunt and it begins to drown out the muffled sound of the supermarket. I speak too soon as something peculiar happens with my senses and I begin to hear everything together in double volume and horrific clarity. Now and again, I will pick up on a particular sentence or phrase that is emanating from something, someone, somewhere and it will ring in my head like an angry child. I reach for my asthma inhaler; I know that this isn't asthma but if I fool others into thinking it is, I don't have to hold it in anymore. Hell, I could go to town and collapse and let my breathing do its own thing and it would be fine because I'm having an asthma attack. That's not weird, that would get me sympathy and maybe even a massive cake and some sugary tea. I'm now aware of my thought processes and I tell myself to stop thinking about massive cakes.

My eyes start streaming and I can see tiny spots of lights everywhere I look. I grab a CD and pretend to look at it--- all I can see is light flashing in and out like a mini fireworks display. I wonder how this is going to end and when I will be able to leave. I am a fraud. I yearn to be Susan Pilchard. I yearn for supermarkets to be the problem and for someone to take me away from the supermarket, give me a massive cake and take me home, where everything will be fine. But I'm now crippled with fear that it won't be fine as leaving the supermarket will not achieve anything but transfer the panic to a new perhaps even more hostile environment.

I kind of want to cry. My breathing is becoming so intense and uncomfortable that I am in severe danger of passing out. I know I must do something or this will become something entirely different. I don't know what could be worse than this but as it's not getting better and with each ticking second, I am developing greater fear, more nausea and more symptoms, I can only conclude that there *is* something worse than this. I momentarily ponder whether this is what it's like just before you die, crippled with fear and things just getting worse until suddenly a switch goes and everything's fine. I imagine if you die in an ugly way, it quite possibly is. I feel no pain, I hasten to add. This again, makes me a fraud. I have time to wisecrack with myself as to what would happen if someone asked me what's wrong.

"Does it hurt anywhere?"
"**My mind feels funny and I can't control my body.**"
"Oh..................um............."

"Give this man some room! He's a bit upset about his life in general and it looks as if he can't handle it and is having trouble keeping his head together!"
"Oh my God! Stand back, I'm trained in this, I'll just use this biro..."

"Oh my God, supermarket manager, what are you going to do??!"

"Well supermarket check out girl, I'm going to take this biro tube, and write 'You are a worthwhile person' on his hand.....wait look, he's coming round."

"It's......it's working!"

I stop joke arseing around in my head because my head is now pulsating with fear and there's no one to fight here so I need to fly. I get up with a jerky motion and walk briskly to the bathrooms, which I know are by the front doors. I pray that the security guard doesn't think I have a pocket full of goodies and intend not to pay. I mean, that's what *I'd* think.

The toilets are empty, but it doesn't matter anyway because toilets have cubicles, people can lock the doors in cubicles and you can spend as long as you want in them because it's private. I quickly splash my face with cold water and then lock myself in a cubicle and wait. Waiting for sanity, waiting for something. I have no idea what I'm going to do now. My heart has almost gone back to normal but I'm sweating profusely, everywhere.

After a while, after what seems to be a lot more than a while and after I have made sure that the coast is clear, I emerge from my cubicle retreat and look at myself in the bathroom mirror. There are massive black holes where my eyes used to be, my hair is drenched and I am quivering. I've looked worse. But only after the flu or a bad night out as a teenager that left me clambering up the walls of a mate's house after a club and subsequent session. Clinging onto any positive, I convince myself that I have looked worse but I haven't. I look like shit and this makes me feel like shit, worse than shit. I *am* shit.

And there it is - my first panic attack in about ten years. I walk back to the car a dishevelled wreck and head home. There's no way I'm going back to work, nor should I expect myself to. I email work and let them know that I've been ill and am going to the doctors. I send a separate email to Charles stating the same but that I'll make it in tomorrow to give him a progress report. He immediately emails back and says there's no need, and that I should rest up and come in only when I'm ready. He asks me if anything needs to be sorted at work while I'm away and I lie and tell him yes. I say that I can do the report from home as I now have all the data I need after I checked my emails.

Thankfully, a lot of my job I can do from home and this has only just occurred to me. I have access to many of the programmes we use at work and I have work email. I begin to wonder why I go to work at all. I make up some lengthy bullshit about a client that is due in on Thursday, that eventually ends with the words 'but it's alright, I can contact them from here and perhaps even carry out some of the work without the need for them to come in.' We swap five or six emails, all of which I could have done with one simple phone call but Charles doesn't seem to mind this, I don't think he's too keen on the phone, just like me.

I apologise about my failure to get a card, to which he replies – "I don't even know who this girl is, George -

someone will get her a card. Just get better and I'll see you soon. Sounds like you've got work sorted your end. If I need to know anything, or you need to know anything, we'll be in touch."

And for that, I love my job because I am not worried anymore. Perhaps it is Charles I appreciate. Sure I appreciate him now because he appears to have empathy and understanding and common sense. If I was still a clerk on level two and pulled this stunt, there would be questions asked and pressure applied. Now however, they need me. They would be unable to get another me if I decided to leave and not allowing me to be ill would be good grounds for leaving (*I think*). But maybe the pressure is good. I try not to analyse his management style and wonder if *he's* worried about the report. I *think* I think my duties are more important than they are. I play them down and for good reason; I *do* worry about their incompletion and how this may affect other people though. Perhaps this is the only thing I really worry about. How anything I do at work will affect other people - be it work, or getting the right birthday card. And that's not because I am worried about them or their work. If this were the case, I would still be going to each department to get their stats rather than arrogantly demanding they find them and give them to me. I am just worried about how this will all affect me in the long run. Will they harbour a grudge, and if they do, do I really care? And if I care, why do I care? I have to stop that trail of thought because I start to contradict myself, and anyway, I have some time off now (I wonder how long), and I need to sort some things out.

After that little escapade is sorted and I'm back in the safety of my flat, and work knows the score, I unplug the phone, put my mobile on silent, and drink tea in the lounge - basking in the monotony of daytime TV. I'm completely at ease now. Mainly because my body feels as if it has done a ten mile run and I have no choice but to relax. This is the calm after the storm, but I'm aware of the storm damage and I'd like to fix all that.

I'm okay but I feel as if I've lost a vital part of myself. At this stage, I'm thinking it maybe my social skills because I don't want to see anyone, perhaps ever again. I'd be quite happy staying in this flat for the rest of my life, texting and emailing and arranging and sorting and maybe even a bit of thinking. I have a messenger thing on my computer and I could say I was ill and it's contagious and so people better not visit. Even if they do, I can afford to be anti-social because I'm ill, it's not like someone new is going to come to the door and I have to make a good second impression. And if they do, I won't answer. I'm planning my Howard Hughes existence.

Over the next few days, I languish in my down time and have made a conscious decision to switch off for a bit. The short-term gain and the immediate benefit I feel from doing so allows me to languish further and I relish in the suspended nothingness and void I have happily, *actively* created. I go in to work on the Thursday with the report and see Charles again. He says I don't look much better, and I don't. My thoughts are no longer constant though and I am able to think on my feet and lists aren't on my mind anymore.

"Thanks George."

"Not a problem Charles. I need to take some time off and I need to work it though with someone, how it's going to work. I haven't checked the diary."

Charles is relieved that I have brought it up so he doesn't have to and I have willingly given him the upper hand. He needed to suggest this and hey, I may have been offended, after all I was only ill. Maybe I had eaten a dodgy curry, or Pauline Hedge from Audio Typing had sneezed in my face (I wouldn't put it past her). He also immediately understands that I *do* need some time off, because I never ask for it. Our skit usually goes something like this:

\>\> Charles reminds me by email that I have holiday I need to take; I grumble and reluctantly pick dates, I take a week off and sit in the flat waiting to go back to work.

I am rarely ill. Even when I am, I still turn up to work because I may as well be ill at work as ill at home. Charles knows all of this.

"Well, you know your work load, what's the deal with new clients? All in order?"

"The Robinson contract is in progress. They have been dealing with me for a month and it would be inappropriate to change handlers. I've built up a relationship with them and I'd like to see that through. I think it could bring the company a lot of business."

"Do you want time off from work, or time off from…..*work?*" I am impressed with his understanding of the situation, and his ability to convey what he needs to say in such simple terms.

"Well, I appreciate what you are saying, perhaps time working in a different environment and also having some time off would be beneficial for everyone." I am not so impressed with my articulation of the response I had in my head. I wonder whether this plan we appear to be hatching would qualify as normal work, sickness, or holiday. It will all come down to pay in the end.

"The logistics of undertaking this may be convoluted." I *think* he knows what I'm getting at.

"Well any work that you can undertake away from here, I am more than happy for you to do."

He clicks his pen as his brain buzzes searching for solutions. He's a great thinker and has a mind like an *Apple Mac*. Unlike me, he is able to soak up information and fuse together ideas and possible outcomes very quickly, and articulate them in a humane concise manner. He moulds his voice to suit each individual situation and his approach is equally unique depending on how involved each problem is, who the problem will affect and how his boss will view his actions. I think his boss is too worried about how the board of directors will view *his* decisions.

He can see that I'm not saying anything. It's an important lesson I learned whilst working at *Rillans*, a manufacturing company in Oxford. State your case, and wait. All social awkwardness goes out of the window here, and I enjoy seeing who will come out victorious; it will be me. It is me. *It's always me.*

"Okay, I don't think there's any need for us to go down the sickness route pal, even if you do look like death," he momentarily breaks from his train of thought - "Have you been to the doc?"

"Yeah." I lie.

He doesn't ask how it went and immediately jumps back on his train of thought.

"Take a couple of weeks. How about we count one of them as part of your holiday. I got the diary out yesterday and had a look at how much you have left and you need to take ten days within the next six weeks."

"Really? How did that happen?"

"Well, if we play it this way, you have another five days if you need to take some time off for Easter, on top of what you get anyway and then the entitlement starts again. Besides, if this goes well, we could very well look into the possibility of more project work away from the office."

"Excellent."

My one word response unsettles him. "Is there anything else on your mind George?"

"I don't think so."

"So you're okay?"

"I think so."

"You'd tell me if you weren't."

"Sure."

I wouldn't, or at least I don't think I would. Two years into this job, I aired a grievance with my then line manager and I instantly regretted it. I had realised afterwards that there was nothing he could do about the situation, and me raising my point was futile. I have worked out that most up and coming grievances can be sorted in more of a proactive way, by attempting to influence someone's behaviour and thought patterns.

Perhaps my grievances are loosely based around the fact that I am aware that other people attempt to influence *my* behaviour, and it gets my back up.

I no longer raise my voice. I now raise my guard.

I drive home. I have decided not to go back to the supermarket for a while, and I've decided to not see my friends for a while. This has happened before, and I begin to worry that this comes in cycles and will rear its ugly head every x amount of years. I wonder what I've done that means this is happening now, and I wonder what it is that is actually happening to me.

When I was fifteen, I went through a similar thing. At that age, your body and mind are drowning in hormones and irresponsibility and it took a long while for me to realise that there could be a problem. In fact, I didn't. I allowed myself to fall apart at the seams and carried on regardless until the *seams* were perished. I wasn't interested in anything my peers seemed to be interested in, and I found everything to be mildly ridiculous. I hated a lot of people and had no regard for social convention. I was also very excited about life. I had panic attacks and withdrew from the things that I was once involved in and became very insular and inward looking. For a short while, I continued to be a part of the scene that I had fallen into *whilst* being insular and watched as friends drifted away and acquaintances became more alienated, the chances of them becoming friends more distant with each silence.

I went to the doctor after three months of convincing myself that I didn't need any help. It was the most difficult thing I have ever done (apart from attending my best mate's funeral). I was initially diagnosed with anxiety. The doctor showed me a nice circular chart with arrows and lines that showed how anxiety feeds off itself, a *vicious circle.* It was the first time I'd seen a *picture* of a vicious circle, and it amused me. I nodded and made the right noises for someone who is anxious and he referred me to an anxiety counsellor. I didn't find this very helpful and was very anxious all throughout the meeting. I felt like I was in GCSE Anxiety class - studying the subject as an outsider. I also felt that the woman thought I was a fraud with no right to be in her class. I remember fumbling on the doorknob as I left the room, and her asking me to stop. **Breathe.** Okay, she hoped she helped. I felt angry.

I went, and was asked if my childhood trauma had ignited the flame of self-doubt. I did my best to explain that I *had* no childhood trauma, and they did their best to convince me that I did. I read endless self-help books that portrayed my situation as a complex web and offered advice and instruction that I found insincere and patronising. I talked endlessly to people about things that didn't matter in a vain attempt to identify something to change, and I ate a lot of healthy food and bought some weights to try a kick start my body into feeling better, hoping that my mind would follow. I became painfully depressed as I delved further into avenues of help that made no sense and provided no answer. The fifth appointment with my doctor was a turning point, if only because he had exhausted all possibilities, and I felt that he was now a little exhausted of seeing my teenage face in his office.

He gave me a course of antidepressants, and I took them. I was convinced that this was the answer and began to acclimatise to the fact that maybe my brain was just wired incorrectly and this was now a purely medical problem that could be easily fixed. Temporarily, even before taking the pills, I felt a little better. The fact that there was perhaps an underlying problem was pushed out of my mind with the promise of easy rectification. I even started to become a little bit more of the person I used to be, and everyone was positive around me and the positivity fed off itself.

I took the pills for what seemed like an age, and slowly became numb to events and people around me. I don't think I was depressed anymore, but I wasn't *anything* anymore. The shows I held close to my heart no longer amused me and I stopped listening to music. When a tune came on the radio I liked, I switched it off. I then put my radio away because not only could I not bear the thought of listening to the radio, I could bear less the notion that they might play a song that I would actually enjoy. I stopped hanging out with mates, *period*. The only thing that remained constant in my life was television and I was absorbed with shows I had never seen before and fascinated with news and current affairs.

I remember coming out of this mire very clearly, and it was if as if being so isolated from the world had taken away all of the memories and upset of why it happened in the first place. I reinstalled my hard drive and was up and away. I had convinced myself that it was the pills that had fixed me, and much to my doctor's regret, stopped taking them immediately. I was told that this was a bad idea, but it didn't seem to have a tremendous negative effect. The action of making that decision was enough for me to embellish that I may now be in the driving seat again.

I still had panic attacks all throughout my youth but as I slowly became more self aware, I was able to pinpoint the things and people that would provoke them. I was very selective about the people that I would associate with and became very opinionated and arrogant around loved ones. Amongst strangers and acquaintances - I held a healthy distance. I wouldn't let anyone in unless they had been vetoed by a list in my head.

I'm back at the flat now. I'm thinking about this initial downfall and putting it into context and thinking how it relates to my situation now and I am identifying things that have changed since my teens. The things I have learnt about myself, and the things I have learnt about other people and how they interact. I don't think I'm analysing, more reminiscing. Although there is now nothing pressing, my first week of not being at the office will be convincingly ordered. I would like to research some more remedies and therapies. I would also like to get a bit healthier and start doing some of those things that I have put off around the flat.

Somewhere in the world of problems that is encapsulated under the term **panic**, lies an answer.

In a nutshell...

OBSESSIVE COMPULSIVE DISORDER (OCD)

I think I have this but I can't be sure.. Basically, obsessive thought patterns and rituals. The most common or at least most widely recognised amongst Joe Public would appear to be the fear of contamination, alongside the physical ritual of excessive washing. It, like many other members of its family are linked to a cycle within which the negative aspects are perpetually confirmed as being appropriate.

It is difficult to pin point when an action can be deemed as being OCD, as everyone has a need to clean, and I have more empathy for those people that sit on the boundary, unable to play with the other OCD people (those unfortunate people who have it bad).

Obsessions: Fear of being ashamed death symmetrical arrangements intrusive thoughts negative body image disaster! Contamination.

Compulsions: washing cleaning measuring hoarding counting repeating washing cleaning measuring hoarding counting repeating washing cleaning measuring hoarding counting repeating washing cleaning measuring hoarding counting repeating.

PANIC ATTACKS

Caused by stress, bereavement, family, accidents, and childbirth. It is what I like to refer to as a gateway problem. Naturally, one associates the panic with the place that it occurred and the fear of reliving the attack can lead to agoraphobia.

The body has a natural fight or flight response to danger. When a person perceives some threat or danger, the autonomic nervous system is stimulated. This helps a person escape from danger. During a panic attack, the body's automatic nervous system is triggered for no apparent reason - a false alarm.

And then there's depression. And a whole world of other things that attach themselves to these three and refuse to let go, injecting them with more longevity. Here, look, I'll make a list of them so you can peruse:

1. Social Phobia
2. Social Anxiety
3. Health Anxiety
4. Self Harm
5. Irritable Bowel Syndrome
6. Agoraphobia
7. *Any* Phobia
8. Palpitations
9. Hyperventilation
10. Chest Pains
11. Dilating Eyes
12. Dizziness
13. Nausea
14. Tight Throat
15. Dilating Bronchial Tubes & Asthma
16. Diarrhoea
17. Increased Urination
18. Tight Muscles

19. Headaches
20. The Shakes
21. Depersonalisation
22. Derealisation
23. Emotions
24. Insomnia
25. Exhaustion

I read the list and do a little research. A lot of it is covering old ground but it's nice to cover old ground. I decide to be forward looking and stay mainly on the side of the remedies. I can sort out the real problems when my head is in a better place. I think working from home and making that work is maybe a step in the right direction, and I'm beginning to wonder whether I should tell Charles about what happened. I've emailed Tom and he suggests that I don't as that would open up a whole can of worms. A *whole* can. I kind of think he's right but I want to prove he's wrong. But he's not wrong, so I won't.

I don't spend long on this research because it doesn't seem to be going anywhere. All the time I'm doing it, I have an undeniable sense of progress but I am not naive as to think that it's real progress. I spy the word hypnosis on one site and I am reminded of my brief fling. In my early twenties, I went to a hypnotist. It was *Neuro Linguistic Programming.* I used to chat to a friend of the family who ran an alternative health centre and I was put in touch with this guy who said that he might be able to help me. It wasn't really a life changing decision and I recall that I just kind of fell into the appointment, without really knowing how I got there.

By just not saying no to a line of casual suggestions, I found myself with an appointment to be hypnotised. My cousin Dylan once told me that I say yes too often.

The hypnosis took place in an annex connected to the flat of the woman who ran the centre and it was a lovely place; a rambling old cottage in the centre of town that looked and felt out of place, until you entered. The first time I *did* enter, I was offered a cup of tea and was asked if I needed an ashtray. I said yes to both. I wonder if I am capable of saying no to anything. A woman is in the kitchen, which you are forced to go through as soon as you enter the cottage. She glances over her shoulder and smiles.
"Do you take sugar?" she enquires.
"Yeah, two please."
"Oh I don't know Hannah." (that's the name of the woman who runs the place, and who warmly invited me into her place of retreat).
Hannah smiles at me to reassure me that this comment was not a jibe, *in the slightest.*
"You'll have to ignore Hayley, she's a reformed smoker and drinker. She's only jealous."
Hannah's voice is soothing, relaxed and quiet. She is slightly anodyne. She speaks like I imagine traditional grannies do, the ones who knit and bake and have cats jump up on worktops. Hayley turns and gives me my cup of tea and lets out a broad smile that makes me melt. God, this is great, why can't everyone be like this, or at least pretend to be. Maybe I'll actually vocalise that thought when I get upstairs. Because that's where

I'm going. Hannah slowly mounts the stairs and I follow her to a serene country room upstairs (to the left).

I sit down without being asked to as I can clearly see the chair that is intended for her and so I simply avoid that chair. She asks me to make myself comfortable (she doesn't say, 'oh, you *have*') and I do. I make myself very comfortable. Whilst she hunts her house for an ashtray, I ponder whether I'm actually going to use it. Half of me thinks it would be rude to as the room smells so fresh and calm, but the other half realises that if she has an ashtray, chances are that she smokes herself, but I have my doubts. She may just have one for smokers and being in the trade she is in, appreciates that it may be rather daunting to go into someone else's house and tell a complete stranger all your problems whilst not smoking. She might just smoke pot. I think she *does* smoke pot.

Quickly all off these thoughts disperse, as she's been gone more than five minutes and so not smoking now would just be taking the piss.

"Here we are, I knew I had one somewhere."

'Yeah, next to your stash' I think.

"Excellent, thanks very much." (More appropriate).

"So, I know this must be quite daunting for you. Your brother has told me a little bit about your situation but I want to make sure that this is right for you and you want to be here."

My brother?! I knew she was a family friend and had been to parties and stuff but when did she speak to my brother? And why speak to him??

"No, no, I definitely want to be here. I didn't realise you had spoken to Paul."

"Only in passing really, he said that you were a little stressed about a few things and it might be beneficial to talk with somebody."

She can see I'm a bit confused. I mean, who the fuck is talking to who here. Is everyone talking to each other about what's best for me and arranging appointments? I realise that by not saying no to things, I could have the tendency to erupt with rage at inopportune moments. I quickly pick myself up on this.

"It was your mother I believe who gave you the details, and I apologise now if it appears like you've been rail roaded into this. I had a spare afternoon and I had assumed that you had talked through everything with her prior to this engagement." She speaks so slowly and softly, I am immediately taken back to the conversation we are having, and random thoughts cease.

"No, sorry, that's fine. I'm quite stressed now to be honest. But yeah, I'm fine with this; I mean I appreciate your time."

She smiles and docks her head slightly. I hope she finds my mumbling and sketchy behaviour endearing and cute, and *not* annoying.

We talk for forty-five minutes. When I find a topic during our discussion that I feel is significant, I notice my language becoming increasingly convoluted and I begin to speak faster, ideas coming in with quicker frequency than my mouth is able to handle. I think I slightly raise my voice too but I realign myself when I see that she is having difficulty with this lack of clarity. I think a part of her knows that this exercise is cathartic, and that she really needn't be there but to prompt me. A part of me knows this too. But she must decide which words from my tirade are the key words. The important phrases that will allow her to ask the next question or raise the next point. I wonder how long it would take her to say the things I've just said. I think we're looking at an hour, at least. I'd like to hear more from her, but my nervousness and desperate desire to tell someone *everything* is stopping me from stopping.

Someone else is going to hypnotise me. She has outsourced someone. I find this vitally amusing, only because it reminds me of work and right now, I feel a thousand miles away from that culture. Every place I've worked since university has pretty much been the same and even at twenty-three, I knew the bullshit that took place. I was just viewing it from a different angle. Now, I guess I'm more absorbed in the bullshit. I've been sucked in, and it's good because I have money, and respect and now I contribute, relish in, and to a certain degree, *control* the bullshit.

His name is Trevor (the only other Trevors I know are Trevor from Trevor and Simon, and Trevor from Eastenders. Was there ever a Trevor in Eastenders? I may have made that up). He bounds through the door with business like confidence, and I am immediately taken back to work mode. This isn't all together a bad thing. I am introduced and taken to the room next door. It is a completely different approach and one that I am quietly appreciating. He's the fixer; she listens and soothes, and then this guy comes in and baffles with the scientific fact that he will be able to apply to each individual case. No more mumbo, or jumbo. He talks for ten minutes about *Linguistic Programming* and how he needs to help me rewire my thought processes and how he is going to help me to achieve this. I am in awe of this man and want to be doing his job. I want to do a lot of people's jobs. Anything I cannot do, I want to do, and anything I can, I dismiss as being insignificant. I am told I can do whatever I want to do, and I want the job of telling someone they can do what they want to do, because that seems rewarding.

He counts me down from ten after saying some words and generally trying to get me into a state of hypnosis. As he gets to four, I'm beginning to worry, not because I am about to be hypnotised but because it's now at three, and I have complete clarity and am nowhere near a state of hypnosis. He gets to one and stops. This is one of the most awkward situations I can remember. He asks me to think about a place where everything is fine, where I am calm and serene. A time before I had any doubts or panic and once I am there, tell him. I desperately trawl through my head for a plausible scenario. I have thought at great length about a time when everything was okay and I can't ever remember one. I had a secure, loving and respectful childhood and there just wasn't a trauma or event that shattered me. I'm just this kind of person. My folks did everything in their powers to provide me with everything I could ever need and for that I am eternally grateful. They couldn't shield me from the outside world though and I as got older, I found more and more of it to be inconsequential and insignificant and unfamiliar. What do I say now? What am I going to say to this man and how the hell am I going to get out of this?

I pick a moment in my early teens when I quit swimming classes. I suddenly remember a story that was told to me that I was good at swimming and then lost a race one week and never went back. That is an analyst's wet dream, surely? I know what it means, everyone knows what it means. But it hasn't scarred me. I don't really like swimming anyway. I wonder whether it was the greatest excuse that could have happened - not winning a race. Just quitting would have made me a quitter but quitting in this manner makes me a perfectionist with emotional problems. Yep, bingo! I'm at the pool.

I'm no longer panicking because I can now work with the guy and tell him what he wants to hear. Never does the ridiculousness of this situation really dawn on me, nor does the fact that I will be paying this man a small fortune at the end of the session concern me. We weave in and out of mixed metaphors and I am eager to wrap this up. I don't think he knows that I'm playing with him, or maybe he does and doesn't care. I wonder whether all his clients do this and that's why I'm not hypnotised. Hey, maybe it's the fault of the first person he hypnotized who claimed to go under because *he* was embarrassed. Perhaps this guy actually can't do it and has never been pulled up on it. This makes me laugh. Shit, I've vocalised my laugh.

He asks me what I'm laughing at – not in an accusing way. He must think it is part of the memory. I say nothing, just that I can hear a boy laughing. God, I'm making myself sick with all the bullshit coming out of my mouth. He counts me back, and "I've entered the room again." He tells me to take a minute to compose myself and then we'll talk. I *do* need a minute to compose myself, because that was stupid. I think the fact that I did that and put so much energy into convincing him says more about me than anything else ever will. And it's the only thing left unsaid.

That was that. I wonder if it's an English thing. Most of the comedies I enjoy relish in the celebration of an awkward situation, and I guess it's funny. Actually, all of the great comedies explore this notion. I've just thought of two great American comedies that also do this so maybe it's not solely an English phenomenon. I am slightly obsessed with England. I'm not really very patriotic and have issues with the flag, *any* flag waving actually. But the times I have been abroad, I miss the place terribly and I enjoy the culture, the weather. Everything about it really. My bugbears lie in some governmental decisions, the tabloid culture, and I think there's a lot wrong with the policies that exist. I also quietly seethe about the intolerance than runs through middle England, and am equally fascinated by our class system. I don't like religion, I don't subscribe to their ideal - let's put it that way. My only thought on the matter is that for a community that claim to be based on love and forgiveness at the core, 'they' do not allow or tolerate any piss taking or derogatory comments, yet allow themselves to dictate what is wrong, that people are going to hell for this and that. I have no time for it, and I view war, religion and politics as three things I try not to think about too much, less vocalise. There are enough people on my side who are far more articulate and keen than I who I enjoy listening to, and there's no need for me to add my two penneth. No need at all. I find myself in petty arguments defending my right not to care. I don't pretend to care. David Seargent never pretended to care.

I think about doing the crossword in *The Telegraph* and winning the pen. *God, I want that pen.* But there are more people who want that pen more than I do so I don't bother. Instead, I check my emails. I only checked them an hour ago and can't imagine there will be much for me. No one at work will email me today, and if they do, I won't open it until tomorrow. I have opened emails before that have had a pop up asking for a receipt to confirm that it has been opened. I immediately click it to allow myself to be able to read the goddamn thing and then immediately realise that I have started a stopwatch and that the sender knows the exact time it has taken me to sort the problem out and reply. So I no longer do this because it kills all my excuses.

I emailed Mary, and I emailed Tom this morning but neither really warrants a reply, so I may or may not get one from them. Tom will be at work and he doesn't use his personal email there. He refuses to give out his work email for some reason. I have lots of spam and some of it is actually rather interesting. Not the content, but I like to research back how it came to me and which company has sold my details to which company. I think I entered a competition last year online and ever since, my junk mail has been almost higher than my normal mail.

Chapter Four

I check my email and there is one from my brother asking for a copy of an album for his friend. He doesn't mention who this friend is, but I guess it's Cathy because he mentioned her last time we spoke, and I'm guessing he mentioned her because he was going to ask me to burn a CD for her.

I am very different from my brother. We're not very close but we see each other often. We do share some similarities even though they're hard to spot. Neither of us can be bothered with fuss and we like to keep things simple. We also share musical tastes. I don't know who he's working for at the moment; he's a Graphic Designer, sometimes freelance, sometimes contracted. I want his job, even if he doesn't. I think he's doing what he wants to do; he's certainly good at it. He designed the pages for the 2003 Norfolk Broads Brochure and that sits proudly in most travel agents in town. Heck, it's probably in every town. He has also worked for a holiday company and designed a sleeve for a local band. I think he's taking on smaller independent jobs now, more credible (in whose eyes I don't know). He's been trying to break into a company for a while and I guess he's growing his portfolio.

I burn the CD and text him to say that I have done so. He texts back and informs me that that is *wkd*. I start to tidy the house. I have a perverse love for tidying, but I have to be in the right mood. Sometimes, I can spend three hours tidying the flat, cleaning, organising. It begins with sweeping away fragments of mess and generally making my living space as it should be, but can quickly morph into an obsession and I am acutely aware of when this change over occurs. It happens when the flat is finished and is at **level one.**

Level one = everything clean, put away and no mess. Level one is when most people stop tidying; it's the base level, if you will. This is the level that the flat is judged by at all times, things are usually one level below this, with a nagging sense of responsibility that things need to be pushed up a gear to crawl back up. It's a perpetual war getting from level two to level one and it can sometimes be a bit of a bore. When it becomes so boring that I get displeasure from the monotony of it, I let it slip to level three. Level three is when, to an outsider (or an insider), it would appear that an event has taken place. As small as a gathering of friends that got a bit out of hand, or a small party that left reasonable detritus. Level three demands immediate action, but if I'm not feeling very happy, level three can linger. My thoughts become a little foggy and I am unable to see what level one will look like. I am unable to relinquish the distant memory of level one and the work involved in getting back there doesn't seem to justify the level itself, because level one is normality and why should I have to work so hard to get to normality?

I will finally snap at this stage and the only thing that will push me into getting to work is the fact that I can take it beyond level one, and create a place so anally clean and ordered, that it will make my mind so crisp and clear, my thoughts so concise, that I will probably go on to achieve something fantastic afterwards. I will go from zero to hero in half a day and I will yearn for friends to come round so I can serve them crisps with dips and guacamole. At the moment, all I see is crisp packets…endless crisp packets (I see three).

I don't like to think about level four.

I decide to get to level A, the one above level one. I actually have to check the calendar today for confirmation of not only the date, but also the day. My mind is naggingly out of synch with the rest of the world and the person I used to be, and it makes me feel unhinged. I check; it's Wednesday. I have become washed up quickly and disgustingly familiar with daytime TV. I have sunk into a new routine with helpless joy and it must be nipped in the bud; after all I need to ring these clients this afternoon and as much as I would like to ignore it and hope it goes away, there are some serious things I need to think about regarding my future and my panic.

I have the tendency to jump from moods and ride an emotional rollercoaster when I crave stability and contentment. I am often very depressed and will retreat into a song, but it doesn't last long. Not like it used to. Then something good will occur and I will reach for it, grab onto it with both hands and sometimes get excitable and inappropriate. An idea will pop into my head that promises to change everything and I will drop all of the sense I have and go off on a tangent, spouting rubbish about how this is going to change *everything.* It often will, but not in a good way. I recognise that these awry thought processes also manifest themselves in my actions and I go from uber mess to uber clean in a day. I will allow this to happen again. I know I will. I can kid myself that I can change but we're all stuck in our ways. The fact that I have been able to quit smoking, albeit temporarily *twice* now, fills me with pride and a sense that I *can* change, but now is not the time. Thank god I managed to quit, it doesn't matter that I'm back on them now because I now have a file in my brain that I can freely access that confirms that I will be alright, if only I had the inclination to be.

I clean for an hour or so and make it above level one by cleaning the oven, inside of the fridge and shampooing the carpet. I don't shampoo the whole carpet, it's a half arsed attempt but it's a step forward so the fact that it's a poor job doesn't come into it. It doesn't, so don't question it.

I'm going to ring my clients in a bit. This fills me with no trepidation as I am in control. I am good with people if I know more than them, and if I have information that they need and I am in control, and I know that I can handle this control. I *excel*. I have all the information they require and I pretty much know what I'm going to say. I also know the questions they are likely to ask and problems that they might be able to identify. I know their names, and the bylaws that are loosely connected to their case. I know what they need to do next and I know what my next step will be once I have finished the call. I know what their next move will be, regardless of what I have told them it should be. I know what they will be thinking as I call and I know what they will be scribbling on a scrap of paper for the attention of their partner as I ask them questions. I can hear that their partner is whispering to them frantically behind their ear; I know what and why they are saying what they are saying, and the significance of it. I know that the phone call will tick off box one in the transfer, and create three more jobs for me to do. Two of which I will not be able to do until the clients have sent me the appropriate declarations. I know when they are likely to send these, and I know what to do and who to contact if they do not provide them by this date. But I know when they will send them from the phone call, even if they don't mention it. I know what to do with these documents, and I know I need to cross reference them with the third thing this initial call has created, which is retrieving a report from another company, with which I will research the day after the first phone call. I will diary all of this on and at a quick glance, I can see the progress of the complete project immediately, and I can see exactly what needs to be done and when. After this phone call, I will send two emails to people who need to be sent emails, and that's it. I don't have to do anything until tomorrow morning. I am being paid for my knack of being able to do this, and never fucking up. My wage goes up, and my job gets easier.

 I ring them, everything is in its right place and I am temporarily someone else, someone good.

The postie comes. I'm amazed with my postie. He is bit of a fool. He's been my postie since I lived here. Now and again, he goes off for a holiday or just off and I am thankful for this as it gives me a break. He's old; sixty?

Maybe he's not; maybe he's a lot younger and is just one of those folks who don't age well. He looks quite haggard, and he stoops when he walks as if his back is giving him trouble. He walks a little like an ape, but that doesn't amuse me. It makes me sad. I can't remember whether he's always walked like an ape, maybe he has. He was off last year for five months and I thought he might have died. I sort of wanted to know what happened to him, but never asked the stream of replacement posties; there was never really an opportunity to. Even when there had been the perfect opportunity and a fresh faced lad knocked on the door for an *Amazon* delivery, I could never be too sure whether this was a *Parceforce* man or if I had taken the care to check the obvious clues, and it *was Royal Mail*, if the guy wanted to tell me, or even if he knew. Even if I wanted to ask him, or if I wanted to know. Someone would tell me if he had died surely? People like telling other people about people who have died don't they? It's something that people like to do. I don't. I don't suppose you do either. Maybe you do.

When I worked assignments for the company prior to this one, I used to be around the flat when he arrived and it frustrated me how long it took him to get to my flat. Sometimes it was midday before I got my post. If it got to 11.00 am, I would be in agony wondering whether I had no post, or if he was just late. The replacements turned up at 9.35 am on the dot, every morning.

He hadn't died, he had been run over. I guess that's as good as dying. I found this out from my neighbours. I didn't speak to my neighbours; don't be daft. I had overheard a conversation between the neighbours and a replacement, and he told her about the accident. She wanted the details, it sounds as if she craved the details. The replacement had no details to tell and spoke matter of factly that he was run over, and that he didn't die and that he would be back soon. There didn't appear to be any emotion or regret in his voice and I deduced that he didn't care. I wondered if I cared. I wondered if I cared enough about anything. I don't even know my neighbour's name, nor do I want to. No wait... I know one of them is called Julie, or something. No, I don't know them. But they have made no effort to know me. Perhaps a polite smile on the stairwell is all I really want out of this relationship. I feel bad for not knowing them and wonder whether I should rectify this but I've been here too long for any contact not to be seen as being weird. Maybe they don't really like other people and could actually be my friends. Maybe they are just like me and are thinking the same thing right now, and they weren't really interested in the postman but just wanted to talk to someone.

Even when I don't see the postman, I know he has delivered my mail. When I get home from work and see the letters on my mat, I know that the last person to touch them was him and I may as well have been here to see him drop them off because I can imagine his awkward monkey frame slotting them through my letterbox.

The times I have been there, at the door when he arrives are more often than coincidence. I can be walking from the lounge to the bathroom at exactly the same time that he walks toward the door. I ought to mention that I have a partial glass door. It is wooden but has three panels three quarters of the way towards the top, meaning I can see who is at the door. I sometimes wonder whether I should change this and get a solid door with a peephole. Or just a solid door. Hell, maybe I should get a chain so I can ask for people's official card before I let them in. Then if a murdering scumbag came to the door, I could run from his presence with his hand grappling and grabbing through the gap. He would then kick the door down, and I would grab a knife, and run around the flat, and probably fall on the knife and die horribly. The guy would kick the door down and panic and flee and I would be on the news for a bit.

My funeral would be arranged, my people would grieve, my loved ones take my possessions and hold them close to their heart and within a couple of months (that's not big headed) things would be almost back to normal and that would be it.

This finality saddens me. If I had kids, I'd live on through them. But I don't have kids. How could I look after a child when I can barely look after myself?

Postie does his thing. I play a game with postie. He manages to make a joke about something related to the mail, or something between us every time we meet and this is intriguing and awe inspiring. I attempt to give him less and less ammo or opportunity for this to take place and the more I try, the easier it appears for him to find something to joke about. I think he's winning 34 – 7 currently. I've kinda given up trying to win, but I always try to claw *some* points back. I *haven't* given up counting though.

I can see him, and he's clocked me. Bring it on postie! I slowly walk towards the door and quickly unlock it before he has the chance to see me fiddling with the key, to which he would say 'You locked me out ya bugger! I know I sometimes bring bills but still.....' Then it would be 35 to him, and that's just embarrassing for everyone involved. I open the door and nod to him and he stops, just awkwardly out of reach and hands me my mail, having to bend over and reach his hand out so straight and stretched, I think that this is a skit, and that he has immediately tried to secure an extra point by just acting mad. It's reminiscent of someone giving a king a document or being knighted. God, is he *bowing* to me? He's not bowing. I think his back is just doing his head in. Either that or he's just being weird. Being weird won't get him an extra point. If anything being weird means points are deducted.

He notes I'm still in my dressing gown and says:

"Alright for some! Good night was it?" Shit. He's won. Oh well.

"Something like that, cheers then."

I have some bills. These immediately go into my incoming tray. I nicked one from work and it sorts me out nicely. I think I'll be treating my home life more like work, especially now I may be working more from home. I will have to separate my home work and my work home though. Not sure how to do that yet but there are websites on that. I don't have much else - a postcard from my parents, which is warm and funny. I also have a letter from a company I once bought something from an age ago and they are informing me that I did this, and I haven't bought anything since, and that this maybe is a mistake because they sell the following things.......

I bin this.

I take it out of the bin and put it in a cardboard box that I leave by the bin. I could recycle that. The decision rather than the action makes me feel humane and progressive and responsible. Let's gloss over the hundreds of pamphlets I have already thrown out in the regular trash and just focus on this glimpse of global sacrifice. Hell, I may even internally curse the waste that this letter and accompanying brochure created and think about the rainforests, or something. I do, and I feel superior to people like the person I was five minutes ago who abandonly threw it in the bin.

I don't care for the plight of the rainforests. I'm also not too bothered about global warming or the melting icecaps. Charities rile me and people who collect for charities I try not to think about because I don't like them or how they make me feel. I have given to two charities before in an official capacity. And I gave a guy in a motorway service station some cash last month, and he gave me a sticker. I wore it for a bit, it was a very commendable charity and I liked the guy who was collecting. I was taken aback that those two things had happened, and that I had some change so I acted upon this set and dug deep. Ha, look at all the other people without badges. Okay, it's a sticker.

I make myself my third coffee and put my feet up and watch telly. It's okay, it's only a break. This isn't what I *do* now. I do just that too, I actually put my feet up on the coffee table in front of me. There's a makeover programme on the box and I am morbidly fascinated with it for five minutes. The team have just bought lots of lime paint, which they are going to use to transform Brenda's kitchen. Brenda isn't happy and I don't think a lime kitchen will make her feel any better. The team is frantically running round the house because they only have twenty minutes to complete the house. They are working on three rooms and they have a team of twelve people who are all hurried. They only have nineteen minutes and they remind each other of this constantly. I feel sorry for Brenda and I turn to the news.

Aaaaahhhh! Information.

The first news story is about lonely farmers and milk cartons in some area that's not here. Farmers who are looking for love will have their pictures plastered onto the side of milk cartons in an attempt to match them up with a suitable....farm hand? I don't know, it all seems like rather a good idea but smacks of desperation to me. I wonder if it really does or I'm just thinking it does because that's how I think. They show an example of this project and I lose interest because it's not funny or sad anymore. The next item is a weather warning. Apparently, we're having very strange weather for this time of year. The time between Christmas and Easter always has weird weather. It would be weirder for it to be normal. But we always have weird weather so *that's* normal, surely? I wonder who is dictating what is normal, and then I realise that they have stats and numbers and files at their disposal so they probably *do* know what they're talking about. People like talking about things that are out of the ordinary anyway so it may just be a big conversation starter conspiracy.

I worry and I am amused by the notion that one day, there could be no more news. Nothing. In sync, everybody just decided to take a day off from doing anything news worthy. Nothing *weird* happened. The news came on, and the casters played cards, or made one of those question answer things with paper on their hands like gloves. Or they tell a story, or talk about themselves for a bit, where they are from and what they fear, who they want to meet. I want it to be uninteresting and awkward and heart warming and I crave for it daily. I also crave for news and secretly belittle those who do not deliver it with concise English, or who make an endearing mistake. I don't find it endearing and am annoyed by how unprofessional they are being. I wonder if I should watch Brenda, I wonder how she's getting on. There's only four minutes until her house will be slightly different and she will be slightly happier.

I don't switch back; I'll only get sucked in. I finish my coffee and get ready to go out. I've got no particular place to go but I noticed the glass box is full and so I'll pop down to the recycling bank in town. This isn't really anything to do with recycling anymore, my bin men are good and I don't want to take the piss. Actually, I'm just concerned that they'll see me one day and pick me out as the person who doesn't recycle, as glass is *obvious* in bins.

More importantly though, it gives me the opportunity to smash some glass. Who in their right mind wouldn't jump at that? Weird people, that's who. I need some groceries, nothing I really need but I could do with a few bits and bobs. I may have a look around town too. I won't go into Norwich today, just stay local.

As I drive through town after my brief glass smash, I am feeling awfully numb. I'm no longer stressed out and my thoughts are under my control again but there is an underlying void within me that I can't shake off. As I pull up to the pay and display in the centre, the numb feeling takes effect mainly on the face and I become aware of all of the tiny little muscles around my jaw. I start to lick my lips to promote some blood flow. I don't know if that's what I need to promote, or if the numb feeling is of too *much* blood. I don't think that's right, but I can feel my blood pumping around my face, at least that's what it feels like. I wonder what would happen now if I had to speak to anyone because I don't think I could, to my satisfaction. I sit in my car for a bit, sipping on the juice I bought last week. I know that it's probably not a good idea, and there's a shop opposite the car park that would have fresh juice. Juice that's not expensive, and not small. The threat of tummy problems later on in the day does not stop me from sipping. I ask myself why I'm in town and try and figure out if I could just leave and go back home. I don't feel like shit but maybe I'm just trying to fill my time doing something productive, and being out of the flat and in town is more compelling and more normal. I make a decision to go back, and tell myself that this is okay and I haven't failed anything because I am doing this. I bet people make decisions like this all the time.

My car needs a wash; I shall do that.

Washing the car is cathartic. I'm outside in the fresh air, I'm cleaning and I get a sense of pride running around the neighbourhood in a clean car - first impressions and all that. It used to be difficult for me to wash my car but our building has got a private forecourt with an electronic lock, and during the day most people are out. Our block is mainly made up of people in their mid thirties, with a few retired folk on the top floor. We've got nice shiny lifts, everyone keeps themselves to themselves and the halls and communal area (the landing) are always clean. I pay a service charge to my landlord. I'm hoping he won't be my landlord for much longer. I want to buy this place from him. Then I can sell it. I'd like to get on the property ladder; I will soon. I convince myself that the reason I haven't is because of house prices and because I am unable to confirm whether my job will maintain its current status. The market hasn't stopped growing, and I'm still working for the company. I'll get on it soon. I make enough money to be able to move into a decent place with a bit of number crunching. I may even enjoy the organisation. Hell, who am I kidding, I'd love the organisation. But I'm not in the mood thanks. And if I'm not in the mood, it's not going to happen because I only have myself to answer to.

Maybe I should get a cat.

I used to have a list.

I had a list of things I wanted to achieve before I hit thirty. I don't have a list of things to do before forty, because I can't imagine ever being forty. It doesn't really suit me. I'll be twenty-five always. I have a very childish sense of humour and find the puerile and inane funny. I find cruel humour and the noises the human body makes painfully funny and have never really grown up. My humour is basic in this sense, and I guess a little surreal in every other sense. I like to be in the company of people who share this mix, and spend most of my time in the company of people who do not.

    Things to do before you die. Quickly do them so you can die. This no longer concerns me, as it has nothing to do with me anymore. I have my own set of rules and morals now and I try not to be influenced by these lists. Television is very persuasive though and I sometimes find myself thinking about them and why I don't want to be involved or yearn for these experiences.

I get back and ring the doctor. An instant decision that I hope sparks off some more instant decisions. I know and trust my doctor and I quite like going to the surgery. This is only because I'm so familiar with it and it has **decorum.** I ring the number from my list of numbers. My book took me a year to compile and it has misc. chapters, colour coding and levels of relevance and importance and just having it near me makes me feel secure. The only thing I'm not too sure about is the fact that I have put people's first names as the frame of reference relating to each letter of the alphabet. Not the surname. This is not how it's meant to be and I spent a while worrying about this. I don't worry about this anymore. I ring the number and it's been changed. I know this because a computerised lady tells me so, and then gives me the right number. I scrawl the number down on a post it note; I shall rectify the mistake in my book at a later date. A date when I've a ruler and markers to hand. Also at a time when I'm feeling neat, and calm. The phone call itself is making me a little uptight.

I ring the correct number and get straight through. I ask if I can make an appointment to see, "Well, anyone." as soon as I can. They ask me who my doctor is and I tell them. They tell me that he has no free appointments today but I am welcome to come in for the open surgery after five o clock. She then informs me that another doctor is available. I say that it's okay, and I'll try again tomorrow. Whether there was something in my voice or whether she just had a change of heart, as I say this, she attempts to find a better solution.

"Mmmm, Doctor Brett is out of the surgery after five o'clock so you wouldn't be able to see him in open surgery. I think Dr. Gallows will be here, he's very good. The only other thing I can suggest..." There is a pause. "Perhaps if you come in at four thirty, you will be able to see Dr. Brett before he goes. Is that okay?"

"That's great, thank you for that."

I'm genuinely surprised at this, I can't work out what happened there, but I don't want to start thinking about that. Maybe I'll save that for something to say to my brother, then he can come up with suggestions about what it may mean. He likes coming up with suggestions for what things may or may not mean.

Much as I didn't prepare myself for making the call, and that went well, I make no preparations for seeing Dr. Brett and don't even think about it until four o'clock, when I have to get ready. I'm going to be getting into a nice shiny new car! Doctor Brett has known me since I wasn't even born. He was my mother's doctor and has a deep Irish voice. I don't know how old he is, but I think he's older than I think he is, even though I don't think he is any age. He was made a senior partner two years ago and he looks like he enjoys life. He does all the things I wish I wanted to do like regularly play golf, go out more than four times a year to a restaurant, go to the football, and be a doctor. I sometimes think he hates me, or at the very least, tires of seeing me. And I sometimes believe that he is not happy with his life and feels put down by something or someone. Maybe he has had to fight all of his life. There's something about him that suggests this; I can't quite put my finger on it but I can't shake the fascination either. He may be a maverick and he may be unconventional. This is not to say that he's not entirely professional. He is a very serious sincere intelligent man and has decorum. Yet it looks as if someone with a lighter view on the world has always stood in his way and he tires of this, and sometimes I wonder whether he has given up his latest fight with bureaucracy, or governing bodies, or whatever.

When I arrive at the doctors, I attempt to enter their car park. As I zoom around the corner, passing two ample spaces on the way, I have twenty minutes before my appointment. I left far too early and have arrived far too early. This almost stresses me as much as it would have done had I been seven minutes late. I instantly regret not parking in those spaces and I immediately feel the wrath of my bad decision as I zoom faster round the block only to find that the two spaces are now full. As if to add insult to injury, I am held up by a car attempting to reverse into one of the spaces. It would take me forty five seconds to walk from either one of the spaces (one: forty five seconds, the other: forty eight seconds). However, the car park would mean I had a three second walk. It's a tiny parking area with room for four cars, with an additional two if they went the other way, so as the park, should it become full, would look like this:

= [
= [

The lines are not to scale, and the four cars are tiny little cars, and the two cars let's say are vans. The car park is full. I knew it would be because the walk in surgery is the most popular time of the day. It's full of people who couldn't make a proper appointment, the losers. And there is a sense of mild defeat in the air when I finally get there, now just about on time. A queue of people who gave their name to be added on to the lucky list and who are getting there names crossed off and putting on another list as they arrive. Hang on??!

You ring up and put your name on the list for the walk in surgery, and then your name is transferred to another list depending on the how early you turn up. I find this ridiculous and hilarious, but as it doesn't affect me, I do not feel angry, or lucky. I enjoy watching other people's reactions who have turned up thirty minutes early, having rang early - assuming that this means, you know, they will be seen early. Only to find that someone who rang up after lunch had come in an hour early, and is at the top of the list. I watch as bemusement and confusion flicker momentarily on their brow and they look like they might cry for a nano second. A look of disappointment and confessed weakness as they learn that the world is not a very welcoming place sometimes and that unfortunate things can happen even when you do the right thing sometimes. The force against you is reasonable.

I tire of being amazed at this and I tire of the queue. People begin to tut behind me, which enrages me. Someone sneezes and I think: *faker.* He's practicing. Someone coughs and I think: Jesus! He's not. I get to the front of the queue and I give my name. She is the lady I spoke to on the phone and I am thankful of this and she knows the score and tells me that if I wait in the second floor waiting room (just up the stairs first on your left, opposite the bathroom), my name will be called when my doctor becomes available. I feel special because she has to break her flow of repetition for me, and it makes me feel important. The feeling I get when I am behind someone with loads of shopping at a supermarket and for whatever reason, a man ushers me to pay my small grasp of groceries at the information desk. I have been chosen and I am special, so **fuck off.** Maybe not fuck off.

The waiting room is minuscule and is reminiscent of a private carriage in a train. I pick the seat closest to a corner but there is nowhere here I really feel safe. This seating arrangement has no clause for me; the arrangement does not cater for my whims and social inadequacies *at all.* Even when it is empty like this. I wonder why the downstairs waiting room is full and this is not and then I remember that this is Brett's private waiting room. Well, he shares it with another doctor but I know nothing of him, nor have I ever seen him, nor is he a partner so I choose to ignore his existence. I stop wondering why I am here and they are there and glance down to my left where I see a small corner table with a dead plant and a hastily thrown pile of old magazines. *Country living* is there, which depresses me. There are no pamphlets or leaflets, as they are all downstairs. The notice board is full of information though and I peruse this with mock interest in case someone else enters and I have to deflect their human need to acknowledge my existence. Downstairs, I could be a chair or a plate or a cup. I am a part of the make up of the room and there is no need for me to pretend that *I* exist, let alone the people around me.

Here, it is different.

Here, I will become instantly involved in whatever the other person is going through and will be forced to adapt like a wild animal in a zoo. I pray to God that no one else will walk in. I don't believe in God. If someone walks in, I *definitely* don't believe in God. There's a poster that reminds me that I need to stop smoking, or I will die. And there's a poster that if I were a woman who was being beaten by her husband, identifies the possible emotions that I may be going through and suggests that these are not valid reasons for not calling the number that it then gives. Endless numbers and facts (*alarming* facts) are sprawled over a small area on the wall. None of them apply to me and this saddens me. To my left, I pick up a celebrity rag and flick through the pages with weak disapproval and hostile embarrassment. I look at the pictures of vacuous celebrities with too much money and not enough column inches and am glad that none of this applies to me, or interests me. *This* interests me.

Doctor Brett pokes his head round the door, states my name and walks up to his room with me in tow. He walks in a very matter of fact way and I can tell that he is in a hurry and has more pressing things on his mind. This immediately panics me as I am not going to ask him for some antibiotics or show him a sore throat that just won't go away. I know he has my notes though and so he will be able to refer me back to some course of action, whilst looking forward to something new and exciting that *Glaxo* or some board may have discovered. A technique that isn't embarrassing or faintly ridiculous, or that *does* work. I stutter and splutter my way through a list of things that have happened over the last weeks and how I am now feeling numb and uninterested, heck maybe even a little down. I make care that I don't mention any key words or talk in clichés. He immediately begins tapping on his computer and I can see the screen. He writes LOW MOOD, and then ticks a box. He informs me that he doesn't want to go down the medicinal route right now and refers me to someone to talk to. He really doesn't have time for this and I feel bad for him that maybe he feels bad for not having enough time for me. Even if he did have all the time in the world though, this probably would be the same process. I must stop thinking that doctors are wizards. He books me an appointment with another doctor, which is in three weeks, and we have a little chat about how I am in general. The lights are off now and the audience have gone home so I'm a little more honest and reflective with him. This isn't my appointment anymore and we can freestyle it (man).

He's a lovely guy, but he's not a wizard.

I remember the feeling I had as a teenager after coming out of that same surgery. I had built up and put off going for such a long time, I had assured myself that when it was over, so would my problems be. The massive disappointment and disillusionment that this actually wasn't the case, and all I had achieved was to get a professional body to confirm my worst fears, and to then shrug as to what the solution may be. It gave me justification to worry about every worry I have ever worried about, and this was a worry. It was a catalyst of the worst kind as it came from the thing that was meant to save me. Everyone was shocked at the rate of my decline after that day. I wasn't as I was beginning to become unshockable.

This time it is different. I have progressed. I diary the next appointment in and get on with my life. I have no nagging suspicion that this appointment will not be of any use and I am not cynical. My work has helped me put perspective on things - diarying things on and searching for solutions, but in their right allocated time. There is a time and a place for everything and now is neither the time nor place for worrying about the next step, because the next step is far away and I am prepared.

I drive home and stop off at the local supermarket, one that I have only been to a handful of times before, but one I feel compelled to visit now. I am stopping here because it's convenient and it's actually the nearest shop to my flat. It's not however my market of choice and I don't aspire to be anything when I'm in this shop. I know this even though they are just serving food and household goods and not a lifestyle. I don't empathise with the other shoppers because the image of the store is not in keeping with the image I have of myself. It's not my brand. I stop here because I have nothing to buy and it doesn't matter that I don't know the layout because I am just perusing, window-shopping if you like. I know that I want something for tea - a treat. Something *ready made* by somebody somewhere that will take all the effort (and enjoyment) I get out of searching and utilising scraps and ends of things and leftovers I find in the fridge and freezer. Most importantly, it is a treat and I don't need it.

I spend twenty minutes in this shop, most of which is spent finding things that are wrong about the own label products and picking up on possible traits of fellow shoppers that may clash with my own. I peruse the cakes and note that these cakes are different from the cakes in the other shops that I frequent regularly. The same for the bread, and the same for the selection of yoghurts. I spy the ready meals section, and find it amusing that they come in standards. Standards of quality and lifestyle, ranging from 99p to £4.99. I enjoy being in this section as different classes and lifestyles come and pick up the meals and make an informed decision about which would suit them best. Some immediately go to their designated section and pick up a meal with ease and familiarity like it's second nature to them, and the notion of changing an alien concept. Some skit between basic and normal, looking longingly and disgustingly at the special menu section. Many pull a wild card that completely contradicts the meal they *should* be buying. I *love* all this shit.

I stand by the one up from basic range. This to me is normal, it's not special and it's not simple. The food is good; I've tasted it many times. I have treated myself to the special range as an experiment and decided that the price increase doesn't warrant the actual difference. Most of the time the difference is marked, but not actually better. When I discover this, and have bought an item for an over inflated price that isn't actually very nice, I have not lost. I feel good, perhaps better than I would if the meal had been nice. Because I am right, and I win. The pretentious nature of the product has been foiled. By me.

I'm not in my normal shop, and this isn't a normal day so I decide not to make a normal decision and go to the special menu selection and pick up a fish pie. It certainly looks special, and I will certainly feel special when I go to pay for it. Unless of course, the person in front of me has a bottle of wine, a whole salmon and fresh prawns from the counter, some King Edward spuds and some garlic. If that happens, I will feel *terrible.*

There's no one in front of me with those things so I still feel special. The check out girl is vitally younger than me and I flirt with her. I leave my gaze on her just a little too long and stagger my smile, making a distinct effort to react slowly and meaningfully when she asks me a question. I take my time rearranging my wallet as she does her bleep and I kinda wish I had done a lot of shopping so I can savour the feeling, hell the *fun* I'm having with this girl. I don't worry about whether she thinks I'm a fool or whether she may be enjoying this banter, as I know I'm not a fool and I know she is. I'm good at flirting with people I am able to flirt with. Someone even told me I was sexy once. My mate's girlfriend had been to a party that I also went to and I wasn't aware of who she was. I don't remember speaking to her and generally recall that I had a bad time, and that no one really cared for my presence. I guess I must have made some kind of lasting impression with her though, and my mate told me of this the next day. I'm certainly no threat, and that's why he felt comfortable that his missus had shown an interest. It catapulted my confidence and I began to enjoy being around her because she thought I was sexy.

I'd even taunt my friend a little making subtle innuendos (is there such a thing?) and suggested that she may one day decide that she wants to sleep with me and this is a distinct possibility that both of us must prepare ourselves for so when the awkward moment arises, we can act with decorum and tact. It's of course bullshit, but it made everyone feel as if they were living in a soap opera for a bit. I wonder if we should ring Jeremy Kyle.

The fish pie was *adequate* - ha! I win.

My brother would always choose the special selection, and I am jealous of his simple logic. He has money, he want the best, that's it. I used to belittle his furnishings and gadgets and food because it seemed awfully pretentious and unnecessary to me. It took me a while to realise that I was using my ethics to mask my massive jealousy, and now I have money, I relish in the disgustingly decadent.

I still hunt for a bargain but I now have a more definable set of pigeon holes in which I can place what is good or bad value. I always buy expensive milk, and I never buy cheap bread. I always buy very cheap yoghurts and value cleaning products. It has taken me ten years, but at any given moment, somebody could name a product, an item and I would be able to tell them which brand and which price I would be willing to pay. I can say this with immediate confidence, and I *love* it. My only pitfall is the intensity to which I follow these rules. I therefore will have difficulty if I enter someone else's domain and they are using a brand or item from either wrong end of the spectrum. If it's shit, I internalise my complaints that they should just fucking dig a little deeper and stop economising, they're proper people now! They have money, **Jesus Christ.** If the product is too expensive and I hold the knowledge/opinion that the product two tiers down in the pecking order is of the same if not better quality, I belittle their pretension and ignorance. *The fools.*

Tom stopped me from belittling their ignorance during a drinking session one weekend. I do drink sometimes. He did this by dramatically exposing *my* ignorance. He asked me what was so bad about my brother owning a kettle that cost over £80 (it cost £85). I spluttered and guffawed at the fact that I had to justify my argument that a kettle worth more than £80 is a problem, and looked at him with contempt. He then looked at me as if I was a dick so I rewound my brain and repeated his line of questioning to myself in my head, allowing the words to permeate my brain this time and wondering whether I *was* a dick.

I spluttered that it is vulgar and unnecessary. Tom brought it to my attention that we use the kettle all day; it's one of the most used items in the house. People converge around the kettle, and it's like an old friend. It's the first thing many of us see in the morning, and if not, it will mark its presence soon. We think nothing of going out and spending £80 on a nice meal for four (three?) in a restaurant, and where does that go? Down the toilet. I shiver at Tom's vulgarity, it sits uneasily next to the valid point he is making, but breaks the seriousness of his point. He is utterly convincing me.

Because I hate my fucking kettle. It works fine, and probably will for years. But my brother has got a chrome stainless steel monster of a kettle that beeps, and has digital displays, and a bar across the top changes from blue to pink when it has boiled. There is a progress bar that allows you to see how the water is doing, it has an inbuilt filter to eliminate hard drinking water and lime scale. This thing cleans itself for god's sake.

Finally, and most important of all, It looks sexy and progressive and impressive. I want it and have secretly wanted it for a year.

So maybe Tom is right. I don't mind being wrong, I quite like it. I especially don't mind being wrong in the company of someone I like and trust, and someone who I rarely, if ever go into battle with because they share my own ethos and outlook. A clash that brings up a possible rebellion in this alliance fills me with wonder and I enjoy having to rethink and rewire my preconceptions. I never tell them this, and usually just stay silent. I think the people around me know me well enough by now for them to appreciate that this, in a way is conceding defeat.

My only concern, before I go to *Argos* and order this bad boy, is that by having great things around you all the time, these become the norm and there's nothing to look forward to or compare yourself or your belongings with. I worry that others will see my stuff as pretentious and I worry that I actually do, despite Tom's comments. I am concerned that I don't know what I think and I'm just a packaged set of one liners and borrowed opinions and guffaws and I'm not really a proper person. This is over a kettle.

Maybe if I get this, I'll get bored with it and there will be no better kettle to buy or aspire to. Tom is trying to take away my aspirations goddamnit. He is trying to identify my aspirations and complete them, and this is not fair. He should know that this is not fair, and that my kettle comment was a sound bite and did not need analysis. Or a solution.

I can't think of anything worse than a solution.

Chapter Five

I rarely go round to Tom's house. He lives five miles away from me and so we don't see each other with the ease in which we once did. Meetings are fun, frequent and enjoyable. Hell - maybe even more frequent and enjoyable than when we were children but arrangements and planning are more necessary. Thankfully, the text message has made this necessity relatively pain free. He lives in a complex of new houses on the new *Bovis* estate across town. He bought a starter home three years ago with his girlfriend, and it's very nice. It's a little boxy, and the security of the world that he now inhabits scares me and comforts me in equal measure.

I don't dislike Tom's other half, and I don't think she dislikes me. She shares his humour, or at least finds his humour amusing so I feel I have a connection with her. I am like family with her and although there is decorum, there is a nagging sense of acceptance and slight resentment. I try not to get involved with his home life as they have a set routine and like to stick to it. I am acutely aware of when I shouldn't be round there, and it usually is when I am. Thankfully, she has work friends that Tom doesn't associate with. No doubt he would be able to charm them and flirt but he maintains that they need their own lives. I think that just as she has her world, I am Tom's other world. She views me as this and over time, I have become more of a slogan, or representation to her. I signify her other half's other world and I sink into my own when I am with her, as neither of us are really talking to each other. I sometimes think that we could talk for hours were we given the opportunity, I have stories about his childhood I would happily reminisce, and she must have stuff she wants to say. But we don't, and I appreciate this.

The times I do go round Toms, Harriet is usually out and we sometimes share a spliff and act like naughty school kids, goofing around and reliving our youth before she comes back from wherever it was that she went. I like going round there because there is a beginning and an end to the evening and I can chose to a certain extent when these things will occur. Tom's house is ace too. He's obsessed with gadgets, but not those that I have. He buys big, expensive products that actually make his life easier and more desirable. To him, and to me. I don't know how he can afford to do this. I know financially how he can - he has a good job. I don't know he gets away with it though.

Our chat flows seamlessly and even any awkwardness is very quickly identified, commented on, taken the piss out of, kicked the shit out of generally. I have different zones in my head for different people and the conversations that may or may not occur. These are well defined and easily accessible (even when stoned), so there's no problem. I don't have to access any files with Tom though and it gives my brain a welcome rest. Also, he was the first person that talked to me at school, and has never said a bad word about me to anyone, and I don't think he ever would. The same naturally is true for myself.

Today I go round to Tom's and we share a sneaky spliff outside before lunchtime. I have brought round bread and fancy dried looking ham from *Marks and Spencers*, and we watch a bit of comedy on the television. I have no plans for the day and neither does Tom. Tom knows the kind of things I don't like to do, and I appreciate that some of things I don't enjoy may be of interest to him. He knows this. He doesn't have much of the spliff and I convince myself that it's okay to have most of it as I am no longer smoking cigarettes and it's my day off today. I've *paid* for *this* day. Of the two-week period in which I currently find myself in, half of the designated time is open for abuse surely? I have already convinced myself of this but momentarily have to remind myself that it is okay. Tom suggests going to a shopping village and getting some lunch. I concur that this is a great idea. I am slightly stoned and this will enable the village to be a little more bearable. If I have any more though, it will catapult the village into a living hell. There's such a fine line and I am thankful that I am with someone who will curb my enthusiasm for soft drugs.

I leave the food at his house. I really had no intention of eating it there anyway. It was a mere gesture and it felt more appropriate than bringing cakes or chocolate, somehow. I like the idea of Tom and his missus enjoying the bread with their dinner, or she takes a piece of the wrinkled ham with her to her place of work (wherever that is) and momentarily thinks about me. I wonder whether I do this with increased frequency so I can become a part of these moments. More often than not, I worry that this is becoming awkward but I don't think it is. Everyone is appreciative of ham and bread, right?

"Are we going to have a nice time Tom?"

"We're going to attempt to George. Or it may be a living hell. Either way...." He shrugs, and titters.

We get in his car and he turns all of his gadgets on. I feel like I'm driving with my Dad. His car has the unmistakable new car smell and the beeps and clicks make me feel secure and comfortable. I'm somewhere where nobody can hurt me.

"What a shit car." I ridiculously quip.

"Why thank you kind sir." He plays dubiously with his *tomtom* and I look on with awe. "Right, South Shields Shopping Village.... come on son, do me proud."

"Are they...good?" I point disgustedly at the tomtom.

"I'm going to have to pretend I didn't hear that. Look at it; it's a thing of beauty. And you haven't got one, because you are living in the past." There is a sense of cheekiness and banter in the air that I am relishing and never want it to end.

"*You* are living in a dream world. You've got sucked in mate. You're a puppet."

"I am, and I fucking love it."

"I know you do Tom, I know...."

We both laugh (a little), working out who won that little round.

Tom drives like a madman, furiously stopping and starting, revving and complaining. In many ways, he mirrors my own style, and I can decipher whether he's better than me. He has a better car, a much better car and I'm sure some of the moves he's pulling are down to

this fact. He exhorts pockets of self-confidence and antagonism when he double declutches and I am dutifully impressed and insanely jealous.
"No need, no need." I fake a serious irritated look.
"You love it, bitch." comes his retort.
"I didn't know you could do that." I say.
"What?"
"Double declutching."
"What are you talking about?"
"Double declutching."
He looks confused. "What's double declutching?"

A driving procedure used for vehicles with an unsynchronized manual transmission.

Before the introduction of synchronizers (1920s) and helical cut gears, double declutching was a technique required to prevent damage to an automobile's gear system. Due to the difficulty involved in learning the technique, and because of the advent of synchronized gearing systems it has largely fallen into disuse. However, drivers of large trucks still use double clutching, as those vehicles are usually equipped with the older, more efficient, and more durable unsynchronized gearboxes.
The purpose of the double-clutch is to match the speed of the rotating parts of the gearbox for the gear you wish to select to the speed of the input shaft being driven by the engine. Once the speeds are matched, the gear will engage smoothly. If the speeds are not matched, the dog teeth on the collar will "crash" or grate as they attempt to fit into the holes on the desired

gear. A modern synchromesh gearbox accomplishes this synchronization automatically.

When shifting up on a non-synchroniser equipped vehicle, the clutch pedal is pressed, the throttle is released, and gearbox shifted into neutral. The clutch pedal is then released. As the engine idles with no load, the rpms will decrease until they are at a level suitable for shifting into the next gear. The driver then depresses the clutch again and shifts into the next gear. The whole maneuver can, with practice, take no more than a fraction of a second, and the result is a very smooth gear change.

However, in order to downshift, engine revs must be increased while the gearbox is in neutral and the clutch is engaged. This requires the driver to shift into neutral, release the clutch pedal, apply throttle to bring the revs up to a suitable speed, depress the clutch again, and finally shift into gear. This operation can be very difficult to master, as it requires the driver to gauge the speed of the vehicle accurately and is often conducted as cars in front slow down.

"Must you *Google* everything?"

It must have been annoying. I read the whole definition from my phone. It's still a magical thrill for me being able to Google things on the move and in a conversation because I now know everything and have access to everything, all the time. I no longer have conversations with people about that thing, you know, oh god, what was it called. Because I Google it. Arguments finish quickly and abruptly as I Google the question and immediately am told of the winner of the argument, or at least of the person with the better memory. My Google still beats their memory, even if they won the argument. I miss those times.

"Put Google away. You can't compete with my gadgets George. It's futile, I have more things that beep than you do, and you must accept this."

I put it away from my sweaty clutch. "You know what double declutching is."

"I do know, yeah but I didn't realise I was doing it."

"That's probably why you can do it. I can't. It's a skill mate."

"I have a skill?"

"It would appear so - TOM!" I shout and drop my phone quickly turning to Tom with my hands outstretched to control the steering, one encroaching on the handbrake. Tom immediately swings his vision to the centre of the windscreen and spies a lady crossing the road near the vets. He has already started to slow down but needs to tap the brakes a little fiercely and dodge with artistic merit this frame that is hobbling over the road. She has made the majority of the distance, and Tom is driving too fast but it's not over yet.

"Oh, you fucking bitch!" Tom has to squeeze the brakes harder than I IMAGINED AND I AM THRUST FORWARD, THE STRAP HOLDING ME IN YEARNING TO SNAP.

It's fine, and we're okay, the car's okay and the lady is fine. We mount the curb though and the car spins a little as it stops. There was no one behind, and few people seemed to see this. Tom starts up immediately and swings back into the flow of traffic so as not to give the event any more credence than it deserves.

"You okay?" he asks.

"Yeah man, I want to listen to some music."

He switches his mp3 on and connects the adaptor, pressing shuffle. It's the exact song that I want to listen to right now, and it's a perfect come down for the small hiccup that just happened. As it grows into the chorus, I turn it up and watch people for a bit before I start talking to Tom again. I am not pissed off with him, but I'd like him to think that maybe I am.

Our journey takes one hour and twenty minutes during which time we stop twice. Once for petrol, and once to buy cigarettes because we forgot to buy them when we bought petrol. Tom smokes whilst he drives and flicks the ash carelessly out of the small gap in his window. Some of it falls into his lap and he begrudgingly immediately brushes his groin and leaves a grey streak. I wonder if I need to get anything from the village and decide that a new pair of shoes may be an idea. I look down at my shoes.

"New shoes?" Tom enquires.

"These? I've had these for five years Tom."

"I know."

"Oh." I pretend to look upset.

"They're shit." with which I laugh.

"You say the nicest things Tom. Yeah maybe I should get some new ones. Is *Clarks* still there?"

"Yeah I think so. I might get some trainers, these are looking a bit shabby."

They're not. They look great.

The village is discerningly busy for a weekday and we immediately go for a coffee. It's an excuse for me to have a cigarette because I have decided that I am allowed to have one with a coffee outside of the house, and a beer or with wine, anywhere (and on holiday). That's two boxes ticked right there and so I spark up without any reluctance (outside on a rickety stool linked to a coffee chain). Tom is getting the drinks in because he's good at that. I watch for signs of banter from outside the coffee house and am not disappointed as he laughs with the cashier. It's rarely about something that is funny, but he has the vital knack of turning awkward situations into socially acceptable 'funny' exchanges.

I have *Jon Brion* on my mp3 and it makes this situation very surreal and warming. I am still slightly stoned and the tones of the song transport me into another world and I feel as if I'm watching the village on television, or I am in the scene of a film. A rather rubbish film. **A film just about thoughts, with no discernable plot, starring me.**

"When are you back at work Tom?'

"Tuesday I think. I don't know, we'll see how it goes. I have some arsehole clients at the moment and they're really fucking me about."

"What's up?"

"Um...they're dicks. They want me to adhere closer to the script, whatever that means. They rang me as they saw my work for North Star last year."

"Oh that holiday brochure? I remember that. That was good."

"It was alright yeah, I was hoping it would have provoked more work than it has done but I haven't really been proactive in marketing since Tina left. They want the same thing that happened to Blinders to happen to them, even though they sell pipes and, god, fittings for things and…things."

"Sounds like bullshit. Just do the work and bill them and move on."

Tom laughs; "Oh yeah, okay. It's like I've suddenly had an epiphany, you're so wise…"

I puff on my cigarette; "I'm only interested if we're talking about me and my problems."

"Oh look, a sale on a teapot world!" Tom slyly grins at me and we decide to traipse around the shops and then go for a pint with lunch a bit later on.

Shops.

We get to the pub just after three and gingerly enter a side door, with all the welcoming qualities of something that isn't very welcoming. The meal happens. It's nice. There are other people there. They're different from us, but they probably share some qualities that we have. It's a pub, what more do you want from me?

<Tom plays with his scampi.>

TOM: What are you going to do?

GEORGE: What do you mean? Regarding what?

TOM: Your job. Are there any openings?

GEORGE: No, oh I don't know. I've been offered a position in the events managements team and it's a little more work and a load more money.

TOM: Not interested?

GEORGE: Not really. You're lucky man, you get to, well I don't know, you appear to have a lot of room to do what you want in your job.

TOM: I have no one on my arse telling me what to do, but I imagine that's the same for you. I just have less structure and that's not always a good thing. I suppose I can take today off yeah. But you're here too. We're in this together. Sounds like you're happy where you are. If you work more from home and do projects and whatever else it is that you do, that's gotta be worth thinking about.

GEORGE: Work is alright. I like to complain about it but it's not that bad. I can't be doing with my colleagues though. I really fucking tire of it.

TOM: Maybe they tire of you.

GEORGE: Maybe they do.

TOM: I think they do.

GEORGE: I think you better finish your scampi. They don't grow on trees you know.

TOM: How's your brother?

GEORGE: He's good. He's taken on some big clients. Have you worked with him before?

TOM: I am aware of his work. I appreciate it.

GEORGE: I'm sure he appreciates that.

TOM: You should become a graphic designer too. We could have a little club.

GEORGE: You mean start a business?

TOM: No. I mean start a little club.

GEORGE: I could be your administration monkey.

TOM: It's not as daft as you might think.

GEORGE: I don't think it's daft.

TOM: Well, it *is* daft.

GEORGE: I know.

TOM: This scampi is shit. How's yours?

GEORGE: It's a cheese jacket potato Tom.

TOM: I see.

GEORGE: Are you where you want to be? You're settled now.

TOM: Yeah, I'm doing what I can do and I'm going to be doing this for a long time. Unless my family dies. Then I may just do something else.

GEORGE: That's a terrible thing to say.

TOM: I know. I'm not even sure what it means.

GEORGE: You know what it means. That reminds me of that advert - I think it was Lloyds. You know the one I mean, with the beach and the hut and the fishing trips.

TOM: I have no idea what you mean. A recent advert?

GEORGE: No.

Here is what I mean:

There was once a man on some island somewhere who leased out boats. He spent most of his time sitting on the beach and reading and sometimes he would close up and go for walks. He loved his job and he pulled in a liveable wage and all he wanted for was in his world. He enjoyed the simple life.

One day, a man came to lease a boat with his wife and enjoyed himself. He came back three times during his two week stay on the island and expressed words like authentic and real, and the men had one way conversations about the boats and the man's life back in the office and how this was just what they wanted and how it was so cheap.

On the last day of the man's holiday, he spent the day on the beach but this time he did not hire out a boat. Instead, as his wife sat reading John Grisham on a mat borrowed from the hotel, he chatted enthusiastically with the boatman. He told him that he could *rather have something here* and that if he had some help, the man could double his fleet of boats and get a franchise thing going. He could work it with the hotel chain nearby and open in the surrounding islands. Both men were intelligent and he subtlety suggested that the boatman was wasting his intelligence on such a small time operation.

Within five years - with a lot of hard work, he could be working from a centralised area, and be in complete control. Within two years, and a little work, the company could be sold – maybe floated, and then this boatman would be set up for life. He could move to an island and spend his days on a beach, doing what he loved.

And that's it; the man is already doing this, and sees no need to go through all that hardship and progression to be able to get to where he wants to be. He's there already. I like this story.

TOM:	Yeah, you like that story because it's a blatant excuse to not have to push yourself.
GEORGE:	-------------
TOM:	You don't live on a beach George.
GEORGE:	Must you live so incessantly in the real world?
TOM:	Must you quote *Peep Show* all the time?
GEORGE:	You're right, that scampi does look shit.
TOM:	You can't handle the truth.
GEORGE:	You're right. Never been able to. It's better living in your own world.

TOM: Make guest appearances in the real world sometimes though.

GEORGE: Maybe I will.

TOM: I think you should go for that job. You'll walk the interview.

GEORGE: I will. I think that's what I'm afraid of.

TOM: You should be afraid.

GEORGE: It's events management.

TOM: Yeah I do that. Or at least I have done. I once did some graphics work for a dog grooming company.

GEORGE: Really? I didn't know that.

TOM: No, it wasn't very involved and I enjoyed it. I probably didn't see you much during that time anyway. I think you were out of action.

GEORGE: I see. What did you do?

TOM: Oh, some grooming woman contacted me for some business card and shit. I convinced her that she wanted me to undertake a revamp of her company.

	She wanted loads of work done that would have cost her more separately.
GEORGE:	And you told her that?
TOM:	Yeah, but what she got in the end with my service charge outweighed her initial costing. But long term, she made huge savings. Everyone was a winner in the end. She's doing very well.
GEORGE:	That's pretty impressive.
TOM:	Not just a pretty face George.
GEORGE:	No, you're certainly not that.
TOM:	Quiet, I haven't finished my amazing story.
GEORGE:	Please, finish. *Finish.*
TOM:	I just did some letterheads and cards, reviewed her pricing and got her to charge by the half hour instead of the job. We got a trainee for her and sacked two of her people who were haemorrhaging cash. We got t-shirts and a shitty little re-launch party done. Her adverts were scrapped in the paper and we got a deal with the local pet shops, and blazoned her name on their

vans. Oh and we got her a website. She didn't have a website. That was what I mainly did actually. Her website was good.

GEORGE: Yeah I've seen your sites.

TOM: Yet I haven't got my own yet.

GEORGE: Yes you have.

TOM: Well not really, it's not interactive. It just showcases my talent. It's basically an online CV, and I know I get work from it, but it's only directing at one form of customer at the moment - those big organisations that want to employ me on a contract basis.

GEORGE: How did you get to know this woman then?

TOM: TV, I had some TV show contact me because they had contacted her to do a programme about businesses, or something.

GEORGE: You've been on telly? Why didn't I know about this?

TOM: I was on television, and it wasn't very exciting. No anecdotes. I was meant to be a cog in a part of a process but ended up running the show, and the telly show ended up being as much about me as it was about her business.

GEORGE: Well that must have increased awareness. You pulled in some work from that?

TOM: No, I don't live on a beach either.

GEORGE: I still can't believe you've been on telly without me knowing it. I watch a *lot* of television, and I suppose I could call you a friend.

TOM: See, it's comments like that.

GEORGE: What?

TOM: That's why you and I could never be friends.

GEORGE: You're such a bastard.

TOM: And on that bombshell...

GEORGE: Yeah, I don't think I want to look at that scampi anymore.

TOM: Me neither.

I like that story. I don't care what Tom says. I kind of like his reaction to the story too. Perhaps more than I like the story itself. The shops here are rubbish because I can't find anything I want to buy. Tom buys three books from the cheapo bookstore, and a puzzle for 99p that I think is meant for children. He also buys a load of misfits; these strange battered chocolate pieces that I can see have gone all white and bubbly on the surface. They are cheap though and Tom relishes in his bargain. I have one - they're actually very nice.

He buys a shirt from a designer place. It looks good, it fits and so he buys it. How simple. We buy provisions for the drive back. He buys trainers. I get a couple of birthday cards that I find amusing. This makes me feel good because I have two birthdays coming up and so it's a job done and will stop me having to endure the torture of searching for an appropriate card at the last minute. I may even write the cards now and file them when I get home. I may even get the stamps.

Tom buys three CDs from the card shop. They are selling CDs, three for £5.99. He buys the best TV themes in the world ever, an awfully short *Beatles* compilation, and an eighties mix, which is a six CD set, but does have the sticker dictating its part of this amazing offer. He sheepishly goes to the counter and is informed that it *is* part of the deal. He pauses and I see that he is thinking about getting two more six CD sets, as that would be better value. He doesn't. We don't need eighteen CDs of eighties music. At least not *this* eighties music. It's not *our* music. Never trust a collection of songs that claim to be the best of the eighties that doesn't contain any *Smiths* songs. Not even *Depeche Mode*. I shiver as I realise that this will soundtrack the drive back. I think I would prefer to listen to the TV theme one. I drop hints that this may be the case.

We rush back with less urgency than when we arrived. It's getting late and I'm hoping that he'll suggest getting a takeaway tonight, and that his other half is going out with her work friends. I want to be twenty-one again and spend days like this every day and think that things will always stay this way. I allow myself to be absorbed in my childhood in the car on the way back and smoke a cigarette in the car like it's okay. I laugh and joke with Tom and I smile at the frames of reference and stories he constructs. I belittle a lot of what he says and he insults all of my inadequacies. I skip tracks I know he loves and he turns tracks up he knows I hate. I much prefer this than the journey up because I no longer have to think about shoes. I look at my shoes and Tom says nothing. Another theme transports me back to when I was a child, and we stop talking and insulting and enjoy the song. It's a really awful song.

My phone has declared the arrival of three text messages since we left the village but it's been on lock and I can't see or remember how to unlock it in the relative darkness of Tom's car. I'm not expecting any one to contact and figure that the three messages are some convoluted explanation of something from my father. He is the only one that sends text messages in pages and he deplores text speak. I respect him for this, and his willingness to pay three times as much in order to strictly adhere to the laws of fine English. I also curse him for wasting my time. I don't touch my phone until we get back to his house, where I trawl though the unlocking process whilst Tom changes. He's always changing, even on a day off, come six o'clock, he yearns to get out of his day clothes and into his evening wear. Not that he goes formal; he does the opposite and goes two stages more casual than whatever he is wearing during the day. I sometimes wonder what would happen if he spent the day in his jogging pants and vest. Perhaps he'd come downstairs at 7.00pm with a dress fashioned from leaves. The image of Tom in a grass dress flashes across my eyes and I laugh.

Oh, well this isn't good. I have three text messages. One is from my brother asking me to ring my mother. One is from my mother, asking me to ring her, and one is from my brother saying that my uncle has been taken ill and that he's gone round to my mothers. I deal with this with slight apprehension and text back 'understood', and before sending, adding 'I can be there at 9, are u all there?'

I have to wait for 22 minutes before I get a reply, and wonder why I'm not phoning someone. My mother calls and tells me that he's gone into hospital with a suspected heart attack and that he's in the hospital with his wife and son. She tells me that there's no panic, but she just wanted me to know because it changes our plans for the weekend, as she'll probably have to go to Oxford to see him. There is no emotion in her voice, but a slight determined edge, and she sounds a little breathless. I forget what we had plans to do but don't mention this. I tell her not to worry about anything and that I will go round to see my Dad tomorrow night with a takeaway and make sure he is okay and has everything he needs. She is relieved as she realises that I have deduced that she has rang me, mainly to get me to check on Dad.

"Mum's off to Oxford, something about my uncle being taken ill so I have to go and check up on Dad."

"What, now? Which Uncle? Shit!"

"No. Not now. Maybe tomorrow night or Friday. It's my mother's brother's, brother in law?"

"Oh right." There is a tone to his voice that suggests 'Oh, well that's not so bad'. I find this weird, but justified. I, after all said 'I *have* to go round'. I didn't even enquire as to how the guy is; he's had a fucking heart attack. I'm more concerned with the fact that *I* have to go round to say hello to my own father, because his wife's brother's brother in law is in hospital. Hell, may even *die.* I am temporarily disgusted with myself.

"Beer?"

"Yeah why not. I'll have one of your - Jesus. Where did you get this from?"

"It's fake *Tiger*. They're actually pretty good. A guy at our solicitors got them for me."

"Yeah, where from?"

"No idea. They're stronger than *Tiger*."

He passes me an opener and we enjoy a beer.

I try to feel sad.

Chapter Six

I get home far too late to think about going to my parent's house. I decide to pop round tomorrow and suggest we go out for a pub lunch. My mother didn't say it, but I am guessing she is either going early tomorrow morning, or she has already left. She doesn't like to hang around. I manage to get to sleep relatively easily, the first time in a long while.

I dream, and it's a bad dream. I never tend to have nightmares, or happy dreams but they are definable in the sense that I can easily separate them into positive or negative experiences. I usually dream about the mundane and usual, and it usually revolves around something that I have been working on during the day, or some comment somebody made to me that I wasn't too sure about the meaning of. I try not to obsess about things like this too much, but if I don't, my dreams pick up the thread and do not always put a nice spin on the situation.

Last night was a bad dream. I dreamt that I was at college and I had boxes of items for my family and friends; things I have borrowed, old wallets and paperclips. I keep on dropping the boxes and one pupil kicks a toy car out my way which is in turn, holding some stones that mean something to someone who felt the need to bring them back from a beach somewhere sometime, probably a long time a go. I feel like I'm being bullied and this is what it must feel like to be bullied. I've never really been bullied. Just ignored or belittled ever so slightly. At primary school, I was a bouncy popular leader and when I went to secondary school, I collapsed and became scared and upset. I refused to let anyone else enter my world and would not socialise or banter with anyone else. Other kids suddenly didn't seem to interest me and I was glad to be unhappy. Most of my bad dreams are about belongings being taken away from me, or losing items I am hoarding. And they usually stem around a school or college. Obviously, after I have one of these dreams, I wonder what it means, and then realise very quickly what it is supposed to mean and wonder whether it actually means this. I ponder on whether my tiny head is complex and cunning enough to concoct dreams that mean something to fool me into thinking I am an interesting person. I also wonder whether I am always only just getting enough sleep and that is due to an insatiable lust to maintain the tightrope. Dreams make me wonder, when I believe they are meant to clarify.

My friend Clare dreams a lot. She also knits a lot and I will be thankful of this if she knitted me something. I see her every now and again and we watch *Gardeners World* or *Miss Marple* and drink copious amounts of tea. She edits the letters page of *Woman's Beacon*, a lightweight publication for mums and housewives. It's the kind of magazine that has a few recipes, two or three stories of something amazing (but futile) that occurred in someone's life (*My husband was a serial killer!* -------- *My Doctor said I had bird flu*. My Story...). It usually involves death or someone cheating on someone. There's a fashion page, a few holiday shots, and advice on which cream women should put on their faces to make their faces less flaky (but not shiny). I grew up with these rags around me so I am aware of their nature.

Clare's job is to decide which letters to print, fashion a short reply (sometimes with an exclamation mark!) and generally make it an entertaining read. She looks after the competitions and I think she edits some of the magazine itself. It sounds as if she is like me in the sense that she has made this job her own, and she maybe even be secretly planning to take it over. She could be editor next year I'm sure. She's not a big fan of the magazine, but relishes in helping create this alien world.

Anyway, on our last meeting, which must have been almost a month ago now, she bouncily entered my flat and immediately told me about a dream she had had three nights prior.

I like it when Clare comes round because I can be childish and it not feel inappropriate. Her job dictates that she maintains her childlike qualities and I am slightly jealous of this. She doesn't appear to make lists, and appears to be fascinated with mine.

I am interested in other people silly lists. One thing I enjoy finding out is who someone would like to share a dinner table with, and one that I have thought about endlessly when alone. I have a slight obsession with Lennon and he is always the first to make an appearance. I then make a small list of interesting and influential people from the past and present, sometimes the future. I make the list from people who have trail blazed, innovated and entertained, and who would have interesting things to say. The only problem lies when I have completed the list and sit back and watch the conversation flow. I always feel awkward and out of place and can't imagine me fitting into the group. I spend most of my time in the kitchen cooking for them.

So I scrap this list and come up with a list that I could never tell anyone about because it doesn't put me in an amazing light, and is not the image of myself with which I wish to project. These normally have lots of quiet people who are just like me and telling other people about this doesn't warrant *anything.* I once met a person from the internet who would ask questions like this randomly, as if he was still on a message board. I didn't find this particularly endearing, but it was fun and we found a lot out about one another in a very short amount of time. It took me five years to ask Clare who she would dine with. I enjoyed knowing that I had yet to ask her, and took pleasure in attempting to decipher which characters she would chose. I also wondered what she might cook them. I wanted to hear about the whole shebang, from the hanging up of coats, to the after dinner mints. I knew she would be able to deliver, and she did.

I arise the next day feeling fresh and alive. I think I'm beginning to reap the rewards from cutting down my smoking as I am feeling less terrible each morning. Today has lots of scope and I momentarily feel young and excitable again. I text Dad as soon as I wake and suggest a pub lunch. He doesn't have to think about this and just texts: *Great! Drewnes lane?* Drewnes lane it is, a pub out of the way and familiar and quite good value.

It's a chain, and it's fine. I don't understand people who have a disapproving sneer at chains but I don't like to reason this too much as I know a lot of people who don't like chains. I can understand the boycotting of certain companies but you still have to exist in the world that has been created for you, and everyday shouldn't have to be a trailblazing *do-good* day. We have people who do that for us. There *are* people out there like this, and God bless them all.

I pick Dad up and we go for some food. Picking Dad up will always be a strange thing for both of us, even if he lives to a ripe old age and me picking him up outweighs the times that he used to pick me up, it will still be special (and a little weird - but weird in a good way). On the way there, I ask him what's been happening and he has lots of news. I sit back and enjoy hearing his voice, and can see that he is genuinely excited about many of the things going on for him and Mum. We don't go into very deep territory in the car; well you don't do you? Perhaps we'll get serious in the bar, we can, and sometimes we do. He once told me that he had a mini epiphany when he went on holiday once and was sat on the beach, and realised that everyone was enjoying the beach together, no matter how much they earned, or their social status. It didn't matter if there was someone claiming income support next to someone pulling in 150 k. There's only so much enjoyment you can muster. He draws things from this, as do I. I like to think about this sometimes, and I also like to think about my Dad thinking about it, and the obvious thought patterns it provokes.

We have a great lunch and Dad has a beer. I don't ask about Mum, as I know he will tell me what I need to know. He tells me that she's a little shaken, and that maybe I should go down to Oxford. There's no need but I let slip that I was having some time off and might go travelling. I hadn't thought about the notion that I could go travelling until it came out of my mouth, purely intended as something to say. Even with close friends and family, sometimes I just blurt something out because I feel the need to say something. That can sometimes get me into trouble if the thing I blurt out is a suggestion that we do something, and the person listening says yes. Because I didn't want to do anything, I just wanted to speak.

I drive back with Dad and I stay at his cottage for a while, chatting and drinking coffee. I give him the selection of food I picked up for him, mainly expensive fish and a few outlandish ready meals. I chose the most expensive things I can so as to signify that I have bought some treats for him, as a gift, and I'm not just buying some groceries because I don't think he can look after himself. He *can* look after himself, but I kinda want to (without him knowing). He tells me that I look after him well, we hug, and I zoom off back home to try and eliminate the possibility that I may just do a bit of travelling for a fortnight.

I decide immediately on the drive home that I'm going to go to Oxford. I don't have any need to and I don't think I'll have a very good time but I'd like to be with my family, and I know I'll end up in the flat mulling under the guise of progress if I stay. I can work from wherever; so long as I have my trusty diary and access to the net, I'm good to go. I don't think I'm going to need to make any phone calls. I make three calls before I work out my trip to confirm that yes, I didn't need to make any phone calls. I also pencil in the date when I am going to go back to work, and set an alarm on my phone three days before this is due to happen, to awaken me from my holiday. Three days gives me enough time to put in place those things that need to be put in place, and allows myself sufficient time to prepare my battle plan. Because there's going to be one, and things are going to get interesting. I'm not planning on anything grandiose or any grand gesture. I used to do that a lot in my early and mid twenties and couldn't understand how ineffectual it was. I now know that everybody used to make grand gestures and now they've grown up. This makes me a feel a little foolish. But there are always fools around me, so I feel less foolish anyway.

I have ten days including weekend days. So I have seven days really. That's a week. The house is tidy and I have sorted my paperwork. Everything is clean and so is my mind. Everything seems suddenly very simple and I can feel waves of calm enveloping my thinking. I have clarity and feel concise. It feels weird and I temporarily ponder whether I should make a spliff, to *ruin* it. I don't. I am pleased with myself that I don't and I celebrate with a coffee, sharpening my mind further until I start to think in shapes and lines. I put *Parklife* on, because it's clean and crisp and I remember when I heard it in my twenties and it signified a shift. I wonder how other people deal with this clarity or whether this is in fact not normal, and just the other side of my scale; one with which I am not altogether familiar. I recognise it and the memories of this feeling stand out like a proud skyscraper amongst the many smaller buildings. The endless other buildings. The scraper pierces a cloud, but it is lost because no one looks up anymore. I don't look up anymore. You shouldn't look at the stars. You really shouldn't.

I put this new found sharpness to good use and write an inventory, and itinerary of my Oxford trip, and staple another page to the back of this to dictate what could happen after Oxford, and think about all the people that I have known throughout my life. I reign myself in from this stupid massive thought and my clarity enables me to do this. I briefly think about some of the people I have known throughout my life because I think I would actually like to see some of them again, and they may even be pleased to see me. I jot down random names I pluck from the ether, where they were living before, and where they may be living now. Some I haven't spoken to in over six years, but I still put them on the list. Some weren't even friends, or acquaintances, and rather just people who shared a place and time, through no fault of their own. I think it was probably my fault actually.

I get as far as Southampton, Oxford, Sheffield, Cardiff, Exeter and Cheltenham and Bristol as places where I could go and possibly stay. But I wonder why I am doing it and seeing the names of these places on paper panics me as all I see is seven massive disappointments, laced with awkward social nightmares. And not only may this happen, I'm fucking planning it.

I still maintain that I should go, and I will, but after another coffee and hearing *This is a low,* I decide to free flow it. Lille flashes across my eyes but it's okay. That demon needs exorcising anyway. Even if it's not France, or Australia. And it's not for a year, and I won't have a backpack, and it's in very safe familiar surroundings. Look, it's a big step forward. I decide that all I need is money really. My life here is sorted and running smoothly so I will go to Oxford and see what happens. I can always come back.

Maybe I'm not coming back.

Money has been my saviour. I hate not having it and I lust over its powers and the security it holds. I appreciate that money can't bring you happiness, and I am reminded of my Dad's beach theory (is it a theory, or a catalyst? It might just be a sentence).

I throw clothes into a bag and chuck them straight into the boot of my car. There is no process or logic to the way in which I do this and it feels kinda nice that I'm not concerned with the repercussions. I am not concerned, as I don't think there will be any, bar maybe the odd crushed shirt. I am pleased with my abandon and convince myself that I may be acting like a normal human being. I get my work bag and put in fifteen CDs, some compilations but nine are from the new albums I have yet to listen to properly. They have been on my computer for months and I have played the singles, and the odd opener but have yet to be forced to listen, like I would have to do if I took the train. Maybe I should take the train? No, I'm not going to take the train. I pay enough tax and insurance on my car for that to be a justifiable reason not to take public transport. Even when public transport is cheaper (rarely) or more convenient (frequently). Also, I put in twenty cigarettes, a pack of unopened. A lighter, a drink and my phone book. I also take my diary and a pad of post it notes and a pen. In case, mainly, I crash the car and have to ask for the other person's details. I put in my mp3 player, some chewing gum and I place my wallet, keys and mobile on top of the bag. I really need to inflate the tyres in my car, fill her up; with petrol, and add some screen wash. All of this can wait. I will stop at the supermarket on my way out. This wouldn't happen if I weren't so damn alert.

I try and sit back down and watch the news but I am jittery and uptight. Ah, yes, clarity also comes with its down side. Maybe I should stop drinking coffee. I pour myself another coffee. I spark up a cigarette and gingerly place my hand by a slightly ajar window as if I am attempting to sneak the smoke from someone. I text my mother and ask her if she wants company by saying *fancy a visitor?* I know that this conveys everything I need to say because my mother knows me well, and I know her well, but perhaps not as well as she knows me because she's known me all my life, and I missed out on thirty years of hers. Thirty years man - that's a long time. That's nearly my age. It won't be soon.

She texts back immediately saying *come down, we're at Brian's flat. Meet me at station?* She knows me too well and is probably thinking I'm halfway to Oxford now and haven't thought to text her until the last minute. She does know me well, but today I am not that person, and I am striving to be a different person. I text back explaining that I'm thinking about leaving tomorrow. She informs me that they'll either be at the hospital or at Brian's. I don't know who Brian is; maybe my Mum doesn't either and has just included me in her confusion. Maybe I should pretend I know Brian, it may be the right thing to do. Maybe it's a spelling mistake. I do know that my uncle's son is called Browne. I never thought of this as amusing until I mentioned it in passing one day at the university bar and everybody laughed. I felt upset and sad that they had laughed, and then laughed myself. I still don't think it's very funny though. I think it's a great name. Why did other people have to make me think that not only is it a weird name, but also that I am weird for thinking that it is not a weird name. Trouble is, their comments weren't weird at all, they're plausible and honest.

I don't care much for honesty anymore. *That's* plausible.

I leave at 8.30 am, as if I am going to work. I decide to get some lunch in a supermarket café, well brunch. I'm hoping if I pull off near Oxford, I can find an out of town market place and sit for an hour or so; re-energise myself. I am also hoping that, as it is a weekday, it won't be very busy and I will get fresh chips. I think that maybe I'd actually prefer it if the chips weren't fresh as I enjoy it when they have been resting and go a little soggy.

I will be going to my brand of choice supermarket and I know what I am going to expect.

I try not to go mad on the motorway and constantly peer over my shoulder and in the mirror when other cars pull in. I think that maybe there could be a police car around and maybe those signs denoting a speed camera are telling the truth. I go a little over what is reasonable in a court of law for some of the time and the rest is spent poodling along at the pace of whoever is in front of me. A couple of cars attempt a race, and I accept their challenge with childish dangerous accuracy. It breaks up the monotony of the journey and I harbour bad thoughts about what I am doing and the effect that it could have on others if I were to crash. I think about my family and friends and the complex web we all weave for one another, and I multiply this by all of the cars and passengers that I zoom past. I slow down - for a bit.

I change my CDs with alarming gusto and irritation at regular intervals, never with the compilations though; I should make more of these compilations. I think if I am going to die soon, it will be from crashing into the central reservation when changing a CD, I think that this is more likely than lung or throat cancer, madness (Can you die from madness?), or a heart attack. I think it's about as likely as dying from a brain tumour. That's how my best friend died. I know a lot of people who have died and now they're dead and I don't think about them anymore, only to briefly lament on how bad it is of me not to think about these dead people. I wonder where they've gone and if they can see what I'm doing and if they know what I'm thinking. I wonder if they have been reincarnated, and I scoff at the notion that they could be. Buddhists think they have been. I like Buddhists. I ponder on whether saying I like Buddhists is inverse racism, and is more of an insult than if I were to say I hated them. This notion is ridiculous and nonsensical and I turn the tunes up.

I weave in and out of cars for fun and listen to Interpol on level seven. It goes to fifteen but the speakers crack a little bit, and I suppose it's good to hear *something* of the road. That's something I need to fix actually, I owe it to myself to install a good sound system in my car. I find other people who do this slightly irritating though, but maybe only because I know they are doing it for different reasons. They must be. Everything can't surely just boil down to jealousy on my part. I must be right, or I face the awful prospect that I could be wrong. My ethos would dissolve into shit and *you* would then have the upper hand.

The supermarket delivers its promise. I text my mother and tell her that I will be there soon and she rings me back. They're in a pub, and it sounds as if my whole extended family is there. Someone who I am supposed to have a frame of reference for hollers 'Hello George!' down the phone from what sounds like across the room, but it could just be my hearing. I hear that people find this amusing and there's a ripple of laughter as people tell the person that said it to calm down, and that gets a laugh too. She tells me that everything is okay, that my (sort of) uncle is not critical but it was a shock, he had a massive heart attack. I am dubious of the word massive as I am sure it's a word that has been bounded around the group and maybe no one even said it, not even a doctor (who is qualified). He knows massive when he sees it, and he wouldn't use that word anyway. I conclude that it wasn't a massive heart attack and convey my general *everything will get better* point of view with sympathetic noises. I sincerely think everything will get better. I like to think of myself as a realist who toys with pessimism, but I do think everything is improving all the time. If you think about all the people in all the world that are currently working on something right now to make things better, then that's a lot of things being made better, all the time. When we go to sleep, the other half of the world get up and take over the shift and look for ways to make everything better. This constant process makes me feel better. I don't like to think about those people that are trying to make things worse, but I'm constantly reminded of them every time I switch on the television. Some of these people claim that *they* are trying to make things better.

    I arrange to meet my mother at this pub, and if they're not there, I will go round to Browne's house. It *was* Browne. I have only met Browne once and we merely exchanged pleasantries. He took the trouble to email me a link to a website that spewed out recommendations on a streaming radio station that you could tailor make to your own tastes. The more time that you spend developing your tastes and likes and dislikes, the more the system works in your favour. When you've been there six months, other people have an opportunity to listen to your radio station and are given an opportunity to talk to you and you can listen to theirs the following week. There are progress charts, news. Google are bound to want to buy this in a couple of years. I was grateful for this and I was grateful that he took the time to email me (at all). I am glad that this happened also because I can talk to him about it when I get there. I could probably talk to only him and only that subject for my whole time at his house. I wonder whether people think I am assuming I will be invited to stay over because I'm really not. I haven't made any plans but I will try and stay with my mother and I doubt that she is going to stay. I sincerely hope that this is the case.

The streets of Oxford are alien to me and I have trouble manoeuvring around town. I appear to have gone round in a circle three times and look longingly at my phone as if the answer lies within that piece of technology, *somewhere*. I have the name of the pub, and I know the street in which it is in, but have no idea where the street is, or even if I'm in the right area. At that moment, a text comes in and I pull over outside a charity shop. I open it and it's Mum telling me they're back at the house. I wish I had a *tomtom*, but then I look at a map and find the address of Browne's house and immediately am glad that I don't have a *tomtom*, and belittle those that do with a self-satisfied breath.

I pull up to the house and see my Mum's car is on the drive next to another car, which needs a good clean. I am hoping mum will answer and take me into a safe place, or at least I wish I knew who was in this house. What if there are lots of people hanging on to one persons every word in a small lounge, and I enter at the wrong moment and he loses his thread and everyone looks at me disappointedly, heck maybe a little disapprovingly. What if there are loads of people I don't know. What if there are loads of people I *do* know and I have nothing to say. I am no longer a child so I cannot be shy or timid. Damn someone for taking that privilege away from me. Shy kids are cute, shy adults are annoying. Actually from my time at university, I realised that many people see quiet people as being mysterious, and I get a kick out of that. Maybe I don't speak so often as others because I fear doing so will only dispel my self imposed myth. I'll start talking bollocks like everyone else does. There are a hundred possibilities of what lies in wait for me behind this door, and all of them are pain crushingly bad. But I am pushing my envelope I convince myself, and that's always a good thing. (Isn't it?)

"Hello, you must be George!"

"Er, yeah, hiya."

"You don't remember me do you?" She faintly touches my arm and smiles lovingly at my face.

"No of course I do..." I lie.

"I haven't seen you in years. You must have been eight or nine."

"Nine I think, you bought me a pencil case, or something."

What a stupid thing to say.

She ignores it; "Come in, come in; your mother is in the kitchen, we were just talking about your brother actually."

She leads me into a kitchen through what seems to be a never-ending twisty hall. It's clearly an extension they've had put on the house and it looks disjointed. But I like the fact that the house appears to be in two sections and I'm going to the section where there are hardly any people. Two in fact, three now I have joined my mum and Auntie Sally. I don't know who she is related to, she's just Sally. I could work it out but it would give me a headache. Hell, she may as well be a friend of the family that I started calling auntie at a formative age. She probably has no connection with me whatsoever. But she did give me a pencil case, or something.

I give my mum a hug and we talk about the journey, and my uncle. She's on top form actually, and I think a change of scenery and people has done her good. I wait for Sally to say that it's such a shame that it takes an emergency before family meets up. She says it. I wait for Sally to comment on how well I'm looking, although if she were to say that, it would be a horrible lie because I spied myself in the hall mirror, and I look *terrible*. She says it. I then wait for Sally to go so I can talk with my mother alone. She doesn't go.

My mum asks me what my plans were and if I had any. I say no, and she grabs my hand and drags me into a heaving lounge. I am glad that she did this because it needed to be done and it dissolves any awkwardness because it gets the ordeal over quickly and relatively painlessly. She will also do most of the talking. It works, and I stand in the middle of the room, smiling politely and shaking hands. She even wraps up the event by saying that we're going to pop into town. She doesn't even tell them why, and they don't even ask. I can learn a lot from her actions, but I won't for another four years probably.

"Sorry son, I had to do that."

"Understood. Do you want to get a coffee?"

We go into town and get a coffee at a small bakery that has facilities out the back. I have a strong coffee and a sticky bun and my mother has a tea a bit of my sticky bun. I ask her what her plans are, and she says she has booked into a chain hotel through a deal my brother got her involved in. She's planning on staying there for another two nights but it could be longer. I don't ask any questions about the welfare of my uncle because I can sense that she has talked about nothing else for the last five hours.

"I'll book another room for you."

"Okay, cool. Just the one night, I've got to be in Southampton tomorrow night."

And that was that, I decided to go to Southampton. I know it a little from when I was younger and we went to the Isle of Wight for our summer vacation. I also know two people there and toy with the idea of just turning up with no invite or warning. Or I may not go to Southampton. My mother doesn't ask why I'm going anyway. She is used to people going places and doing things and meeting people, she doesn't need to ask anymore because whatever the reason, it's going to be plausible isn't it, and that's all that matters.

We go straight back to the hotel and book in and watch television and read through the pamphlets that have been left for perusal by my bed. I love hotels like this.

There's no comfort but there are little things to expose and enjoy and I dig the tackiness. Mum goes to sleep in her room and I arrange to ring her at seven to go down and get some food. We are told that we can't eat in the restaurant because it's for patrons only, and we are not patrons because of the deal we are on. We say that this is fine and that we appreciate them offering us bar snacks. We're allowed bar snacks, and I take advantage of this allowance and grab a toasted sandwich before retiring for a telly fest. I go immediately for *Sky One,* as that's the treat. It used to be wrestling when I was a little younger and Sky was still a pursuit of the lucky few. Then it was *The Simpsons*, and now it's just the channel itself.

We go for a bite to eat later on, and I get back to read though a magazine I picked up at the foyer. I check my emails and think about what may or may not happen tomorrow. I decide that maybe I will go to Southampton, and I email my friend Alan who lives there with his brother. I haven't seen him in three years but have no qualm in emailing the guy. We were a part of a close-knit community in our twenties and circumstance and age dictated that we probably wouldn't see each other as often, and this turned more concrete with him moving away from the area. I forget that he is always online and am shocked, pleasantly surprised, and then understand, as his reply comes back with refreshing immediacy. He says that he has a few days off from work and that I should come down for a beer tomorrow afternoon. I wonder if making lists and plans is really necessary, perhaps ever again. Things are going nice and smoothly so far. *So far.*

Mornings in hotels are great because you are forced to get up because of the threat of missing breakfast, or a maid entering the room. Yet you can lounge around early on, because breakfast can be on your terms, and you can always put the do not disturb message out. I have to check out today, breakfast is included in the deal though and I force myself up and trundle down the corridor to wake my mum. I knock on the door but there's no one there. I figure she must be downstairs already but then it occurs to me that she wouldn't just start breakfast without me. I knock on the door again and begin to worry a little. What if she's in there, and not well and unable to come to the door or tell me of her discomfort? How very British of me to stand here thinking these things but not do a goddamn thing about it. If I were to raise the alarm and I was wrong, that would possibly be the worst outcome. Surely there's nothing worse.

My mum opens the door with a breezy smile and we go to get our breakfast. I say my goodbyes and she gives me a hug, leaving me with "I hope you find what you're looking for in Southampton." Damn, she knows I'm looking for something.

Southampton I am more familiar with, and the place where Alan lives I feel at ease in. I've been here a couple of times before and it's good to be back. I have no foreboding sense of doom as I approach this area; just a nagging sense of irritance that I haven't ventured down before now. When I knock on his door, I am greeted with a cockney smile and news that the kettle has just finished boiling. We shake hands, and it's like the three years apart never happened. We immediately strike up where we left off and chat flows aimlessly and effortlessly. He asks me why I'm in Southampton and I tell him I have no idea. I say that my job was getting on top of me and make a few gestures with my face and hands, and he gets it.

"So you're doing a magical mystery tour?"

"Something like that."

"Where's next on the list then?"

"Um…probably back to Norfolk?"

"Nice!"

"Heh! Yeah, I don't want to wear myself out."

"Well if you have no plans, stay here for a bit fella."

"Cheers man. I will take you up on that offer tonight if that's okay."

"Of course. No problem, stay for as long as you want. It's pretty boring round here though. We're not getting up to much."

"When you working again?"

"Oh next week sometime. I work from home mostly these days."

"Excellent."

Alan rings one of his friends and suggests we go for a drink and maybe a game of pool at the local. I dread what this local will be like and Alan sees this dread and reassures me that it's okay. It's George friendly. Alan is George friendly too, so I think it probably wouldn't matter if the pub wasn't. I can absorb myself in someone else's company if they are the right type of person and it allows me to undertake things that without them, perhaps I'd find more difficult.

We have decorum together and our relationship is a million miles away from that of Toms and mine. We don't score points off of one another and I can spend longer in his company. He asks after Tom and I relay his latest mischief. Alan laughs and tells me stories about his friends, which are funny also.

I could happily stay here for a week but decide to just stay another day. I relish in a very late night and an even later morning, which coincides with some good television and a cooked breakfast. I remind myself that it is Saturday morning and that I haven't seen Alan in years, and that this behaviour is okay for someone who isn't Twenty-Four anymore. We ponder on what to do and I feel no awkwardness because he doesn't seem to have any plans for his weekend. I think that perhaps maybe he did but now *I* am his plan, and this makes me feel good.

I leave on the Sunday morning. I head for the South West as I know it well and have family there. As Sunday morning looms, I fear that my road trip maybe over as I no longer have a sense of excitement or an idea where I'm going to go next. I'm not sure if continuing will achieve anything, but I do. I decide not to go to Bristol, or Exeter where I would be able to meet up with my cousin, and a friend from my apprentice days for a telesales firm. Both meetings would be plausible and fine, but neither would go as well as the last two stop offs and I am painfully aware of this. I ponder on whether this actually may be a good thing to factor into my trip, but on reflection, decide to do the next thing on my own. As I get older, my ability to mingle increases and I am able to pick out a possible kindred spirit from a face in the crowd. Yet my instinct and gut feelings hold me back and I no longer have the recklessness and abandon of youth to push me past my comfort zone. It's not very stretchy at the moment, and I remind myself that this maybe the purpose of the trip.

   I head for Glastonbury and Street, and decide to stay there for a bit. Wind down, maybe get a bed and breakfast in the town and then do some walking. I tell Alan of my plans on the Saturday night and he tells me that my plans are cool. As I leave on the Sunday morning, I hug Alan and say we should keep in touch. I think we probably will. My driving slows down as I begin to enjoy the journey. For the first time in years, I am enjoying a journey and feel like I am on a train. I reflect on why this is not usually the case and it makes me a little sad, wishing my life away on the motorway.

When I finally arrive in Somerset, it's already getting a little dark. The day has been quite gloomy and not full of expectation like I expect days to be at this time of year. I lament on this as I weave through country lanes. I took the wrong exit from the M4, and find myself in the wrong place, but going in the right direction. Again, this would usually irritate and upset me but today I relish in the adventure. Nothing much has happened since I left Southampton; a couple of drivers cut me up coming out of the one way system, and I stayed well back and let them do their thing. I see them look up three times to their rear view mirror as they speed off, with perverse annoyance and slight confusion as to why I didn't beep, and now I'm slowing down. I kinda like this, and vow to do it more often - refuse to play the game. When I owned my first car, I used to put a lot of effort into beating people at lights, or climbing the hill in second for as long as possible so the engine would cry out with discomfort, and then quickly go to third and fourth in an attempt to beat those cars that had a higher engine capacity when the road turned into dual carriageway. I sometimes did, but only if the other car wasn't really paying attention, and it was pretty dangerous to be honest. I never really thought about death, and after my friend died at such a young age, began to view death as just a consequence, but never a direct consequence of my own actions. And with this in mind, I came to the perverse logic that I may as well dabble in those things that might be dangerous and reckless as I'm going to die *anyway.*

As my car improved in luxury, power and status over the years, my need to prove some form of primitive masculinity at the lights has dispersed. I sometimes think that as this avenue has been shut down now, I internalise whatever it was that was released on these mad bursts of self-destruction in a very unsafe vehicle. *It* was intense hostility. So I've been hoarding up at least fifteen years worth of intense hostility? No wonder I have problems. I look at my contemporaries and those that I have grown up with and Graham springs to mind. He's a very creative guy, he's in a band. I think he's signed to *Wolfstar Records* but that was ages ago so I guess a bigger company may have picked him up now. When he was younger, I used to see him now and again and he was rather cheeky and opinionated. He was hopelessly endearing and sketchy and didn't seem to care what anyone thought of him. Our group all pretended that we didn't care, but in actual fact, we probably cared more than anyone else. We spent an inordinate amount of time attempting to convince people that we didn't care what they thought of us. Everybody thought Graham was great. Graham *was* great. He's still in a band and he's still the same person, but he's got two kids now and a lovely wife and all the things that seemed ridiculous to him at twenty. He's toned himself down and he's the most extreme example I can think of this phenomena. It's simple I guess, it's called growing up.

I wonder if you have to find other outlets when you get older, in order to distinguish the flames of irritation. Or maybe the flames of irritation are just embers now. Maybe when you get to forty, you've seen it all before and reacted to every idiot and scenario and have come through the other end. Perhaps it's just time to join in with this circus. Comedians walk the tight rope between alternative and mainstream throughout their careers and more often than not will fall onto the comfy mainstream mat, at some point. I wonder whether those people that refuse to evolve are amazing, or pathetic.

My friend Pete once said that for every stupid thought you can think of, there are at least one hundred people in the world with that viewpoint, and a great deal of those people will have more energy than you to prove you wrong. Ignore them. I took this advice on board with enthusiasm and reaped the benefits for a little while. I think he realised that there is a time and a place for that attitude, and for me, the time and place is everywhere and always. I enjoy arguing about my right not to argue. Refusing to join in winds people up. Hey, maybe that's my outlet for irritation - irritating other people.

I crawl through the streets of Street and find a pub that fits my requirements for a pub. It looks discerningly ramshackle, warm, and inviting and they have taken care with the chalkboard on the front. I can see that there is an elderly couple eating ham and eggs by the window, and it looks dead, but in a good way. I am confident that I won't be part of a film scene here. I am convinced that this is not a local's pub as I have passed little housing for the last ten minutes. The road ahead looks as if it is also bare of life so I cement in my head that this won't be for locals. I must be on the periphery of Street. This must be the outer ring. I timidly walk in and my correct reading of the establishment pleasantly surprises me. I am immediately greeted by the bar lady who asks me if she can get me anything. I peruse the shelves and peruse my mind in order to establish whether I should get an alcoholic drink. I spy the whiskies and they remind me of rum, so I order a single rum and coke. She gets a shot of rum and asks me how much coke I want. I don't know how much coke I want so I just say 'Halfway is fine." She pours it to halfway and slides me the glass over the counter. I get a ten-pound note ready and wait for her to finish her bleeps. There is a pause, so I fiddle with my wallet for a bit and reach for my cigarettes. The pause gets longer and she is bleeping too much for there not to have been a problem.

"Oh not again." She comically sighs.

"Problems?"

"This thing is useless." She gives me a smile, coupled with a minuscule shake of the head. The combination amuses me. I vocalise the amusement. "Sorry about this Sir......Keith............*Keith*!"

She goes, I guess to get Keith. I'm sure Keith will know what to do. I wonder what would happen if I downed the drink and scarpered. Probably nothing. I would have a free drink and a story to tell. Do people actually ever do that? I wonder if people spend their lives doing things like this. I guess you do that when you're young, and it's a little endearing. Even thinking about what would happen if I did this, at my age is probably a bit pathetic.

Keith comes up from wherever it was that he was.

"This bloody thing!" he says with determined accuracy.

"Oh, whilst you're here..." What a strange way to start a sentence. They'll always be here as long as I am. "I don't suppose you rent out rooms?" I know they do because it says so, right in front of me on a small placard.

"We do yeah, have a word with Sandra when she comes back. We're not so busy at the moment. It's quite lucky for you really. Next week we're almost fully booked."

I wonder whether I should enquire why he is fully booked next week, but I don't.

"Oh great, I'll have a word then. Just a night would be good."

"Aye, aye. We do a breakfast too. Sandra will sort you out son."

Oh so now I'm son. I think I preferred sir.

BLEEP CHUNK READ EXCHANGE CHANGE BLEEP CLUNK.

Sandra doesn't come back for ages. I've almost finished my cigarette before I spy her polishing the jukebox. It's more of a quick dust but she pays particular attention to the screen, which I guess is littered with fingerprints as people fumble and attempt to point out good or appropriate songs to their friend/partner. Something fitting and appropriate with which to soundtrack their evening. I catch her eye and signal that I may want to talk with her.

I book a night and order another drink. It's only seven and I kind of wish it was later. My initial relief that this place appears to be in the middle of nowhere has now turned to slight disappointment, as there is nowhere for me to wander before I sleep tonight. I decide that I will leave the car here anyway and that my time allocated traveling has ceased temporarily until tomorrow morning. I am glad that I have net access on my new phone and I quiver with mock embarrassment at the thought of asking if this place had internet access as I know they wouldn't have, I mean just look at this place. There's no one else here to agree with that point and so I realise that it's unnecessary. It is perhaps a little wrong.

I have a beer as my second drink as I know it will waste a good thirty minutes. I have some papers around me and although they're not my paper of choice, they are rather entertaining and they are giving me plenty of ammo should I meet some normal people on this trip and have to talk about normal things. The paper is also suggesting how I should feel about these stories, which is good because I will be able to feel things about these stories if and when I meet some normal people whilst I'm on this trip.

Chapter Seven

It's 9pm and I have turned in. The room is tiny. It's on the right side of cosy not to be claustrophobic and is littered with quaint touches; an awful seascape, a tray with a massive doily, and a very confusing convoluted mat on the floor which doesn't quite fit the space and doesn't appear to lend itself to the décor of the room. I think I like it. It's got a telly and I can make tea so it's all I need, or could expect for the bargain price. It's anally clean and everything is in its right place. I don't want to mess this up so I sit on the chair under the shackled wooden board that I presume is meant to be a workstation or some sort. I make myself a cup of tea and watch Sunday night telly. It has the desired effect of sending me a little docile, and I sit for twenty minutes half watching BBC2 and half doodling on a page of scrap paper. I am attempting to write a plan of the next couple of days but I am just getting mod targets and squiggles right now. I wish I had a red pen so I could do the middle of the target with the correct colour. I don't though, and this little design could be anything without it.

I switch over and learn that *The Wicker Man* is on in half an hour and my evening suddenly has cohesion and clarity. I decide to take a bath and think about who I should contact next. I shall have some tea and individually wrapped shortcake in the bath, and then email and watch the film. I might even get a whisky from downstairs, and see if they can fix me any food. Hell, crisps will do. I ought to eat well tomorrow though. My guts are beginning to complain at the endless snackage that is going on. They are also complaining a little about the fact that I am on this road trip, with no definable plan.

I leave the bathroom door open whilst I bathe because I can. It unsettles me at first and then I enjoy the breeze that is coming in from the open window. I'm going to get the room as brisk and fresh as bearable, and then turn on the gas heater and watch the film. I don't recall much of the film and grow tired of it very quickly. I text three random people on my phone that I'm watching it, and ask whether I should prepare to shit myself. I put my phone down and wait to see if I will get any reply. All three reply within ten minutes and give me a witty quip and this pleases me. I look to my address book and check my email section. I like to have email addresses written down as well as having them on various databases floating around in the ether, in cables. It grounds me ever so slightly.

   I decide to email anyone I haven't seen in the past year with a general open ended 'How are you?' and I intend to trawl through old attachments to see if there's anything appropriate that I could send. It takes me a good half hour to find some people that I could do this to, and an additional ten minutes to work out each email. It shouldn't take that long, but the film is holding enough of my attention for it to be a slumberous affair. This I think is a rather ridiculous desperate thing to do but I continue and do so for most of the evening.

Someone gingerly knocks on the door halfway through the film and I am startled, a little disappointed. It can only be something official, or inane, and I get the horrible event over as soon as I can. It's someone from the bar asking me if I want anything, drinks, a sandwich, whatever. I find this a little disconcerting, but utterly charming and endearing at the same time. It looks and sounds as if I'm the only one staying here, and I kinda like that too.

I order a double whisky and some cheese sandwiches. I hope they're going to be big door step sandwiches with big slabs of cheese so I can remind myself that I'm in a pub. I toy with the idea of getting chips, or at least attempt asking for them but the notion is so ridiculous that they may be cooking fat and potato at this time that I stop myself. I don't actually remember going to sleep or at what time, or any of the usual stuff I remember. I remember chomping down a thin cheese slice sarnie, and I remember the whisky but I spent most of the night in varying degrees of undress, achieving small parts of the going to bed routine sporadically throughout the evening. It was the early hours before I went off and that was because I found the room very disorientating. I lost track of time completely. The television had cable and so there was a comedy on somewhere, always. The light also didn't dim and I wasn't concerning myself with what tomorrow would bring. I was just plodding through my evening and reluctant to let it go. I collapsed on the bed around 4.am and awoke three hours later with the unmistakable sound of life in my ears. I curse myself for not having brought earplugs. I can hear a vacuum cleaner. I am very tired. I need another five hours sleep. *At the very least.*

I get up and have a shower and wash away my need for more sleep. I have two coffees watching the local news and I get dressed and lounge about for a bit. I wonder what the protocol is in a place like this and when someone will come knocking for me. We're all waiting for someone to come knocking for us in the end. I wonder what life would be like if there was nobody who came knocking and when we would miss them. I decide as my mother did to nip these thoughts in the bud and I wander downstairs, where I am greeted jovially by Sandra and a young barman. Sandra immediately asks me if I would like a coffee and I accept, although my head is still a little buzzing from the two I just drank. I sit on a chair in the corner and read the local rag. I decide that I'm going to drive to South Devon and go over some old stomping grounds. I went to university in Exeter and have cousins who live in Totnes. I love that part of the world and feel a slight connection with it. I can see myself retiring there when I get older. I would have to move Tom down of course. I don't know where I'll stay but I'm realising with greater confidence that this really doesn't matter anymore. Staying overnight somewhere is pretty easy and other people seem to appear welcoming. My gut instinct appears to have done me proud on this occasion so there's no reason why it should fail me today.

I talk to the bar lad momentarily, he attempts to engage me in some talk about football but I'm not really able to play ball, so to speak. I enquire as to when it is that I need to leave my room and he says he doesn't *think* it matters. I tell him that this is great but that I'll be off in an hour or so. I know that it will be sooner than this but his lack of reaction buys me as much time as I need. Hell, I may even have another coffee and stay for a bacon sandwich. I am offered both, but I decline the coffee. I wonder if I am being offered coffee again because I look like I need to sleep. I wonder why I'm not being offered a bed, as that surely would be more appropriate.

I pack up my things and leave, making sure my exit is swift and polite. I used to have a tendency to hang around a lot when making exits, attempting small talk and not really wanting to leave if something had gone well. Suddenly, an event that went well is over and the next event has yet to happen. This next event may not be as successful and it may involve people not as nice as these people. I hang onto the last dying moments of a good time with regret and desperation. At least, I *did*. Now, I like to jump out quickly and I convince myself that the moment is still with me.

I drive slowly out of Street and find the actual town. I don't think I'll stop, I have no plans if I do and I'd like to get to Devon as soon as possible. I know where I'm going now and I take a quick peek at the petrol situation. I know I can get to Devon on this amount and feel no need to top up again as I pass endless small garages offering me inflated petrol prices. Actually, I have no idea if their prices are competitive; I am just assuming that they are not because of their location. I pass the boards with the numbers on and stare vacantly at them, wondering what they denote. I don't ever think about petrol. Friends, family and colleagues who drive raise their concerns with me almost daily about prices and the best places to go, and tax and the budget and I recoil in confusion and apathy. I need to buy petrol and I'm blowed if I'm going to worry about the price, or compare prices as the petrol consumed in running around town in search of a good deal kinda outweighs the saving surely. I don't like to think about petrol. I think maybe I should think about petrol now though as I have less than half a tank and I'm going to need to fill up at some point. I forget whether it is good to run it down to zero, or if that is actually the very worst thing that you could do to your car, and again my brain fizzes with all this conjecture about petrol prices and usage. I turn on the radio and forget about petrol for a bit. Now it has become something that I'm actively not thinking about.

I get onto the motorway at Taunton as the winding country lanes are beginning to wind me up. I feel like I need to blow away some cobwebs. I stop at Taunton to use an Internet café as my phone can't do everything I need it to. There is a nagging sense that I should be doing something else and that my world is falling apart back in Norfolk because I'm not there and although I know this not to be the case, I feel the need to send some emails and make some calls to ensure that this *really* is not the case. I have no trouble in finding a place, and it serves coffee. I spend an hour in Taunton, mainly surfing the web and chatting on *msn*. I sign in and am pleased to see that three people I know are online. They are all working but my brother pops into my world and asks after our mum. He also asks where I am and I tell him. I make up some plausible reason for me being in Taunton and he asks me to get him some rock. I'm not sure if he actually knows where Taunton is, as rock doesn't seem appropriate. My brother has just asked me to get him some rock from Taunton, in spring. I don't belittle him, and inform him that I will do my best. I have already done my best, and decide to get him some fudge. I think about presents and whether I should get some, and who I should buy them for. I also think about my uncle.

My uncle Ted is a lovely man. I don't know him very well and don't recall him being a big part of my life as a child. I sometimes crave for the kind of life where extended family and friends are around me in a small town and I have made that my world. I like the idea of going for a walk from my house and seeing frames of reference, memories and firsts had here and there. I went to four schools in and around Norfolk, my fifth school from the ages of eleven to thirteen was spent in Swansea as my Dad had to take a contract which meant we had to move. I didn't enjoy my time there to be honest and look back at it with regret and sadness. I think I first met Ted at a very early age, perhaps before my memory kicked in. People are always interested in new arrivals and I think we probably visited him as a unit. He was always there at big functions and gatherings. Christmas was an intensely private affair and was just the immediate family. But Easter for some reason went beyond our little sphere and I felt more comfortable with this and it turned into a real celebration of family and of life itself.

I think Easter 1988 was the last time I saw him. I must have been sixteen and was transferring myself to a different building in the school grounds to go to their sixth form college. I yearned to go to a different college but general laziness and the comfort of being swept along in the system dictated that I stayed; I suppose I'm glad I did (Tom did). He came down with the rest of his clan because my mother had invited them. I was deeply resentful of most things at that age but I found the onset of this section of our family to bring hope and happiness to me. There was something significant about the slight change in weather, my own new dawn that was about to happen and the chocolate eggs, buns and turkey that came with it. I don't remember talking to the guy much, he's quite quiet and there were more powerful personalities at work so I didn't get to know him very much. I don't think I got to know anyone very much at sixteen though. I was perhaps even more self-obsessed than I am now and would generally mumble something about my A levels and stomp around in an arrogant stupor, appearing endearing and young and foolish.

I don't know what he does, and I mean that. His name never crops up in conversation, which now I think of it, is a little strange. I wonder if he has a dark secret and that my family doesn't like to talk about it. I wonder what the secret is. I attempted to trace my family tree last year but didn't get very far. I got past four generations and then there seemed to be a full stop and a line that I couldn't break. I needed some cooperation from certain members of my family who were less than willing to help. I still don't know why, perhaps on somebody's death bed, someone will tell me.

Or perhaps everyone's just too busy with their own lives to worry about what other people who are now dead did with theirs. I'd like to know my history though and where I descend from.

When I was initially **diagnosed**, I took great solace in finding more about my family. Initially as an analytical medical response, I wanted to know whether anxiety and depression ran in our family. As if *that* would have made it more bearable. I found out no connections or clues as to why I am like I am. The only semi-interesting thing I could find is that it appears everyone I have researched comes from the south. This may be purely geographical, but I'd like to think otherwise. We have clumps of activity in the South West, South, East Anglia, and Wales. And it's not just that people have grown up and continued to live there, individual people with individual minds have moved to and from these destinations under their own steam, their own guise. There must be something in that, but I doubt there is.

I notice I have an email from Cath as I surf the web. I like to close down my email and just have it on the bottom of the page. It lights up if I have a new message, and it's like getting a phone call or text message. But obviously a lot safer. Thank the lord for email. Cath is someone I spoke to last year whilst on a chat site for those that suffer with panic attacks. The site was a blessing for me and I'm glad that there were other people willing to listen to my shit for a few evenings. It was far more than a few evenings actually but I don't want you to think it was. I remember going on the site one night and listening to other peoples horrific and sad stories. Jane from Birmingham hasn't left the house for seven months and wonders whether she will ever leave the house again. Tina is having difficulty coping with her job and is in an abusive relationship. Simon is fifteen and thinks he has every illness under the sun. He informs the room that he knows he hasn't got every illness under the sun, but whenever anyone mentions an illness, he panics that he may be a good example of somebody with this illness. I used to think Simon was faking it and just having a laugh, much in the same way I fear people thought; maybe still do think that I am faking it (whatever it is). I dabbled with this site for five months and Simon was always on there, like clockwork, Six pm. I guess he may have thought the same about me. His situation filled me with despair, and I would chat to him sometimes to reassure him that he didn't have bowel cancer, and being schizophrenic was a complex thing and he shouldn't worry about that either. I knew my words were futile but I took some solace in watching him write, *Okay I will*, or *Thanks*. I sometimes wonder what Simon is doing now, but only momentarily. I don't go on that site anymore.

Cath came into my life with refreshing ease and there has yet to be any awkwardness. Having said that, we haven't yet met and words on a page are one thing, but meeting someone is entirely different. I wonder how much of a guise she has developed and whether she is anything like I picture her to be. Not her visual image - I know what she looks like. She eagerly sent me a picture, but only via her msn, where everybody gets to see her picture. This was less weird because I wasn't actually given a picture, just pointed in the right direction to where anybody can view her picture. It wasn't weird, and I thank her for doing this. She looks very nice, the kind of girl I could go for a coffee with anyway.

Our relationship developed over time and it entered the sphere of mickey taking and surrealism. She doesn't take her conditions very seriously as she says it doesn't warrant serious discussion. I like this approach and feel comfortable in talking to her because I know any quirks or inadequacies I display won't matter. Her email breezily suggests a coffee in Plymouth next week. I don't really want to go to Plymouth, and I don't know where I'll be next week. I would imagine I'll be back in Norwich and things will go back to normal. I should slot back into my routine with ease. She lives in London with her cat and her sister. I guess she's in Plymouth with work, and has suggested it because she knows I'm heading that way. I email her back and say that I'm not in Devon, and will be back in Norfolk next week. I worry that she will view this as a snub, a rebuttal, but send it anyway. I don't add, "but we could do this...." or anything along those lines. I just wait to see her reply. I don't think she is going to reply immediately so I close down my email and get ready to leave the café. I've been here just over my allotted time, and have to pay an extra five pounds. The affable man behind the counter suggests that I stay for a bit if I have anything else to do, but I say no, and he gives me my five pounds back as if he is doing something charitable. I sneer, and leave.

As I walk back to the car, I pass a *Big Issue* seller. I catch his eye and get ready to say, "*I'm alright thanks mate.*" It's too early to say it at the moment, and I must wait for him to ask me first. I mustn't presume that he's going to ask me. I don't know why I'm so insistent that I'm going to say no anyway. I have bought the paper twice in my life and both times I have got back to the flat and read, absorbed and enjoyed the majority of the magazine. Paper. Magazine. It's a battle though and I don't intend to lose. I just want both of our dignities to remain intact for the next ten seconds. The moment passes, it's fine. I think one of the reasons I dislike this process is because a guy called me a dickhead once because I said no to a copy of the paper. The whole event was mildly ridiculous but I find myself distrusting every Big Issue seller I see now. I replay the event in my head over and over trying to decipher what I could have said to come out on top. I rarely think about what is was about my walk or look that gave him cause to call me a dickhead, but I sometimes wonder if he was right, and that I *am* a dickhead.

I now have empathy for people who have one bad meeting and it colours their common sense and judgment to other people in the same genre, area or minority. I have empathy, but I also have disgust. Which in turn makes me disgusted with myself, and maybe even a little disgusting as a person.

When I get back to the car, I check my emails on my phone and notice two new in my inbox. One of them is from a company that I bought from eighteen months ago and has an attachment I can't open with the phone I have. I delete it and this automatically opens the next one. It's from Cath. She suggests that we meet in London after I get back. This is when I get back so it's far from my mind's grasp. Time wise, it's probably only ten or so days because next weekend would be ideal to go down to London. I love London and I have friends there. But my mind is no longer thinking in time, but distance. I have Taunton to Devon, maybe to Wales and back before this meet becomes a reality. With this perverse logic in mind, I reply with an *Okay great* and a smiley face. She knows I use my phone for emailing and have yet to get a keyboard phone or one of those little electronic sticks that makes everything so much easier. She will therefore appreciate that's it difficult to write a long email on the phone. And she knows I don't do small talk, so everything's okay. As I have a plan for next weekend - well, the weekend after next, I feel a little more secure. I can see where I'm going a little. The more about the immediate future that I become aware of, the safer I feel. **I panic at the quiet times.** I have yet to be hit with the full implications of agreeing to this meet, and I won't until about twenty minutes before when I will become cigarette dependent, and intolerant and be buzzing like a fool.

But now, I must continue with my adventure and I am looking forward to this part. Maybe that's a bad sign. Getting to Exeter seems to take minutes; perhaps I am driving a little too fast. I head straight for the town of Totnes and as I arrive, I am immediately taken back to an old world full of memories and conditions. My cousin lives here, and I used to visit the Cavern Club in

Exeter when I was at uni. He introduced me to the cafes and record shops here. I am slightly disappointed that I have missed market day, but find a parking space on the street and look for somewhere to eat. I'm surprised I have managed to get here actually. My petrol light has been on for the last five miles, but the supermarket is at the bottom of the road, and hell I'll get some points for a full tank. *Must* check my points.

I enter a little coffee shop that has signs outside informing me that they serve baguettes, jacket potatoes, soup and toasted sandwiches. That sounds perfect. I think it's organic, or something. It's a very ramshackled cosy place. I am drawn to places like this. Tom isn't. Tom hates places like this and this baffles me.

We once went into town after a very indulgent film night where we got through a crate of Stella. We got up early and washed our cars (and faces) and then foraged for food. We passed many places like this, but he didn't want any part of it and we ended up having egg and chips in the back of a chain bakery. It was very grimy, but I liked it. I couldn't work out whether I would have liked it more had we gone to a place like I am in now. Tom is like me in that he can quickly identify pretension and his pretension alarm goes off with cunning accuracy and increased frequency. Maybe it doesn't, and I'm just becoming more aware of it as my tastes fall in line with my wage, and age. I guess he could be right, I mean they're serving sun dried this and that, and it looks as if their sandwiches are ciabatta. But what's wrong with that? I guess maybe the price; in this case, it *is* expensive.

I toy with the idea of going to a chain bakery and having egg and chips. I don't though and I sit down and wait for a hint that I should be doing something. There are laminated sheets on the table with a very simple selection of food. I like this simplicity and immediately decide to have a fluffy *BLT*. That's how it's written - *FLUFFY BLT, CRISPY BLT*. I guess it's meant to be endearing, but all I can see is the marketing implications and the way in which the local paper could put a spin on the place if they choose to do so (an 'I'll scratch your back' exchange). I look around and decide which ornaments shouldn't be there and what they could do to make the business better. And I think about a big fluffy bacon lettuce and tomato roll. This is the thought that stays with me the longest thankfully.

The roll is great, as is the atmosphere and the general *'It's okay to loaf'* attitude that both waitresses and diners seem to be promoting. I'm even finding the smell of the cigarette from the next table quite comforting. Usually I find the idea of mixing food and tobacco abhorrent. I knew a girl once who used to do both, *at the same time.*

I order a banana milkshake with my roll and the girl doesn't flinch, not even a knowing smile. This makes the final arrival of the milkshake even sweeter. It's got ice cream in it. It's not pathetic that a thirty four year old man is drinking a milkshake here. I stay here for a few hours. I've heard about, and have seen a few people that read in cafes and I think that it could be for me. I then realise that it is *not* for me, and stop rummaging in my bag for a suitable book. It would only be for show anyway. Which book do I want people to see me reading? I guess it would too much of a cliché to be sat here reading *Catcher in the Rye*. Maybe some Graham Greene would be appropriate. But not *Brighton Rock* because that's obvious. Something like *Our Man in Havana* should do it.

I look up and there is an atlas, which makes me feel small and unable to cope momentarily.

"Can I interest you in a taster?"

What's this now?

"It's hot chocolate, we're developing a new range, would you like to try?"

"Yeah sure, thank you."

"It's hazelnut. Have a taste and I'll be back later to see how you liked it."

"Right. Well, thank you."

I sit and look at this small cup of brown sludge and feel a little down. I shouldn't, somebody has just given me some hot chocolate. But I didn't want it and I don't really want to taste it. I feel like I've lost a point because I didn't say no to her.

I leave the café after telling the nice lady that the hot chocolate was nice, but maybe a little too sweet for my tastes. This seems to be of some significance because she says *"Aah!"* I leave, as I don't want to become any more involved in this palaver. Maybe I have a face on me today that says *speak to me*. And maybe that's a good thing because I'm on my own and it could get awfully lonely without people offering me hot chocolate. Life is full of people offering each other things to find out things about other things. It drives me mad.

I drive down to the riverside and smoke a cigarette on a bench. People walk by me in an effortless flow, some acknowledging me with an awkward smile, most walking by and not giving me a second thought. I put my mp3 in and listen to *James Yorkston*. I am transported into a completely different world for the duration of two songs, and kinda wish I had a spliff, and that it was okay for me to smoke it here. The songs conjure up images in my head and I feel happy for a bit. I see children, dogs, a sailing boat and a family eating sausage rolls from paper bags. I see birds and conversations. I try to lip read and decipher what's going on in other people's worlds. I hear James Yorkston. This is nice. This is costing me nothing yet I would happily pay for it. Maybe I will one day.

I leave Totnes and toy with idea of doing my round robin trip I used to do with friends as a teenager - Dartmouth, Slapton Sands and Kingsbridge. The trip was always enjoyable and I feel that it's the kind of thing I should want to relive. I have decided that reliving some things though is a mistake.

When I was a child, we used to go as a family to the wild woods five or so miles from Great Yarmouth. It was basically a small National Park, with two small car parks, a couple of huts where you could read about birds (and other things), and a walk way surrounding a massive lake. It wasn't that massive. All in all, you could waste a good hour or so in the park, more if you had brought some lunch. It took about an hour to get to from our house and my mother would begin to lay down the possibility that we may be going weeks in advance. Just enough time for my head to begin buzzing with excitement. It was originally trepidation and anxiety, but as we went more often and I knew what to expect, the mere mention of the wild woods would get me over excited and playful. I would nag and pester for a specific date and time, and people around me would tease and prolong my sense of expectation. And it always (still) delivers, which to this day baffles me a little. Because it was just a park, there were little to no amenities. If I were a little older, I could attempt to say that this was a golden age, but it wasn't. No time is - it's just a memory that has been influenced by a hundred other experiences, and it's not to be trusted.

I can say that it's not to be trusted because I went back to the wild woods for my thirtieth birthday. I went with friends and they enjoyed themselves. Hell, I enjoyed myself. But the new way in which I enjoyed myself did not warrant the banishing of all my old memories and the remaining thought that the wild woods was this big mystical world. It was a crippling disappointment that I wish I had experienced at an earlier age because it didn't fit into the already alarming *notion* that I could be thirty.

Since that day, I have vowed never to go back to a memory and attempt to relive it. I believe that this is what will happen should I attempt to make this round robin trip, and I now believe that the same may happen if I now go to Swansea, although Swansea does not hold any good memories for me so I begin to believe that this may be a good thing, as it could exorcise some demons.

I get onto the motorway as soon as I can, taking short cuts, long cuts, and roads I traipsed in my youth. I have plenty of music on board and my random shuffle generator (*in your face*, Tom) has selected *How to Disappear Completely* from *Kid A*. It makes me feel a little weird and I feel a million miles from home. I feel as if I am stranded and clutching at straws. Looking for something that doesn't exist, that never existed. I wonder where everything has gone, where the life I once led is. Where all my old friends are now and whether they think of me. A weird sensation of hate flies through my brain and I know I have to leave.

I head for Wales. It's early days and a quick stop at a garden centre before I hit the motorway provides me with sustenance and a better take on my situation. I sit down and eat my toasted sandwich, fascinated with the people around me. My mp3 player envelops my slightly fuzzy brain. The lady brings me mayonnaise and I smile and express my gratitude with a nod. I make no attempt to take my earphones out and can't be bothered with thinking about whether I should have done, let alone actually doing it. There is an old lady sitting on a plastic chair on the table opposite me. Hell, everybody is sitting on plastic chairs apart from me. I automatically analysed the room and chose to sit at the wooden table and chairs, which now I look a little closer, appears to be a set that is for sale. Everybody else spied this immediately and avoided it for the risk of some sort of polite reprisal. I didn't realise, and now I note that my fellow diners have picked up my error. They probably wish they'd sat here; it is a rather great set up. I spy the tag and see its £295. This means nothing to me.

I peruse the rest of the centre before I leave. It's full of films and cacti and CD compilations, and actual gnomes. There's a great deal of side-lines and stands with strange things people wouldn't want to buy from a garden centre, but they do. They lap it up, as do I. I see a lighter with **Tom** written on it and it looks cheap and nasty and as though I haven't made any effort at all - this is perfect for Tom. I grab it with gusto, and think about getting a basket and filling it with inane tacky gifts for everyone back home.

I leave the centre and get on my way to Cardiff. I know Cardiff a little and depending on the time may stop off and see how it's changed. I learn that the bay has been refurbished and it's quite the place to be now. It doesn't take long to get to the bridge and I get some change ready as I see the tolls ahead. I wonder what would happen to me if I had no money, but then realise that I have a credit card so that situation would never arise. I'm sure that there are procedures in place for that eventuality. There *must* be.

Entering Wales is enjoyable. There's something about the air and the sights and smells that always makes me smile.   Until the memories of Swansea enter my perceptions and I feel a little sick. Thankfully, the ghosts of Swansea were partially exorcised when I went to uni in the late eighties. I spent a lot of time in Bristol, Cardiff and Plymouth, mainly because my friend had a car, and cars were still toys back then. We spent inordinate amounts of cash on petrol, and inordinate amounts of time in the car - skinning up, eating and generally being young and foolish.

I drive around the racetrack entrance to Wales, feeling the gaping fields and making the road signs flicker with my accuracy and dare devilment. I follow and am being followed by fast expensive cars with fast arrogant drivers and I pull in and pull out, turning the safety of the world into a computer game, clutching the corners, melding the car into an artist's impression. I listen to the *Sonic Youth* and fall into a fast dream. As the road straightens and the cars behind flow past with intensity and flourish, I pull off at the Cardiff exit.

The Welsh signs amuse and intrigue me and I try to remember some of the names in my head. I forget them quickly. I ride down to Cardiff Bay, and drive round my old haunts and remember faces and conversations. I don't really think I want to stop anywhere and I am quite enjoying just driving. I wonder what's next and I have an overwhelming feeling that it may be time to head home. I don't really want to stay in Wales overnight and nobody has texted me or emailed me to suggest that I could. I feel a little as if I'm in a void, and begin to wonder whether this was one of those things I shouldn't have returned to. I pull into a fast food restaurant and grab a couple of burgers, merrily chomping them in the car whilst fiddling with my radio. It's meant to pick up new radio stations and frequencies automatically as I move into a new area but it's endlessly scanning airwaves and maintains its position that this fuzzy station is the end result of its search. It's clearly out of station but I listen momentarily attempting to decipher the tune and work out why my radio is not working to the manufacturers' standards. I get a text from Tom enquiring how I'm doing: **Where**

am I? I regret the fact that I'm not with him, talking nonsense. I then relish slightly in the fact that I am somewhere else and for all he knows, I could be having a good time. I don't know if I am. I mean, I'm eating a burger in a car park with no discernable plan and I feel a little sick. Alarm bells ring in my head and I decide to head off. The Welsh section of the trip has been far from satisfactory and I cling onto the hope as I smoke my cigarette that a magic text may appear telling me what I should do now. It doesn't.

As I pull away and get onto the long road ahead, Radio Bristol flickers into audible range and I'm informed of a tailback on a motorway north of here. I won't need to go onto this road and the local DJ cuts into the report with some banter relating to something he said to a previous caller. I become aware of the choices I need to make and whether I should be stopping at Bristol as I had at first intended. The alarm on my phone has yet to chime to alert me that I need to get my head back to thoughts of work and figures and organisation, and I await its arrival. It's not due for a while yet and this fact deflates me a little. Perhaps I'll just go back home now. With that in mind, I shuffle up my CD changer and drive past the turn off to Bristol.

As I am nearing my destination, I stop at a service station for a break from the boring drive. I pull up and immediately spark a cigarette, as some sort of sordid reward for getting another thirty miles, forty miles......I don't know how far I've travelled today and haven't been attentive as to how many I have left to go. Normally, I like to look at the speed I'm going, clock a quick blurred look at the miles I have left to do and make a quick informed idea about the time I will arrive. This gives me a good indication of whether I will be more hungry and where I could get food, how much my gauge is likely to be down so I can work out where and when I need to refill with petrol. It also means I am able to decipher whether this is a good trip or not, and whether there will be any nasty surprises on the way. If the time of day and the music I'm listening to and the sights I see somehow tally with a past memory of a similar journey, I find myself lingering in and out of the feelings I had on that other journey, regardless of how appropriate those feelings are. I like to file up as many frames of reference for as many parts of my life as is humanly possible. Pushing the envelope is scary, but if you know what is likely to happen if you do and know you will be able to deal with it because you've dealt with it before, well that's good. That gives you the upper hand.

I hate service stations. But they are a necessity and I know they will always be a part of my life. I feel safe in their clutches though; there is something very ethereal and anodyne about them to me. I should find them to be ghastly places - endless beeps, caffeine and plastic signs and rubber food. I don't though. Don't get me wrong, I *do* hate them, but they have everything you need, under one roof. And you can park, and you feel better after you've been. You're either relieved as a bodily function is allowed to perform, or satiated. It's a perfectly packaged and well-organised event, and I love it.

This one is particularly big, but you can't stay over. It clearly states that as you enter, and I think there are warnings that this is the case on the signs ten miles back on the motorway. Perhaps it isn't made clear, because that would take a lot of words that probably wouldn't fit onto a sign, and certainly would prove difficult for motorists to read, perhaps it would even be a little dangerous. Perhaps there is a logo or picture that denotes this. Perhaps I made it up. It does however say that it is open twenty-four hours. Because it doesn't have a picture saying it *isn't.*

I go to the bathroom and it's packed. I urinate and look up at a poster. It's meant for me, every man has an individual poster promoting a certain service and they are all unique. I've seen this one before. I look at it and read it three times whilst I piss. I look around the whole centre, reading and digesting menus and wondering if there's anything here for me. I don't really want anything but order a coffee from a stand and sit on a bench opposite the bathrooms, sipping my coffee and playing with my phone. I check my emails again - nothing. No plan and no progress. I spy Cath's last email, one that I have already seen and digested, and dealt with (*I think*). Oh yes, yes I have.

As I position myself in the driver's seat once again, and spark up another cigarette, I see a guy out of the corner of my eye who is clearly walking toward my car. He has vicious intent and I turn momentarily and catch his eye. He raises his head slightly and nods and smiles. It's that very thing everyone does; the recognition nod. It's ridiculous, and life saving. He gets closer and leans himself slightly too early. He is going to lean over and say something to me. My window is half down already, so I flick the engine and put it down fully, just as he has actually started his leaning. His face is wrinkled and if I had only spied his face, I would have made an effort not to have got myself into this position and pretend that I didn't sense him walking over here. I may even have zoomed off, but probably not. He looks like he does this a lot, whatever this is going to turn out to be.

"Hello squire. I hate doing this but I'm out of fags. Can I half inch one?"

Alarm bells scream out to me. I immediately say 'Yeah, no problem' and hand him a fag but my mind has already scanned my files and come up with the following:

1. He is wearing good jeans, not expensive jeans but jeans that fit him well and a top and coat that match, and he looks good. His face I distrust and my instincts tell me that this man is not to be trusted. He is not worthy of my trust. Perhaps this guy is a guy just like me who is just having a rough time at the moment and is out of fags.

2. We are in a service station. If this guy were to walk twenty-four seconds to his left, there is a shop that sells cigarettes. He doesn't live here, he must have come in a car. There are no coaches here. Why has he no money to buy his own fags? Maybe he has no money and stole those clothes.

3. This man is not a murderer. But this man *could* be a murderer. Think about it, murders occur, crimes occur. The people who commit these crimes are rarely caught. We like to think they are, but the ones that aren't caught are humanoids just like us. They eat, and have to go to the post office, and interact with people they see. Why is it so difficult to believe that this guy could be a murderer? People are always saying 'Oh, why me???!' Well, why the fuck not you? What makes you so fucking special that it is such an abhorrent and illogical notion that it could be you? It *could* be you.

4. He's older than me? I think he is. I have a baby face and I can never tell with other people. You know this already.

5. He clearly has an ulterior motive. He has spied me and today, I must be looking vulnerable. I probably am a little vulnerable today actually. He has clearly picked up on this and plans to exploit me.

He lights the fag from my fag, even though I have offered him a lighter. I find this a little strange.
"No need son, I'll use this."
"Oh, okay."
"So where you heading?"
"Oh, London."
"Yeah, which part?"
"All over."
"I'm heading for the coast, me."
"Okay."

"Yeah, it's been a bloody nightmare on the roads today, I got stopped by the police back there a bit."

"Really? Shit."

"Yeah, nightmare. Turns out my lights weren't working or something. I don't know. Cheers for the fag anyway."

"That's okay."

"Not really my brand, I'm trying to cut down."

"Right."

"Bit late for New Years resolutions though."

"Yeah, right."

"You're not listening to me are you?"

"No, not a word."

"I'm just talking away and you've switched off haven't you?"

"Yeah, I find you to be very boring."

"You're in a weird daydream now aren't you? I could be saying anything."

"That's right, it's got to the point in the conversation where I know I can get away with just saying yeah or okay because you are leading the chat."

"That's clever, so we're not having this conversation?"

"Well we are still having a conversation, but it's not this one."

"That's mad. So am I part of your daydream now, or is this my dream?"

"Does it matter?"

"Well yes, it's a little weird."

"Look, I don't mean to be rude but I doubt very much that you have the ability to daydream like this. It's taken me years to perfect."

"Well lar dee dar!"

"Look, it's my dream and so I can say what I want. I could tell you to fuck off."

"You couldn't hit me though."

"I don't want to hit you."

"Well if you're so sure that this is a daydream of your making, then you have control over what I say next."

"Maybe this is what I want you to say."

"You're a weird man."

"You need to buy some fags and stop scrounging."

"Yeah, like that's what you're going to rehearse in your head on the motorway, as if we'd ever be in a world where you could say that, to me."

"Well it's definitely my dream. You'd never say that."

"Wouldn't the world be a better place if everyone was like you, eh?"

"Okay."

"We're coming round? Okay, I'll finish this fag and thank you for it and be on my way, because I had no ulterior motive, you prick. I just wanted a fag. My wife has been in hospital for the last two weeks and we're driving home. I've had no sleep and I gave up fags two years ago and am desperately stressed out and unhappy. You looked like an amicable chap and I thought I'd be able to talk to someone normal about everyday things for a bit to have a break from the atmosphere that is currently suffocating me in my car. I was hoping for a pleasant exchange. I was afraid you may think of me as weird for approaching you but felt I better push the envelope. I'm *so* glad I did now."

"Okay."

"Cheers for the fag mate, bye now. Safe journey."

"Oh, yeah no problem, you too."

I drive. I don't like what just happened. I decide to get home as soon as possible as this is safe and I can forget about Wales, and that man. My brother texts me three times asking me where I am. I pull off just before the main sprint to East Anglia and inform him that I'm on my way home. I don't think to ask why he would want to know where I am, and don't give the exchange a second thought. My main concern now is to get home and do some washing, ironing and organising.

Paul suggests I drop in for a coffee when I get back. I figure he's bored at home. I don't remember if he's working on anything at the moment, but his additional *'Bring biscuits'* message suggests that he's not. When he's working, he doesn't have time for biscuits. *Or me.*

Entering my home sphere again makes me feel better and as I get in range of the radio frequencies, I hear the annoying comforting voice of the local DJ I hate the most. Her name is Julie Fletch, and she's abhorrent. I rarely feel secure in fully writing someone off because I know a few people who have ended up working in media, and I think they probably appear like dicks when they do their job. I don't think many people in the public eye are perceived to be how they really are. This woman though, I don't think she can be putting on an act. She is a horrible gross inflated version of a parody of herself. If she was an actress, she would be revered for her appreciation of the human condition. The way things stand though, she is merely a massive annoyance. I enjoy the outlet of hate and listen intently as she takes a call from someone who has rung in, in an attempt to win something. I don't think the caller actually knows what he is attempting to win, nor can he really believe that he is on air.

I don't know why I don't like her. I find myself disliking her so much sometimes that I actually have to stop myself and try to find something that maybe I could learn to even accept, or put up with about any small particle of her personality, such as it is.

I listen to Julie Fletch for another ten miles. She is discussing one of her infamous hot topics and the majority of callers appear to know nothing of the subject matter. I wonder why they are calling at all, but she does seem to be treating them with a degree of respect, and she has taken their call. Perhaps she is the first person to have taken their call in years, or perhaps she regularly takes their calls. Today's subject matter is immigration and it appears to be merging with gay adoption, and the general state of society as a whole. This swerve is mainly down to Taylor, from somewhere, who is attempting to engage Julie in a deep politically motivated rant about our Labour Government. This is making Julie a little uncomfortable; not only is she taking a call from someone who appears to know more than she does, or at least is saying so many words with so much passion that it would appear to be the case to listeners. But it is also a serious call. I relish in some of the points that Taylor makes and find many of his sound bites to be amusing, if not a little unacceptable. Julie has someone say something in her ear and she politely terminates the call with the words:

'Taylor there with some strong views on the subject, perhaps you have similar views or perhaps you disagree with Taylor. Let us know what *you* think. *This*, is Roxette.'

I turn over and decide to take a pause from the endless speech and tunes and noise that I have subjected myself to over the past couple of days. It feels a tad awkward for the first few minutes, and I am amused by the fact that I am able to feel awkward by myself, in my car, on the motorway. I look around; this isn't a motorway anymore but a dual carriageway. I wonder when this happened, and start thinking about the time that I will arrive at Paul's house, what he will be wearing and the mood that he is likely to be in and what I am likely to say to him when I get there. He said to bring biscuits, so I better stop off somewhere and bring biscuits, and cakes. I stop off at the local supermarket and peruse the aisles with disinterest and confusion. I'm usually quite productive and eager if I have a big shop to do as I can formulate my plan of attack, and I usually have a long list, with colour coding. But if I just have a couple of things to purchase, and especially if these are not solely for me, my thoughts become compressed and I feel as if I have tunnel vision. I am walking down a dark cave with a small light at the end, and minute-by-minute, the cave gets darker and deeper, and the light fades further and becomes more unobtainable. The importance of the correct purchase becomes paramount and the pressure unbearable. I stand longingly by the bakery stand, hanging back enough for the man to realise that I don't want him to ask me what I want, but near enough to view the prices and cakes, and near enough for the man to think that in a minute, I may possibly edge forward and enquire over the price of apple doughnuts, or cookies.

I spend too much time in situations like this, worrying over the possible outcome of a wrong purchase. I know where this stems from, and I choose not to talk about it with you. This is a little bizarre because I have chosen to regurgitate the bilge of every other thing that goes through my head. I wonder how much of my life has been wasted in supermarkets, agonising over this and I wonder more what I would have done with these hours if they were rebated. I sometimes wonder this whilst I'm in the (fucking) supermarket and the trip becomes more ridiculous than usual. I buy a small packet of biscuits surrounded by thick chocolate, which are expensive, and look expensive. If I buy these, I will not have to buy anything else as these are great and it looks like I've made an effort. Well shit, this *is* becoming rather an effort. I also pick up some milk for myself, and some crisps. I put the crisps back and pick up some doughnuts. I'm not sure if Paul likes doughnuts but I decide that it doesn't really matter because I do, and so do people who come to my house. There's no one due at my house but if Tom drops by, he can have a doughnut. Yes, buying doughnuts is the right thing to do.

My brother's house looks achingly clean and perfect from the outside as I pull up on his drive. I'm not sure how this is achieved but I guess that it may have something to do with the fact that all the houses are uniform and looking a little closer, even the flaws appear to have a rustic rambling quality, rather than the decaying rotten quality my building seems to spell out. I think he knows this, even if he doesn't think this himself, he knows I think it and he relishes in this. I think I should perhaps stop buying the most expensive biscuits when I go round because it only reaffirms both our beliefs that he might be on a higher plane. I don't think he is, but it appears that he is, so must be.

"Hello Sir. Or should I say traveller..." He spies the bag in my hand, from our supermarket of choice. "You have biscuits."

"Yeah, you should be able to taste the difference, *apparently.*" I scoff at the notion that we will be able to, even though I buy them, and we do.

"Come in fella, how are you? Tell me aaaallll about it." He says as a reference to a film (I think), or television show and I decide not to tell him all about it.

"Saw a few people I hadn't seen in a while, all good fun."

"Is Mum with you?"

"No. No, I guess she's in Oxford. I was only there for an evening. I just said hello and that was it really. I stayed in that hotel you sorted out for us."

"Yeah that was a good deal, how was it?"

"It did the job."

"I thought Mum would be with you."

"Why?"

"Hang on, when did you leave Oxford?"

His face suddenly looks different, as if his brain has just fizzed, and realising that there maybe is a missing piece of a jigsaw, and he now has the means to put the jigsaw into place. When he does though, the jigsaw may not be a very nice picture. I immediately know that my uncle must have died, and begin to feel very awkward as I do not like where this conversation is going.

"I take it there were some complications in Oxford then?"

"I figured you must have known. Yeah, well he died." There's no emotion in his voice, and I am glad.

"Shit, well Mum didn't ring or anything. Did she ring you?" I stop myself because I realise I am caring more about the whys and wherefores surrounding Mum's first port of call on hearing bad news than her actual welfare, or the welfare of my uncle. Jeez, let's not forget that someone has died here.

"I got a call from Dad. She's sorting out a few things in Oxford until the end of the week. I think she's concerned with her brother's sanity to be honest with you."

"Yeah."

"So you didn't know?"

"Er, no." There is an eerie silence, but it's not awkward because Paul has the hindsight to put a music channel on the television. I presume that he did this for my benefit and that he hasn't been watching it all morning. I kinda like the idea that he has though. "So, what happened? His heart? I mean I know he had a heart attack but I was under the impression that he was no longer critical."

"Oh no, it wasn't his heart."

Mogwai come on the television, and immediately our collective response is to turn and watch the video, transfixed on the sounds that are coming out of his system. For the duration of the song, nobody speaks, which should be weird because he needs to tell me how my uncle, his uncle died. But it's not weird. I wonder why this song is on rotation as it's an old song. I think they must have re-released it as it has recently featured on an advertisement.

Paul regains his composure as the guitars die; "It was an allergic reaction to a drug he was on. Carliium or something."

"Carliium? What's that?"

"I don't know. Trilliium?"

"That's an anti histamine isn't it??"

"Actually, I think it's a building firm." We both shake our heads and let out an exhausted laugh."

"Jesus, he died from..." Paul stares through my thoughts and grabs my meaning with his intent mind.

"No, it wasn't an error on the hospital's part. That's the first thing I thought of."

"Hmmm, it doesn't sound so straightforward."

"Just one of those things it appears." I believe it when Paul says this. I think if pretty much anybody else would have said this, I would have questioned this statement. It's such a woolly and unfortunate thing to say but I know that Paul has researched and questioned and examined everything and so it is not a flippant or throwaway comment coming from his lips. I know this, and it makes time in his company very easy for me. Years of calculation and stress are dissolved.

"Who was that?"

"Mogwai."

"I like it, burn me a copy." I will, in time.

"So when is Mum coming back?"

"I don't know, give her a ring."

He offers me his mobile. He always presumes that I am still on an expensive rate on mine and this slightly irritates me. He is right of course. It would be cheaper to use his.

"I'll give her a ring tonight. I haven't got much to say to her right now. Nothing particularly genuine anyway."

"You should ring her though."

"I will."

Evan Dando comes on MTV and once again we are momentarily transfixed. His words are impressive and humorous and make me think less about myself and more about my mother and my uncle. I wonder why I am not feeling sad yet, or if I will ever feel sad for the man. He was a lovely man and I am beginning to wonder what it will take for me to shed a tear, for anyone, for anything.

"How's work going George?"

It's less of a question and sounds more like a statement. The fact that he uses my name after it makes me feel a little sinister.

"Good."

"Really? That's good. What are you doing these days?"

"Same shit, underpaid and overworked."

"Any plans?"

"Well I've been offered a job in a different department, but that's been offered to me twice before."

"Oh, that events management gig?"

"Aye. I should no doubt give it a go, but something doesn't feel right about it. Anyway, the company has allowed me to work from home more now."

I laugh slightly, mainly because it's such a ridiculous sentence. The company haven't decided anything, the company rarely does. It's just somebody in a department deciding that he or she may be able to get away with doing something because something has gone a bit awry in another department.

"Result mate."

"It is, isn't it?" His simple two-word reply makes me feel quite elated and I realise that this *is* a good result, and I *am* his mate.

He shows me his latest portfolio. I am genuinely interested and a point in the conversation has occurred that allows him to talk about his work. It's very impressive and I can see why he excels in his field. His work is concise and informative but has the welcome touch of creativity that is required. I never really thought of him as a creative person because the part of his character that shines through the most is his business acumen and determination. That mix doesn't fit comfortably in my head and I like to think of people as being creative, but flaky, or decisive and business minded, but closed-minded. As the years go by, I am offered more and more reasons to change this belief system, but never really do. Perhaps I will change this view in a couple of years. We'll see.

It's getting near what I would consider other people's tea time, and I think he may have plans and more importantly, his evening life will begin soon and I know it to be very regimented. I don't think I want to be involved, nor do I really want to be invited, nor do I think I will so I make my excuses and get ready to leave.

As I get into my car, I check my alarm on my phone and notice that it failed to go off two hours ago. I look at the phone with blank apathy and sit in my car for a bit, watching people come home from work and enter their evening mode. I watch a couple get out of their car and wave to another couple getting out of *their* car. They mouth something to one another and both parties laugh, and I feel a little sad. I want to get out of my car with my partner and mouth something to someone else and laugh.

"*No, you don't.*" Tom says in my head, and he's right.

On my way back to my flat, I think about stopping off at the post office in the local one stop shop. I still have packaged CDs for Cath that I need to send off, but if I'm going to see her, if I'm really going to do this, then there's no need. I stop anyway to get milk. I left the milk and doughnuts at my brother's house. This shop doesn't sell doughnuts so I pick up a treacle tart. I can't imagine as many people like treacle tart that like doughnuts, and you can't just leave a treacle tart around the flat. People won't help themselves, and I will have to become involved in the cutting of the treacle tart and it will all get very complicated. But this place does not sell doughnuts and that is a fact that I have resigned myself to.

I return to the flat to find my neighbour in the corridor talking to someone in a baseball cap and a puffa jacket. I haven't seen a jacket like that in years. I nod to her and she nods back, her guest seems agitated and irritated that I have arrived. There's no need for him to be, and I enter my flat as quickly as I can having to remember to use both keys this time. I expect to be awash with mail as I walk through my hall, but I'm not. In fact, all that is waiting for me is a client report that has been forwarded to me from work and a bank statement.

There is very little sorting out or organising for me to do on my return, and this saddens me. All that lies in front of me now is the crippling realisation that everyone is right and that I must accept this job offer in Events Management, because this is progress. I cannot afford to continue this endless bickering, complaining and dissatisfaction when there is a solution in front of me. They're right and this is incredibly irritating. I'm not sure I like the idea of them being right, I'm very set in the notion that I am right and things will not get better, and that this is my life. I suppose I should contact work and enquire about this new employment opportunity and go for it, and earn a bit more money and have new things to do. I could then tell people about the new things that I do and be stretched for a bit. This would then become normality and I should strive for something else, something newer and something better. The road ahead of me is not exciting though. Instead, I feel a suffocating list of things I don't want to do or achieve, and a bigger list of people I will have to schmooze on the way. This all makes me a little sick.

I check my emails. Before I had email on the move, this used to be a rather exciting exercise and I would look forward to the click that catalysed all the new information. Old friends, new friends, companies, questions. I would file, discard, forward. On completing this exercise, I would feel free and safe and unhindered by anything, anyone. But now I check my emails at least twice a day. Most of the time, it is a perpetual exercise anyway; my emails are usually on in some form and my account will automatically inform me of a new addition to a conversation thread. Although this means I am always on top of electronic mail, it doesn't bring me any joy or satisfaction. I am unable to go a couple of hours without checking them. Perhaps this is a problem that I should address; I can think of worse addictions. Smoking, for one. I'm not addicted but I will have another one with an espresso right now.

I sit and watch the rolling news on the twenty-four hour British channel. There's still news about the war and I have become numb to its meaning and significance. I became numb to most things years ago. I am no longer passionate about the things I used to be, and feel safe in the knowledge that there are enough people out there who will fight my corner. Will Self, James Whale (to an extent), Charlie Brooker. Perhaps these are not the people I relate to, and they are actually the people that I want you to think I like. Maybe I spend so much of my time attempting to be a visionary maverick that I forget myself. I'd like to be a part time revolutionary. The kind who just spends five minutes each day on his cause, if that.

There's a news report on a Government leakage and a media cover up, a few more deaths, and breaking news that we do not need to panic yet, but the flu pandemic is progressing, and we are responsible for global warming now. It's pretty much a fact and official looking men with letters after their name are pointing to the culprits. It's us and we should be worried.

"Should we be worried?" the newscaster asks the other newscaster.

"Well quite possibly, yes." says the newscaster.

I decide to postpone my worry until next month, or whenever. I cannot commit right now to that concern. I am sure that next month, I will have something more pressing to think about.

An advert comes on in between the local update and the weather for a news special pencilled in for Friday night. I decide that I am going to watch this, and I hope that nobody will invite me to some place or even contact me, perhaps ever again. I am intent on watching this special in two days time. I have a very small plan now and it would be great if I could fill the time in between now and then with other things. Let's say that half of them should be things I have to do, that have a definable result, a quarter to enjoy myself, even if I don't. The remainder of the time can be held for miscellaneous, and the art of living itself.

The programme is an extended news report concerning a drug that I took in my youth. The drug has been a bone of contention for years and I have watched endless reports on the dangers of taking it under the wrong circumstances and the ease in which it is prescribed. I have extensively researched the drug on the Internet, and heard a thousand horror stories about its effects. I was seriously considering joining the bandwagon a couple of years ago and confessing to the fact that I may be a part of these statistics and that for me, the experience was also a nightmare. I thought long and hard as to whether this was a good idea but concluded that I wanted, needed to move on and put it past me.

Every year or so since, a news report comes out that adds to the already massive list of worries and concerns, and **facts** that surround the drug. I'm not sure what I plan to gain from watching yet another programme about this but I will watch it and I will absorb the information. The people who need to watch the programme are informed of its nature and broadcast date and doubtless they spend a few minutes contemplating their move. They probably have a set of statements ready to rebuff the evidence that is laid out before them, and I am not naive as to think that this airing will make an ounce of difference. I am not so cynical though that I allow myself to think that the making of the programme is a pointless exercise. I believe that it needs to be said, over and over again and that maybe in ten years time, something will happen that will start to change things. We're talking Government funding though, and the NHS, and huge companies that have bigger profits and untouchable directors.

When I first took the drug, I was taking recreational drugs as well and I was young, frightened and searching for answers. I suppose the same could be said of me now, but I'd like to think that the twenty or so years that have passed in the meantime have counted for something; some kind of increased awareness of something or other. I'd like to think that I am now an advanced form of what I used to be, and maybe that's half the problem. I don't know.

I remember taking the drug willingly and expectantly and paying little attention to the list of side effects that were laid out in front of me. I mean - every drug has side effects. Some people are allergic to some things, if you have been told by your doctor that you have an intolerance to some sugars, you should probably contact him before you take a lozenge to ease your throat. If you have a really bad sore throat, and asthma, you shouldn't really take the really good lozenges that work within your lungs to provide immediate relief. You shouldn't take aspirin if you have, or have ever had stomach ulcers. Also if you have had blood clotting disorders, or gout. Perhaps you have liver or kidney problems or are allergic to aspirin. Well that clearly rules out taking aspirin. If you are taking a different kind of anti-inflammatory drug, or develop a runny nose or itchy skin after taking your aspirin, you should stop taking it. Your pharmacist should be informed if you are taking blood-thinning medicines and there is a possible association between aspirin and *Reyes syndrome* when it's given to children. Oh, and children should be given a smaller dosage.

After you have decided that taking aspirin may be a good idea, you have to consider what could happen to you. Your headache may disappear but it's not over. It can sometimes cause indigestion, nausea and vomiting. In which case, you could take some indigestion liquid, or chew on some ginger. Rarely, aspirin may irritate the lining of the stomach, and can sometimes cause bleeding. You can see if this is the case by examining your stools. You should probably do that. Your face may swell up, your mouth and lips will probably be the first to go. You may have difficulty breathing. If you have kidney problems, and you ignored the advice not to take the pills, you may notice swelling of the limbs, but if anything unusual happens, there's no problem. Just consult your pharmacist or doctor and they'll be able to help.

I don't look at the back of the packet anymore. My doctor is a good man and I trust him implicitly. I wonder though whether I am just the last in a long line of people trusting each another implicitly and whether someone needs to break this cycle. I am a patient though and it surely isn't up to me. Anyway, I'm young and I don't know much about anything yet.

Within a week of taking the drugs, I slowly became numb and helpless. I am unable to articulate the true state I found myself in and I am confident that this is a good sign. My ordeal (such as it was) went on for six months and I remember little about it. I spoke to no one during this time, bar a psychologist who I saw once a fortnight to see how the drug was affecting me and whether I needed more, or less. It was always more and I would always have to go to the chemist to pick up a bigger pack. I tried my best not to look depressed as I entered the chemists as it felt like a cliché.

'Oh here's the depressed boy picking up his pills.'

I didn't want anyone to talk to me or acknowledge my existence, and I certainly didn't want anyone to talk *about* me. I severed ties with everything and everyone.

I have probably talked about this before. The whole experience leaves me cold to be honest. My saving grace was television and I think my continued fascination with it lies somewhere within those six months. Sometimes, suddenly whilst watching a programme in the early hours after a late one of a weekend, I can be momentarily transported back to that nightmare and this I see as an alarming wake up call to ensure I never go down that road again. In a nutshell, the drug numbs your senses and though you find it alien to think of negative thoughts, you also find it impossible to think of positive, or even neutral thoughts. I was a walking shell of a boy and it went on for such a long time that I feared, and perhaps still do fear, that it has had some lasting damage. The stories I hear from other people and their experiences only add to this concern.

I watch the rest of the news for half an hour, and then realise that this is twenty-four hour rolling channel and that the news will never end. I'm quite happy absorbing news for the minute and so make myself a long coffee and sit back, ready to be informed about anything and everything. Sometimes I feel like that robot in *Short Circuit* and just wish I could take it in as fast as his robot brain. Jeez, he was a nice robot.

I need to go into work tomorrow and I need to discuss some things with Charles. Things are going well working from home but without the need to fool other people and fill the working day, I realise how easy my job is and how little time I actually need to dedicate to it to pull in my wage and keep everybody happy. I don't think I'm bored (yet), but maybe I am. I need to know what this events job will bring and I need to know what's going to happen to me. My contemporaries all seem like they're going places and have broken free from something and are now on the their way somewhere. Perhaps they think the same of me. I doubt they give me a second thought though. Perhaps they're as self-obsessed as I am.

I walk down to the local post office on a slight caffeine buzz. I see a few people from the building outside the shopping complex and gently gesture a nod in their direction. I am too tired to wonder what their reaction could possibly mean and I enter the post office and join the queue. The queue is long but I don't mind waiting. As I wait, I glance at the shelves to my left and see if I can see any feature films that will excite me enough to invite Tom around. There's a couple actually; perhaps I'll get one out. I spy a deal that makes it impossible not to rent two at once and make a mental note that this is what I shall do next after sending this parcel off. Because I'm not going to London. That's a decision I have made and a decision I am sticking to. I'm not ready to see Cath. Maybe I'll never be, and this is as ready as I can ever get, but I don't think I'd be very good company right now, especially meeting someone for the first time. A tie just ain't gonna cut it and our second meet might not be for months, years. It may affect our online relationship and it will definitely be a fucking nightmare.
   My attention is brought to the man who the lady is dealing with five humans ahead of me. I join it half way through and have missed the bulk of what is going on.

"Well I just refuse now out of principle."

"I don't blame you. People ask me how they can do it and I should tell them but I don't. You can do it online but..."

"I can't be doing with that."

"I know, I know."

"You'll need to fill out this form, and then I can process it for you."

"More forms?"

"I'm afraid so."

"Look, I'm causing a queue here."

"Perhaps we should do it online."

"Yeah. It's all progress." He laughs. She laughs. He leaves. She waits.

"Hello, I'd like to send this to Birmingham please. It has no value."

"Okay, pop it on the scales for me."

"Right, like this?" The old lady pops it on the scales for the slighter younger old lady behind the counter.

"That's going to be eighty pence, first class."

"Yes."

"Okay, and you say there's no value?"

"No no dear, I wouldn't say it's worthless though ha ha."

"......."

"What's the petition for?"

"They're trying to close us down."

"Oh no. That will never do."

She doesn't sign the petition.

"Pop it through the hatch for me."

"There you go."

The chats get boring now, I am aware that popping things on things and through things is the done thing though, and I get my package ready to pop on the scales and then through the hatch when it becomes my turn. If it ever becomes my turn. I am annoyed at myself for being annoyed at being in the queue and decide instead to concentrate on the two films that I am going to rent. I think momentarily about leaving the queue and looking at the DVDs and then joining the queue in a minute or so. Two people have arrived after me though and I am reluctant to lose my place. I wonder how feasible it would be to ask the person behind to save my place and deduce that it is *very* not feasible. Very not feasible indeed.

When I get back from the post office with two films that promise to entertain, I text Tom and suggest that he might like to come and watch one of them with me. It's Thursday and I know he has Friday mornings off. He may even have the whole day off this week, and even if he doesn't, he can swing it if the mood takes him. He doesn't reply for an age and by early evening, I have forgotten about the films, and my invitation and take an early bath. I know I have to go to see Charles tomorrow and I have no idea what I'm going to say, but after the relative success of my road trip, I decide not to plan anything and take it easy. I like playing games with Charles and I think he views me as a bit of a challenge. I'd like to think he does, and not an annoying flaky loser. This is how I often think other people view me. I still don't know how I look upon myself; I spend too much time lying to other people to have an accurate truthful version of myself in my head. I lie to myself and I do it well. In this sense, I am a success.

Tom doesn't text and I am reluctant to ring him. I start to watch one of the films but it quickly bores me. I find films that are formulaic either fascinating, or tedious and it will often depend on whether there is a saving grace actor somewhere to maintain my interest. I usually go by Directors for films I know I will enjoy. I still only have a handful that I know and trust and branching out from this comfort zone has lead to many a wasted hour.

I switch it off after forty-five minutes having given it a fair old chance; perhaps I'll pick it up again tomorrow (the offer is for three nights). I used to trawl through the net and go on film forums in an attempt to find out the classic films and the films that I need to see before I die. I used to collect videos and each Christmas as a youngster, I would give my friend Ben a bunch of videos and a copy of the *Radio Times*. I had circled those programmes that I wished him to tape, and underlined those that were essential. The essential ones were usually films, and I seem to recall he missed *Terminator* one year. Maybe it was *Predator*. I can't remember. Ben was the first person in our sphere to get a video recorder, and it was massive. I don't remember buying videos that weren't blank for years. I remember my cousin had a *French and Saunders* video that cost £17.99, and contained three episodes. It also developed wavy lines at the top and bottom of the screen very quickly, and I would be fascinated as my uncle would fiddle with the tracking for what seemed like hours.

Charles is waiting. I sense that he has been waiting since Wednesday for me to give him an update on the progress of a couple of clients, and an update on how this whole working from home thing is going. Maybe he also wants an update on my general well-being, and anything else I can think to update him on.

"Are you free at some point today to have a quick chat Charles?"

He looks startled as I poke my head round a half open door, and see him looking confused, eagerly staring at a spread sheet with his finger tentatively hovering over his mouse.

He drops his composure and gives me a warm smile.

"George, come in, sit down." He pauses. "You any good with *Excel*?"

"Well I use it."

"I don't know what this fucking problem is. I can't get this macro to work."

"I don't get involved with macros."

"Neither do I." He suspends his thoughts momentarily and makes an instant decision to send the problem elsewhere. "Oh, James can do it."

I don't sit down. "Still ticking along then?"

"Jesus, we've taken on two new trainees downstairs. They're good but it means the Kingman lot are having to send most of their workload across town."

I have no idea what he is talking about.

"That's not good. I've managed to secure those clients for a six month contract and they've provided me with some valuable leads."

"Excellent, excellent." He offers me a seat and I gingerly take it. "How are you, in yourself?"

"Fine."

"Good. How do you think this is going to pan out? Are you happier working from home?"

I search my brain for frames of reference. There is something in the tone of his voice that is eerily familiar. I decide to keep it formal, even though I yearn to break out into blatant honesty. Not with Charles.

"I can dedicate more time to clients from home."

"Hmmmm....."

"I don't get bogged down with office procedure."

"I understand." He flicks the top of his pen.

"I'd like to get a little more definition though." I am wondering whether he'll pick up on what this means.

"A more definable role?"

"In a way yeah, I'm doing a lot of things that... well let's put it *this* way, I'm doing things that other people could do more effectively."

"I see."

"Do you?" I nervously laugh.

"You're very diplomatic, George. You've been here a long time and you've developed your own style. Do you think maybe that style has come round and bitten you on the ass?"

"I guess that's what *you* think."

He pauses and smiles, and lowers his voice a little. "I don't think anything mate. What can I do to make things better?"

I am disappointed in this, it feels like a cop out, but I'll play ball.

"I think a lot of procedure can be given to others. I am happy to chip in and do my bit but I waste an inordinate amount of time on unnecessary things. That's something that can be done immediately..."

"You're right George, but I'm not sure why you are telling me this. Just get someone else to do it."

"Well I'd like things to evolve."

"I know. Look, are you saying that you'd rather not come in to the office at all?"

"No." Maybe I am.

He looks concerned. "I am glad you've come to see me and I am glad you're raising these issues with me George. There's only so much I can do. That's one of the reasons I suggested you go for the events management position. The salary increase is obviously a nice carrot, but it's a very definable role, and gives you a lot of scope. You would have people working under you and you'd be able to steer the ship."

"It's not available anymore though is it?" I don't know this for sure, but sense that I have missed my chance.

"Joanne has taken on the position for now, but only because there was no one else. She's a busy lady."

"She can do her job *and* this job?" Charles looks tired of this conversation, so I give him the opportunity to wrap it up. "Okay, look, get me some information from head office about the events management thing. I'll carry on with the projects and start delegating some of the bumpf to colleagues. If they complain, I'll say it's down to you."

I give him a wink and he laughs nervously.

It's at this point that I decide that I will view my position as being paid on results, not time. Perhaps the board will view this also, and I will be rewarded appropriately, significantly. With every job I have had since school, I have found it very hard to break away from the time equals money ethos. The more you do, the more you earn and if you work like a monkey, then you will reap the rewards. It only started to occur to me a couple of years ago that you could develop a skill and be paid for a result that could take you a couple of hours. This is okay. One man can get paid more than another and it is fair. I still feel regret and a little bad for those people that are paid less than me, and that I am somehow a fraud, but I feel equal regret that I have wasted all these hours feeling like this. I also have decided to stop seeking permission to do things so much. Charles doesn't have the answer.

I sneak by my office and check my mail. I have a few reports that need looking at but most of my mail is stationery booklets. I decide to take the bull by the horns in a very placid insignificant way and I grab the brochures and take them down to Sam who looks after most of the orders after she has opened the post. She normally leaves at around midday but if she has a large order come in, sometimes she can be here until four. This is slightly ridiculous as she doesn't get paid overtime. She likes to complain about it, but I can't see how things will change. Sometimes she leaves a load of boxes in the first aid room and locks the door. Nobody knows they are there, until a couple of days later when she gets a trainee to help her lug them down to Accounts. What Accounts want with stationery I do not know. But it keeps Sam occupied, the trainee feels as if he is helping; maybe even progressing, and the company that sent them tick along.

I get out of the lift and see Sam and she gives me a tired comical look. I like Sam a lot, and I think she might like me. She's slightly older and I flirt a little with her, just staying on the right side of bawdy, toying with suggestions and generally *"being awful"*. If I was somebody else and heard myself talking to her in this manner, I may well think that I am a cunt. Maybe people hear me and fail to realise that we are friends and *do* think of me in this way. I don't really care.

I pass her the brochures and tell her that I'm not dealing with the companies anymore, and enquire as to whether I could use her services (should the moment arise that I should need any more stationery). She groans slightly, then smiles. I shouldn't have given her the brochures, I realise she doesn't want, or need them. I chat inanely to her outside the lift and help her with what I can help her with.

I venture upstairs and check the board outside the cafe. There's no scampi today, or at least it's not being advertised as a scampi day. I survey the seats through the decrepit glass door, and see the coast is clear. Judy is working hard behind the counter. I'm not sure what she has just made but it looks like a lasagne. That won't sell well, I know that much. There are chips though and they always go down well. They're very social and I think most departments get a plate of chips at some point during the day. I order a toasted sandwich with salad and Judy tells me it won't be a minute. I believe her, and pay for it, then hang around the large window that overlooks the courtyard, it gives me an eagle's view of Sectors 4 and 7b. There's not much work going on, I can't see people running around working.

I take the sandwich down to my office and smile at a young girl who works in Promotions. She smiles back. I think she is smiling because I am holding a plate of food, but maybe not. I check my emails and make a few calls and surf the web for a bit. The usual suspects are pulled up and I check a few forums I sometimes post on. This is what I do at work. If you count the hours during the day that actual work is undertaken, it barely pushes one. Yet this is a scenario that I have created, and perhaps now Charles is right. Perhaps it is going to be my ultimate undoing. For the things that rile me now are the things that I have created. Rebellion is all well and good when there is someone or something to rebel against, and there always needs to be a goal or reasonable purpose. Otherwise, it's just a little sad.

I go home, knowing less than I have ever done about my job and where I am going. The excitement and youth I once felt from somehow beating the system, whilst reaping the benefits of being a part of the system is gone. I was kidding myself; I *am* kidding myself than I'm anything more (or less) than anyone else. I think Charles is beginning to realise that things are beginning to grate. I wonder what would happen if I handed my notice in, and the repercussions that this may have. For the life of me, I cannot deduce who would be affected. I think they would be temporarily riled at my actions as they would not be able to employ another me. Charles knows that I do more than is expected of me, and less than I am able. I hope I have planted some seeds in his head and I hope he is now in fear of something. I finish my day, emailing Charles before I leave stating that I will back in on Wednesday. He doesn't reply.

Tom still hasn't replied. This is not unusual. Once we went four months without seeing one another and it wasn't deliberate or weird, neither was it an issue when we finally met and shared our woes and anecdotal evidence over a warm pint. We tend to just slip in and out of social expectation and if he is off doing his thing and I am doing mine (whatever that is), we just drift in different directions. I think maybe this is shaping up to be one of those times, and perhaps it's for the best as I appear to be in a place where change needs to be implemented. I think I should treat my life more like work right now. I think this more than ever; it's the only way I can solve whatever it is that needs solving.

Monday is my appointment with the doctor. I am not seeing my doctor; he has referred me to someone who is apparently a specialist in the area within which he thinks I fall, and I am seeing this man at **3.00pm.** He is young, perhaps only a few years older than me and I am aware of his existence because I have seen him pottering around the surgery looking earnest and sympathetic. I know that I won't get on with him. My guts are telling me this, and I am not altogether sure why I agreed to go as I know pretty much what he will say, and what I will say in return. In a way, it is the hypnosis all over again. However this time, I am paying no monies, and it's normal so I will give it a go without fear of reprisal. I have a whole weekend to worry about this man and the things that he'll say to me and the things that I will attempt to say to him. I fear that I will look weak and he will feel superior. I don't know how I'm going to act with him. Our ages are close and I think we may be as intelligent. Perhaps I am a little more. I think maybe I have more social intelligence anyway.

I have no plans for the weekend and for the first time in ages, this saddens me. I have a backlog of seven books that I have assured myself I will read (and enjoy) before the year is up. I also have the second half of a film, and a whole film to watch. The house is full of food so I could quite easily cook, and I have a phonebook and email account with people I could contact. Yet somehow there is an unweilding emptiness about the days ahead and I can feel a dark cloud approaching.

Chapter Eight

The weekend is spent in limbo. Saturday I have pretty much written off as I rise nearer afternoon than morning. I don't know what time it is, nor do I take the time to check. I want the day to be over but I also want it to have started earlier, and better. When I was taking the antidepressants, I used to pray for night time and sometimes get up as it was getting dark. I would wait and fill the hours before late night television with rudimentary actions, things that would keep me alive somehow. I would take great care in the things that before I would brush over, brushing my teeth became a grand event and one with which I would linger on, not wanting it to end. I would not want anything to end. When the time came that I was fed for the day, clean, and the television shut down beyond reasonable doubt, I would sink into my bed and feel safe at last. The threat of having to do it all again loomed over me like a giant fog, but I was helpless in the hands of time and the fact that tomorrow would come, sooner than later.

Now I fear that happening again. Not right now, but generally that fear is always with me like an extra layer of clothing as it gets hotter. If anything, right now the opposite is occurring and I am dreading the evenings as I try in vain to lull myself to sleep but know that it matters not the time at which I retire or how tired I am when my head hits the pillow because I will rise with standard panda eyes mid sleep. I always feel as if I need another four hours and I probably do. My body and mind are pushed to their limits every night as I fight the thoughts that are still keeping me awake.

And so that's half the problem as I weave into my weekend. I feel absolutely shattered and on edge. I need to let some of this adrenalin out, but exercise is out of the question. I think about going for a run and immediately rule it out for some reason or another. Maybe I should go for a walk but without a purpose, I feel fraudulent and wasteful. I don't need any shopping and the thought of reading the headlines in any paper doesn't fill me with much hope. I feel a little trapped and once up, seem taut and ungrateful. I have a couple of coffees which enable me to think more concisely, but hinder my progress in getting away from this building panic and looming despair. I have to put the television on to remind myself of other people and look longingly at my phone. My mind begins to buzz and I feel as if I'm on drugs. I wonder whether I should counteract this feeling and actually take some. I have a little puff left over from Southampton and am starting to wonder whether this would be a good idea, even though I know it wouldn't be.

I look for my keys because soon I will have to leave the house. I can't stay in this place much longer and the keys are the most important things to enable me to leave. I think they must be in the coat I was last wearing, but I don't know where the coat is. I know where my wallet is because I saw it in the bedroom about half an hour ago. My phone is in my pocket and that's probably all I'll need. I'm not sure where I'm going yet but as long as I have my phone, my wallet and my keys, it doesn't really matter, I'm prepared for any eventuality. Unless of course, I go for a drink with someone, in which case I need fags. Then I will also need my lighter and my chewies. The likelihood of that happening is very low but I must find these things just in case. I probably need a plan too and so I need to find my post it notes, and a pen. They should be in the same place so I go to the kitchen and look for them...they're there. I grab a post it note and take it with me to the lounge, where I put my shoes on in double quick time and move my phone to my other pocket so when I put my keys in that pocket, it won't scratch the screen of my phone. I take my phone out and ensure that it is on lock so I do not ring my friends whilst my phone is in my pocket. I get up and look in the mirror and look like shit but probably look okay actually and as I'm not going anywhere special, I can probably get away with looking like this. I finish tying my shoes laces and go back to the kitchen where I pick up another pen and go back to the lounge where I try to think of something to write on the post it note. I can't think of anything so go to the bathroom, and stop momentarily at the hall mirror checking what I look like. I remember that I look shit, and go to the bathroom where I attempt to make myself look better. I wash my face and go to the bedroom where I find my keys. My keys are on the table next to my bed and not in my coat. I grab my coat and put the keys in my coat and then go back to the lounge where I sit down and wonder where my fags are. I go to the kitchen and look for my fags and then go back to the lounge and put my coat on. I check my coat pockets and my keys are there and then I put my mobile in my trouser pockets and wonder if my fags are in my bedroom. I've just looked in my bedroom but go back, getting another glimpse of myself in the mirror on the way. I spy my fags in my drawer and open all of the drawers one after the other in case my chewies and lighter are also there. I go back to the lounge and pick up the post it note and pens and go to the kitchen and place them back from where I got them originally. I walk to the hall and take my coat off and rearrange my clothing because my shirtsleeve hasn't fallen correctly. I need to redo my shoelaces and so I do, and then walk to the lounge and sit down. My heart is beating very fast and I need my asthma inhaler. I need to find it first.

It takes forty-five minutes to get out of the flat.

I drive into town and pass the bottle bank on the way; I am saddened as I remember the box of bottles sitting by the back door. A perfect opportunity to sort something out and tidy up loose ends is missed and I lament this. I've always loved going to the bottle bank. I think I get a little kick out of the organised destruction and satisfaction from hearing glass smash, but I also enjoy the ritual. It's one of the few chores that still requires me to drive somewhere. The journey there is laced with expectation and slight nerves, and the ride back is full of job satisfaction and contentment. Most of my chores can be undertaken from the comfort of my flat these days. The Internet means that I can now pay the majority of my bills online and most of my shopping is now done with a click of a mouse. I somehow miss my life before the Internet but I am glad I am not living it anymore.

Sometimes, I will go to the local library and book myself in for a half hour session on their computers. I like spending time in a library and feel serene and calm amongst all of the information and culture. People seem friendly and open hearted and I feel as if I somehow fit in. I only feel this because everybody around me looks as if they don't belong, and we can be strange together. I don't think I'll stop at the library today though. Although I have decided this, I still anticipate any sudden moves as I approach the turn off to the road that the library is on. I am prone to split second decisions and they are never based upon a gut feeling (or any form of logic it would appear). I pass the turn off and look at my healthy petrol balance. I wonder whether I should drive around to waste some petrol so I would then have to buy some petrol, as buying petrol is an achievement. As I pass over the shopping precinct nearing the centre of town, I wonder how long I would have to go to use up enough petrol to warrant having to fill up the tank. I guess that it would be twenty miles or so, but I doubt that would make a significant dent in the tank. My tank has a large capacity. That's a sign of my success.

I recall other times I have felt like this and remember my course of action for those times. One time was three years ago, I had received a call from my cousin that she was in town and was coming round to see my brother and I. My brother was staying with me for a bit as his relationship with his then girlfriend was hitting troubled times. I was in a very strange state of mind and could not face staying in the flat, let alone seeing someone out of my inner circle, and having to act normal. I took the car and drove to a car park near a set of hotels on the coastline. It was a long drive and took me a good forty-five minutes, maybe more. There was a definite goal and purpose to my journey though. I was going to listen to an album on the way there and an album on the way back that I wasn't that familiar with. I would get there and sort out my diary, smoke a few fags and take in the scenery. I should point out that this car park is not merely a place to park the car, but more of a set of spaces alongside a steep hill that overlooks the sea, and lies adjacent to a long strip of brightly coloured hotels, lights, restaurants and closed down surf shacks. I call it a car park but I guess it's just open road spaces. It's rather strange actually as the spaces are length ways on and it appears like it's a park with a road running through it. One of the great things about this place is that a lot of people go there to eat fish and chips, or park up and then go for a brisk walk in the early evening. Just being sat in your car and doing nothing in particular is not viewed as weird here and I can safely hide in my metal cocoon listening to tunes whilst chomping on snacks, or more precisely smoking endless cigarettes.

I feel warm and secure as I recall this time and instantly decide to go back. I have to turn around to do this and chose a suitable petrol station. Probably the same station that I will have to use later on this evening to fill up for the days ahead. That is presuming of course that I will need petrol in the near future. I can't really imagine a time in the near future that I will need to leave the house, bar from the doctors and maybe if this feeling crops up again anytime soon.

The drive down is enjoyable and I listen to a *Calla* compilation that someone has left in my car. I don't know who has left it here or how it came into my person but it seems to be sound tracking the journey rather well. The end result is as familiar as I recall. I park with ease and turn off the engine, sparking a ciggie and clambering to reach the half-finished bottle of drink that is rumbling around under the passenger seat. Life is predictably active and there is an elderly couple gingerly encouraging their dog to leave the relative comfort of his haven in the boot of a car to brisk the early evening breeze along the front. It's Saturday night and there is a feeling of hope in the air. I can see shadowy figures as I look to the horizon and as I open my window to let air in and ash out, I can hear muffled conversations and audible agreements (and possible arguments) carried on the wind. I wonder what types of people are staying in the hotels that are laid out in front of me and what is showing at the theatre at the bottom of the road. I think of all the plans that must be being fulfilled as I speak. I ponder. I'd like to stay here for as long as possible before I start to feel that this maybe is weird.

I make up a story in my head that I am picking up my parents from a birthday bash in the hotel and this makes me feel a little better. Should a work colleague see me and come over, this is what I will tell them. And they will believe me, because people don't lie about that sort of thing. People don't drive all the way out here to sit and park and ponder and smoke. Because that would be weird. But I won't see any work colleagues because I am deliciously far from home and nobody knows me here. I am completely at ease because of this and wonder whether I should weave this theory into any future plans I might have. Perhaps I could become a nomad and travel from place to place. Meeting people on my own terms and leaving places when I want to leave. Learning things from previous encounters and relationships and improving and getting better each time. Then maybe when I am about fifty-five, I will have found a set of rules that I can live by and I won't feel weird anymore. Perhaps that's what I am really, a nomad. For someone who craves order and times and structure, I sail very close to the wind and constantly appear to want to sabotage my own interests.

It happens though, it does become a little weird after a while, and I can't really stomach any more tobacco. I am feeling a little nausea and head back. There are only so many cigarettes I can smoke in the name of normality, and I can't smoke whilst I drive, as you know. I get back late and stop quickly for a bag of chips that I devour mostly on the drive back, naively clutching at the open bag when a given opportunity rears its head. Mainly traffic lights but I help myself to a fair few outside the chip shop. On my return to the flat, I have only a handful left and reluctantly put them in the oven, as if it warrants heating up the stove for such a paltry amount.

My weekend is slowly becoming a mess. The minute I get back to the flat, I am stricken with a lack of knowledge. I have no idea what to do with my evening. I know I don't want company, but I don't care much for my own this evening. I am not tired and do not wish to be entertained, in any way. I am clean, and satiated so there's no task to be performed. I am bored, but edgy enough to not actually want to find anything to do. I stand at the kitchen sink for a good five minutes, holding on and hoping that something will pop into my head for me to get on with. Something that will make me competent or at least feel normal again. I make myself a cup of tea and a joint. I can only think that numbing my senses further will send me into some state where my consciousness does not need to play a vital role. I'd like to watch some shitty television, but not the shitty television that is on offer to me this evening. I hate Saturday night television. In fact, I hate Saturdays. Well, at least I hate *this* Saturday.

Monday comes round with stern precision, almost as if Sunday had never existed. The usual comedown before the new week is lost and I greet the day with reluctance. I am not too worried about going to see the counsellor, yet I am concerned that I will have to make a decision to look for answers along a different route than I have been up to now. I don't think he will be able to help. I know he will not help me, but it is the only course of action for me at present. I suppose I should be thankful as I enter the day with nothing on my mind but this appointment, and even though this clouds any decision I make on this fine day, I have perverse clarity as my thinking becomes tunnel focused and consumed with fear. I'm okay when I am consumed with fear from a solitary source as the fear acts as a catalyst. I know what I am fearful of, and I know that the fear will cease once this horrendous thing has taken place. It's comforting in a way. I have distant frames of reference from when I was at school and developed butterfly stomach before an exam. I recoil with additional memories as I think to the times when this fear became perpetual as my teens progressed. These thoughts are reigned in frantically as I am reminded that today, I am going to see a counsellor. I should learn to say no.

I leave the flat with only fifteen minutes to get to my appointment. This is presuming that everything will go like clockwork, there will be no misadventure and all of the lights will be on my side. I am a little disappointed with myself for allowing this to happen but am then pleasantly surprised when there *is* no misadventure and I pull effortlessly into the small car park with a couple to minutes to spare. I did kinda jump a red light at Tamworth Junction, and the lanes out of my complex were rushed a little. I fear I'm developing a lack of fear for the things that I should be fearful of as the fear of the appointment becomes fiercer. It always seems to happen this way. The greater the panic, the less fear I have for my own safety and well-being and I toy with my knife's edge. They say stress does funny things to people and they're right. We all need a little stress to push us and to realise the bad times and search for those we deem to be good. I have researched this. I am living proof of this - *barely*.

The surgery is empty. I am surprised by this because it's very cold and there's a flu going around. Most people at the office are sniffling, *snivelling.* There are three people in the ground floor waiting room, I don't know about upstairs, and I'm not going to find that out.

For I am exploring the new building today. They spent five months building an extension to the existing structure and it was finally opened last week. There was a slight furore to this decision as to accommodate the new block, a tree had to be cut down that apparently was an important cultural point for the town. It was called *"The Big Tree"*, and it was big. My only knowledge of it is that it marks the boundary from the town to the suburbs, and it is very tall. It is also a good meeting point; I would often meet a friend at the big tree. I don't think it's that upsetting that it has gone though. The surrounding houses are now drenched in light for parts of the day and it was pretty ugly anyway. I remember reading groups of letters in the local press complaining that it should be saved. And that was it; they were complaining, they weren't being proactive or positive. They didn't mention that it would make way for a surgery. Thinking about it, they may not have known that when they wrote their diatribe. I wonder what kind of people write into the local rag, I sometimes flick through the pages on my way to the television guide and see a familiar name. It wouldn't surprise me to find out that it is the same people week after week. Perhaps they do good, perhaps they just need to vent. Either way, that tree has gone, and I no longer meet people at the big tree.

There is no queue but I still have to wait. The kind looking lady acknowledges my existence with a smile and holds up a finger to denote that she will be with me in, I presume - one minute. I look around the walls whilst I wait and spy a black and white picture of a group of people that reminds me of school photos. On closer inspection, it is a group of doctors, perhaps the founders of this surgery. It's not really black and white, but brown - sepia if you will. I look at the other patients and try to decipher whether they are seriously ill and whether they are likely to give me a nasty bug or not. I wonder what I may contract if I stay here too long. I decide not much.

I am informed that I must walk through the awkward tunnel to get to the new waiting room area in the new building. The tunnel looks as if it was an afterthought. Perhaps the builders erected the new block and then realised that they had not extended the building, merely built a separate surgery. The tunnel looks rushed and temporary, and I honestly believe it has been meticulously designed to look like this. It's not modern and it's not clever, and I like walking along it. The ground below my feet is slightly sloped, and it makes you feel like you are in an airport; perhaps that's the look that the designers were going for.

The new waiting room is very nice. There are comfy sofas instead of chairs and a television playing on a stand in the corner. Mental patients are allowed to sit comfortably and be entertained. I am mental. *This* is mental. As I sit down, it dawns on me that I have nothing to say, and wish that I could tell him everything that I have told you, and he give me a pill that makes all that I told you okay, and not weird. I wonder if a pill like that did exist, where it would put me. What kind of person I would be and whether the free time and brain space that would be allotted to me be could be spent on more worthwhile pursuits. Maybe I would be a famous artist, or writer. Maybe I would be very academic and not analyse things so much. I may even have become the person I wanted to be. The doctor opens the door and looks me up and down. This is a very bad start and I despise him for doing this. It's such an arrogant rude thing to do and I am immediately beginning to put down my shutters. I can feel them securing. The locks in my brain are tightening and my body is desperately trying to evacuate any badness in my body.

"George?"

"Yes, thank you." I thank him for saying my name.

"Come in, do."

I follow him into a small pokey room, and look at his face nervously. He has yet to make eye contact with me and when I offer him my hand, he begrudgingly gives me his, and it is clammy. He must have known it was clammy, but I didn't mind. I don't mind other people's clammy hands for some reason. But he did not mention the clamminess or feel the need to apologise.

I think this guy is a dick.

"Okay, take a seat." I do. "Before we start, I'd just like to you to read through this set of forms and quickly fill in the boxes that are appropriate."

He hands me a sheet of paper with six attachments stapled at the right hand corner. I tick and ignore, tick and ignore. It's all very basic questioning and I shiver at the final one, enquiring as to whether I have ever had suicidal thoughts. I mean sure I have, I've thought about everything at some point. I'm not going to kill myself and never have thought that I would, but I've thought about what would happen if I did, how it would feel and the massive repercussions it may have on the people around me. I only think about this because it's perverse and I enjoy pushing this button in my head. When my best mate died and I was at the funeral, Tom was by my side and he looked fascinated with the event, the speeches and the rows of mourners. When we got to the pub afterwards, he told me that he had to stop himself from saying something ridiculous and hurtful so all around could hear. He questioned what would happen if someone had just blurted out that they never really liked him, just to provoke a reaction and see peoples worlds fall apart again. I wonder what would have happened, whether people would have put it down to grief and put an arm round the abusers shoulder, leading him away to a black BMW on the forecourt. Perhaps he would have been lynched and no one would ever speak to him again. Perhaps that's what he would have wanted. Perhaps that's what my dead mate would have wanted. I can see him looking down upon us finding that quite amusing.

"All done?" he says with alarming efficiency.

"I think so."

"Good." He doesn't read it, but glances at the last box. He is clearly relieved that I have ticked **N** (no) to suicide, and he is now in the clear that what he says to me is not of paramount importance. I can read this man like a book. "So, what brings you here?"

"Um, I don't know what to say really, I've had a lot of panic attacks, and I guess I'm quite...." I can barely bring myself to say it. "I'm quite depressed I guess. I guess you have my notes."

"Yes, yes. Let's take a look." He glances at the massive list of drugs and comments from the last twenty years and I am thankful that records exist so some form of paperwork is outsourced to someone else.

"I'm not on any medication."

"No, I know." He still is reluctant to give me eye contact and talks to me whilst playing with his mouse clicking in and out of drugs. I know what he is doing as I do the very same if I have a computer in front of me and a client and I'm attempting to work out what to do for the best. "You say you're depressed."

"Yeah."

"There's a marked difference between what we call depression and a low mood. Would you say you were in a low mood?"

"Um, yeah I guess so."

"So we would agree that you're low, and maybe not depressed."

"I don't know. I mean I'd say I was depressed. I don't want to take medication but...

He cuts me up critically with a swift rebuttal; "I don't think there's any need to go down that route right now. Can you tell me a little about what has brought you here?"

Oh fuck. Well this is it. I clam up. I can feel my throat tightening and he chooses now to give me eye contact. And it's not just brief contact or a friendly welcoming glaze, but intense interest. I don't think he is interested though, I think he thinks he has me over a barrel and that maybe this is a game. This *isn't* a game.

"Um......" I desperately want and need to say something but as I grasp for the words, all that I can do is produce mucous and I realise I have no thoughts. He stares confusingly into my eyes. I'd like to think that he's trying to decipher the kind of person I am and the thoughts that may have attributed to what is fast becoming my downfall. Surely he can pinpoint something from his years of training. Surely this isn't solely down to me. This is so fucking hard I can't believe it. "I guess I'm not happy in my job, I'm very low. I'm not really seeing friends anymore, I don't want to and just feel numb all the time."

"What do you do?"

"I work in an office."

"What do you want to do?" Clever.

"I don't know, maybe that's the problem."

"Are you working now?"

"Sort of, I'm working from home but it's project work. I'm not.....engaging."

"Do you feel this way when you're working, or do you find you haven't got the time?" I am disgusted by this comment and the final shutter comes down and he is now blocked out completely.

"Yes, I feel that way all the time."

"What do you do with yourself?" He is now blatant and disinterested, blatantly disinterested.

"Um, well...."

He cuts me up again, "Stamp collecting, skiing??" He lets out a little laugh, but it does not forgive his attitude. I laugh though out of politeness.

"Um, well, I don't know. I manage to fill my days but I couldn't tell you with what."

"Sports?"

"No I don't play any sports."

"None at all? You exercise?"

"Not really no."

"Well it sounds as if you need to occupy yourself more. That would be my advice."

"Right."

"I can only do so much George."

Jesus, this guy is a cunt.

"Yeah yeah I understand how the system works. I am eating healthily and keeping busy. I'm doing all the things I know I should be doing but I can't shake off this thing, whatever it is."

"No, no." He plays with his pen and I can see him looking at his appointment schedule on his computer.

"I know you haven't got much time." This startles him and he makes a sheepish look as if he has been found out. Perhaps this is what needed to have happened because he changes his tact slightly. I know that he knows I know Doctor Brett, and he knows my family have some standing in the community. I don't know whether any of this makes a blind bit of difference to the way in which he chooses to treat me but I'd like to think that it does.

"Let's take things as they are. I mean are you sleeping?"

"No, well yeah but. I'm waking up insanely early and I'm probably getting three or so hours a night."

"That won't do, your body needs to replenish. I think you need to take a look at a few things in your life that you could change, and we can help you with that." God, is he wrapping this meeting up? "Perhaps looking at your job would be a good start."

"I've thought about that a lot."

"Well maybe you shouldn't. Is there any way that you can make your situation at work more bearable?"

"Probably."

"Is that something you can do?"

"Um, maybe."

"Well that's good. Look, whatever has happened in the past has gone. You're young..." Yeah, younger than you. "Do try and get some exercise, it's a wonderful drug." I want to tell him it's not as wonderful as cannabis, and then slap him and walk out to an inner orchestrated theme, drive maniacally to the coast and crash my car. But then, I'd have to fill in loads of accident reports and try to get a new car and deal with insurance claims. Or I would be dead, and that would be a terrible inconvenience for my family and friends. "I'd like to see you again."

"Right, that would be good yeah."

"I'm sorry I can't spend more time with you today George." He clicks on his schedule and spends a couple of minutes toing and froing and generally making productive noises with his mouth. "Same time next week is good for me."

"That's great yeah."

"In the meantime, I want you to make a change at work, it doesn't matter how small but just one change that will make things a little better. I also suggest that you walk, or if you're feeling adventurous, go for a run."

"Yeah, well - we'll see." He says nothing to this.

"You know George, life can be a very complex thing but it needn't be. Go get 'em!"

"Um, right yeah." I begin to stand up and he remains seated. I wonder whether he's going to see me out but it's clear that it is not on his agenda. I shake his hand, which is still clammy and take my piece of paper with the time and date of my next appointment. I have gained nothing from this. Or so I would argue.

Chapter Nine

You join me in the summertime. Since I left that doctors surgery, four months have passed by.

Lots of things have happened since that day and I feel a little better. Five days passed and I took it upon myself to ring the surgery and ask to be put through to the counsellor. Predictably he was not available to talk. I presume that he is never actually available to talk to anyone, and this is the way it should be. I liaised with the receptionist who was surprised to hear that I wanted to cancel the engagement. I informed her that I didn't want to reschedule and that there was no need for me to remain on the books. The phone call itself was rather easy to make as I was aware that I did not have to come up with an excuse or let her know anything surrounding the reasons why I am choosing to put a line under this experience. I was in the driving seat and it felt rather wonderful making the call and crossing out the next appointment date on my diary and on my calendar. I hadn't put an alarm setting on my phone; there was no need to because history tells me that there is no point (as it can't be trusted). But I also think I knew the minute I lay eyes on the guy that there would be no reprise of the meet.

Many things have happened since that day. I can tell you about them now, but I'd like to get myself comfy and organised before I do so.

It's Saturday today. Mid July. The day begins at 9.30am. One of the reasons I am up so early is because I had left my curtains open the night before and was woken gently by the sun poking its head into my domain. I have taken to opening the curtains in the lounge and bedroom before I retire to bed now. I no longer read before I go to bed as it was beginning to feel like a chore, and I have discarded the television that was once in my room. This means I tend to stay up later in the lounge, but I have no form of entertainment when I decide to sleep and somehow, this is working for me. I ensure that I don't enter my room before I am shattered and more often than not, I am in bed and sleeping by at least eleven thirty pm. I am amazed at how such a simple thing has affected me in such a positive way.

I have a shower. This is another change. I have always had a bath in the morning, for as long as I can remember. In the flat I was in before this with Dylan (my cousin), the shower was a part of Dylan's en suite and although he persuaded me to use it for the first month, and I did, I felt incredibly intrusive walking through his slumber to shower myself. I would get up half an hour before he did and wondered whether he silently appreciated this time that he was gently awoken by trickling water and the sound of his flat mate and cousin washing himself, or if he was intensely annoyed. I never asked him but I lasted only three weeks and then I started taking baths. This then became the routine - the habit, and I began to reap the little rewards from doing so. My days began in a very peaceful manner after having relaxed in a hot steamy world. I would also play my radio whilst I washed because I knew it was far enough away for Dylan to be unaware. Often I didn't even really wash and just lay there amongst a cloud of bubbles, momentarily glancing at the clock and deciphering how many more minutes I had left before I had to dress.

The reprise of the shower has left me a little more invigorated as I rise. It is a quick process and I go from being asleep to awake and ready for action very quickly. I have started to eat yoghurt and drink just the one coffee as a form of breakfast, and I no longer reach for a fag the minute I become aware of my breathing. I constantly convince myself that these small changes are nothing to do with the fact that this man in that surgery told me to put them into place. I will not even accept that he may have planted a seed.

It's been muggy and close for the last couple of days, but on Thursday night there was a big storm that broke the darkness. It didn't keep me awake but I was aware of its presence and I think it entered my dreams in a way, influencing the way in which they progressed. The result of the storm is felt fully this morning as the air is clear and crisp and there is not a cloud in the sky. Moments like this fill me with anticipation, expectation and hope. I'd love to go driving today and have a result to attain. I have no real plans, I'd like to go into town at some point and I need to collect some things from the post office, but apart from that, I may just waste some time outside.

Things that have happened in the past four months:

1. I am now Client Liaison Manager for Sector Four. Charles spent a few days developing a new title and role for me and he did a good job. I went to see him a week after the doctors and explained that I was not happy and gave him my notice. He said nothing at the time but asked me to come back two days later. I did so, and he asked me why I wanted to leave. I tried not to go into detail, but the main gist of my point was that I felt under worked, and overworked. My mind was not being pushed in the right direction, and I was bored. But I didn't have time to be bored because I had an endless list of pointless procedures to wade through on a weekly basis. He was right; the job that I made for myself had bitten me on the ass. I let him know that he was right without actually telling him, and he promised to make some big changes, and leave it with him and so I did.

   Charles did the following things for me:

1. (a) He gave me a title with which I can now happily tell people about if they choose to ask me. I now have an occupation, and as if to cement this fact to onlookers, and myself further, he printed me new business cards and I now have a private email address, one not connected with the company itself.

1. (b) I have now got an assistant. The trainee that was employed two months ago is now directly under me, learning how to become me in future years. Most of the small annoying jobs that I once complained about are now his domain, and I even had a say in his salary. He is a good lad and ten years my junior. He, like me, doesn't seem to have any discernable skills, and I joked with Charles that it must have been easy for him to work out where to put this guy when he came for the interview.

1. (c) I work from ten in the morning to three in the afternoon in the office, and have to be in the office for those times, unless I have a meeting or have to see clients. I now field more calls and only half are for me. Charles has developed a client liaison team now and there are four of us who manage various groups of people. I don't mind doing this as I like to see what the other teams are getting up to. At present, I only have one assistant. I think Charles is hoping that I will fast track the trainee and he will become one of my team, and then I will employ other people. The other teams have already got four people each and I feel that Charles may be pushing us to increase our numbers. I explain to him that everything is in hand, and I am not concerned as my trainee is great and at the moment, both of us are enjoying being pushed. I joke with him that if we keep this up for another couple of months, we can secure some more clients (maybe steal some off the other teams) and then once he's completely up to speed (he pretty much is now actually), I'll employ

another two team members and he will be able to work closer with me, and maybe even get a pay rise.

2. I went to the funeral for my Uncle. It was dignified and a little horrific.

3. Clare has been made editor of Woman's Beacon and I think she has gone a little mad on the power. She comes round more often than before and she has become very opinionated. I haven't seen many changes in the publication since she became editor, but she informs me that she doesn't intend to make any. I guess she is concentrating on maintaining the magazine for a while. She wasn't sourced to make a change; the previous editor was headhunted by a newspaper to look after the entertainment section. Clare slotted comfortably into her new role but she is changing as a person. I guess everyone is. We're all influenced by our experiences and I guess some people evolve quicker if they have had a bigger experience.

4. I went to the grave of my mate with Tom.

5. I have stopped smoking spliffs. This is not strictly true but I no longer reach for the smoke if I feel I need it as it only covers up whatever it is that I am choosing to ignore. I smoke now as I drink, rarely but controlled.

I am sure that lots of other things have happened but those are the things that stick. Oh, I have yet to see

Cath, but I did send her an email explaining why. I decided for the first time in my life, to be brutally honest with somebody and see how it pans out. Cath was a prime target for this honesty as I know a lot about her, and she knows a lot about me, but we haven't yet met, and there is no pressure to actually meet. I could easily delete her from my email contacts and never talk to her again. She doesn't know what I look like and there would be no repercussions. Because of this lack of consequence that I would be aware of, I don't think I'd feel bad. It would clearly be a bad thing to do and it would maybe make her upset, or at least confused as to why I had severed all ties, but as I would never be reminded of this, I wouldn't think about it. I wonder what would happen if there were no consequences to any of my actions. I then remember that I lived my early twenties with this ethos as a large part of my life and remember it to be bad. But I was given the negative consequences; they were laid out in front of me, and I still didn't stop.

Cath texted me a further three times over a period of ten days tentatively suggesting times we could meet and each time, I would quickly rebuff the suggestion with what I deemed to be a plausible excuse. By the third text, I started to realise that I needed to act one way or another. I either needed to be honest or be brutal. As it is not in my nature to be brutal, and I didn't know how to be honest, because I honestly didn't know what I felt or why I didn't want to meet her, I decided to email her and bare my soul. It was one of the hardest things I have done.

I told her everything, the fact that I had been having panic attacks frequently and that I had been afraid, upset and unwilling. This email is purely for my own benefit, and it is seeping with massive self-indulgence. On reading it back to myself, I feel a little sick and unfeasible. I edit it over the course of two weeks and the final result is unrecognisable from the initial draft. It sits in my draft box for an age, and each day, I take it one step further to being sent. I have told my parents, friends and various professionals about my fears and inadequacies and have taken a lot of medication and felt a lot of emotions. I don't think I have ever been this honest though. To me, it sounds a little desperate and needy, but I have every intention of sending the thing. If I were to receive the same email from someone, I am not sure whether I would delete it, and the person from my life, or whether I would read it with fascination and empathise. I think I know I would delete it. But either way, it's fine. She is going to stop contacting me, that is the most likely outcome, and for that, I will not have to travel to London and meet her. This can only be a good thing. I have the upper hand. And she didn't see this counter move coming a mile off. Maybe I should start playing chess.

I did once; it's not a very good story though.

I mention this now, as I only sent the email three days ago and coming from the shower fresh faced and eager to face the day, I switch my laptop on and it informs me that I have a new message from Cath. This surprises me a little, and I decide not to open it, leaving it for as long as possible before I decide to venture in. It's a fucking gorgeous day and I lament that I have no garden to sit in. Instead, I spend some time in the kitchen as at this time of the day, the sun streams through my small kitchen window, lighting anything that lies in its path. I decide to do the washing up and clean the worktops. I then clean them a little too much and use two different sprays, an antibacterial spray and a polish, because it smells nicer than the spray. Had I bought a decent spray from my supermarket of choice, I would no doubt have no need to take two bottles into the kitchen. The sun glistens on my face for twenty minutes or so and I wonder whether it is worth it to bring a chair into the kitchen and lay there to get some more rays. Even this is a little weird and I know I won't follow through with this deceptive plan. I want sunlight, I crave it but I do not really want to go outside yet. I could go into the communal gardens, and doubtless this would be acceptable to my neighbours, but I don't like the idea of people watching me. People tell me that this is my over inflated self-importance and people couldn't really give a shit about what I do. Although I know this to be partially true, if I spy anyone outside the flat, from inside the flat, I immediately check them out and sometimes can watch them for minutes, just transfixed on their actions.

Worse still, they may choose to join me and then I'd have to talk to them.

I put Devendra Banhart on the lounge stereo and wander round the room, looking at books I have and ornaments I have been given and painstakingly arranged. My mind feels vitally clear. I am not concise quite yet but I feel as if a new era is being ushered in. I can sense a new dawn and I am excited, yet calm. I have foresight and I am concentrating on the day. Today will be a good day. Devendra tickles my happiness and I let a little of it out in the form of a small smile. A glimpse of light is being attracted to the lounge mirror from somewhere. It projects beautiful light across the room and hits a crystal by the fourth wall. The room hasn't had the smell of stale tobacco for months, and I wish somebody would buy me flowers so I could have some flowers. There is no dirt beneath my feet and no cobwebs overhead. The screen of the television sparkles and creates a shiny tempting pulse in my eyes. My tongue feels clean. My tongue never feels clean. My hair slips into my eyes for the first time in years and as I flick it across my face, I decide not to cut it. Perhaps ever again.

   I haven't had long hair in a long time. I wonder if it will change me for the better.

The email is still there. I still haven't opened it.

The phone rings, and I answer it. Oh that's another thing you should probably know. I no longer screen my phone calls and I haven't used my usual technique of 1471 redial for months. I have decided to do this as this is really pushing the envelope. The minute the phone rings, my heart misses a beat and my forehead becomes hot. I usually get a slight whiff of my own smell and I am stuck on the spot. It's worse than ever but that's only because I know I'm going to answer it. I'm hoping that the more I do this, the less frantic my natural response will become. The first time I did it, it was a fucking nightmare. Tom had slept over and it was early morning. I knew that he wouldn't be up for hours and I was amusing myself by tidying the flat whilst watching a music station on cable. The phone rang and I answered immediately, trying to act all cool and natural in my own company. It turned out to be a phone company who was attempting to sell me a new contract. I had no frame of reference as to what I should do if such an event occurs, and he kept me on the phone for over five minutes. When I felt like there was a natural break, I declared that I wasn't interested, but he didn't stop and continued his pitch. The more I heard, the less able I was to stop him, and he knew that I was vulnerable and the perfect candidate to aid him in reaching his monthly targets. He had the upper hand.

I remember just putting the phone down after what seemed like twenty-seven apologies on my behalf. He seemed irritated and upset, which added to my panic. I ended up slowly putting the phone away from my head whilst simultaneously (tentatively) pressing my thumb onto the red button on the phone. I put it back on the holder with precision and disgust. The phone immediately rang again and it was my mother. I had a quick conversation with her, about what I cannot remember. This probably means that it was a positive phone call about happy things and questions, because these are the exchanges I remember the least about.

So who is at the other end of this call? Whatever it is, whoever it is and whatever they want, I can handle it. I can say no, and probably will, regardless of whether I actually want to do it. I have come full circle with this now; **no** is now my default setting and I take great pride in seeing how quickly I can say it, and how immediate their acceptance of this is. It's usually pretty immediate these days as I have mastered a definite tone of voice. I have transferred the skills I have from work to my personal life. I have transferable skills. Check it - it's on my CV.

It's Tom. He sounds alarmed. I figure this is because this is maybe the first time I've picked up my phone in - shit, maybe years. He doesn't mention the significance of it, which I am thankful for. He asks me what I'm doing and I tell him nothing. I pronounce nothing fiercely and he laughs. He informs me that he is on his way over, and I comically say that this is most fortunate as I am here, and bored. The call lasts about twenty-six seconds, and I am glad I do not have to do 1471 only to see its Tom's number and spend an hour or so wondering what he could want; whether I owe him money or a favour, or whether he has a party he wants me to attend. You know, I probably would go to a party tonight. Maybe I could push the envelope even further. I yearn for a party to test out my skills. Oh yeah sure, I say that *now*. I text him 'Bring biscuits' and he texts back saying 'Type?' and I text back 'Use your imagination'. He doesn't continue the exchange and I wonder if he is painstakingly working out which type to buy. I do hope he is. I hope he's suffering in the supermarket, but I bet he's not. I wonder if we'll taste the difference together. I also wonder how long it will take him to get here.

I killed my best mate.

I didn't mean to do it. I was young and naïve and didn't know about repercussions or appreciate the consequences of my actions. Nobody else knows, or at least I don't think they do. I wonder whether everybody knows and nobody states it. It makes me feel confused and sick when I think about it, and I think about it rarely. Tom helped. Well, he didn't not help.
I never mention my mate's death with Tom and I don't think he would want me to. I know I wouldn't want someone to. We talk about things we used to get up to and reminisce as people do, but the actual death is never touched upon. I guess this is healthy, but I sometimes yearn to talk about it. I never have. I know people who have talked to people about it, and in the thrawl of a drunken evening, have confided in me that they have done so. I believe that in me they see a kindred spirit for the small part of themselves that may have an emotional disturbance. I am not annoyed, or pleased that they do this, but I appreciate their honesty and I guess it makes me feel special in some perverse way.
Tom arrives looking worn out and dishevelled. This is not my usual Tom, and he appears to have a black eye. He gives me a look to denote that there's no need to mention his appearance and that he doesn't want to talk about it. I concur with a raise of the eyebrows and ask him if he wants tea. Of course he wants tea. He has barely put his foot in the door, and he lights an embassy.
"Where the hell have you been?"
"Where the hell have *you* been?"

"A disagreement. I'll save it for later."
"Fair enough. I've been here."
"You're always here."
"Do you want a shower?"
"Are you saying I smell?"
"Yes."
"Well actually yeah I could do with a wash. Maybe not a shower."
"Where have you just come from?"
"Oh I slept at a mate's house." I don't ask which mate; Tom has an alarming amount of friends.
"Late one last night?"
"I've just got up."
"You'll be wanting a bacon sandwich then I presume?"

Tom spends the rest of the day with me, but I don't see him for most of that time. He falls in and out of sleep on the sofa. When he realises that he is awake - he has a cigarette, and I sporadically bring him things to eat, magazines and coffees. We haven't really got much to say to each other today, and I'm happy pottering around the flat, re-potting plants and taking old pictures down. I sometimes wish I knew how I could steer the chat to the subject of our best mate. I guess we'd have to be drunk, or stoned. I want it to progress naturally but simply having the thought in my mind means that it can never rear its head in this manner. Even when we went to his grave recently, it was only because we were shopping in the complex opposite the cemetery. And then we only popped in and looked at the stone, said "Well, there it is." then left for some burgers. Not entirely enlightening, nor great. I don't know what I was expecting though.

Tom falls asleep and I go to my laptop to open the email from Cath. I wonder if after I open it, I will tell Tom about it. I open it and read it intently.

Chapter Ten

No Worries, speak to you soon x

That's it. That's all she has written. Within those six words, and one kiss lies something else and I look blankly through them, attempting to decipher a greater moment and work out whether I am pleased or disappointed in what I see. This was meant to be my epiphany; wise words were supposed to be exchanged, words which may even change the way in which I think other people view me. The ways in which I view the world, and all of the other people that inhabit it.

I know she cares about me, and I know that this is her way of telling me that it is no big deal. She knows that I suffer from panic attacks, and we have talked at length about each other lives and our fears. Perhaps I need to tell someone that doesn't know.

I realise that this quickly becomes more than it was before. This is no longer about Cath and excuses, and conformation of social gesture. This is now about wanting to provoke a reaction from people when I tell them my woes. I suddenly feel disgustingly self-reverential, and indulgent and immediately begin to take a disliking to myself. My own self-importance fills my head with bile, and the fact that I recognise this, and abhor it turns my head from matter, to shit. I get a sharp pain in my head and I close the email down. I wonder what I want from other people and whether telling everyone anything ever again is a good idea. My words become jumbled in my head and what was initially a simple day turns to be one of mass confusion and upset.

I'd like to tell someone the truth for once. I'd like to be able to tell someone who doesn't appreciate the panic or depression that I don't want to go to this party (or that meal) because I have anxiety and really have trouble in this situation, or that situation. I then want them to either be like Cath and say "No worries." or ask me about it. If they are arsey about it, then I want to know. Then I can justify to myself that they are nasty people and that *that* is the reason I am not going to go to any further engagements with them. Hang on, then that would mean that *that* is the excuse, and not panic. But maybe panic is the reason and them being bastards is the excuse. Maybe both are excuses and I'm just lazy.

I wish I knew what the fuck was going on and how this trail of thought started so I could finish it.

I am repeating myself.

I am repeating myself. I am repeating myself because two years ago, I sent a similar email to my friend Katie, who I also met on the Internet but through a music site. It was pretty much the same situation actually. I didn't want to meet her, and to be honest I put my panic and anxiety down as a reason for not wanting to, but it was really because I was safely in my box and didn't want to brave the new experience. I have just realised that I am repeating history. I'm choosing to ignore things and I may even be lying a little. Everything I've told you so far could be a lie. Or I may be fine and just made all of this up to amuse myself. Wouldn't that be weird? Would that make me a bastard? I guess if I don't suffer from anything, then I have no right to make fun of it. I don't think I have though.

The familiarity of my actions and my complete denial to accept the repetition clouds my judgment. Attempting to relive something perhaps, I don't know. Anyway, the reply from Katie was great. That was an epiphany.

Reply to all → Forward↶ Print↶ Add Katie to Contacts list↶ Delete this message↶ Report phishing↶ Show original↶ Message text garbled?

Lol. It certainly does not freak me out, in fact it hits home a lot closer than you could possibly imagine. I know I've never told you, but I guess it's not something I really brag about when I first speak to someone. 'Hi my name is Katie and I suffer with depression and panic attacks'. Not that I've tried that as an ice breaker, but I'm sure it would have an amusing result, namely road runner I should imagine.

Now I'm not going to go into too much detail about my panic attacks because they are quite few and far between, but I know what you mean about the embarrassment, I once had one on a train from Hereford to Birmingham, they stopped the train and everything, it was mortifying! The worst I think was the attitude of the nurse at Dudley Hospital, she actually told me that I was acting to get attention; I nearly hit the closed minded cowbag. But I do kind of see her point of view, I mean I don't know if you've ever felt the same, but sometimes I really think that I could stop it, you know when you're in the midst of 'must calm down, must calm down, can't feel my fingers, must calm down, think I'm going to have a heart attack' I do wonder if I could just stop it cos it really does make me feel so stupid. What I'm trying to say is I guess is that you're not on your own, there are a lot of us out there, all you have to do is google panic attacks and you'll find a whole community of sufferers.

I know that you must feel quite isolated, that's what happens, you feel like a complete pillock, but I found, and whether you want to take advice from a strangerish person hee hee - that talking to complete strangers was possibly the best remedy I could do. So it would be my honour to be that sounding board for you. But do try not to isolate yourself too much, have some me time of course but the more you hide away the more you will build up anxiety which will prevent you from ever leaving the house, and that leads to a completely different can of worms.

And as for meeting me, I will not pressure you into that. But I still want to meet up, but only on your terms and when you're ready for putting yourself into that situation. I will be here for you to send random bollox to whenever you seem fit, and I won't think any less of you, cos that means beating myself up and I'm not in a habit of hitting myself, padded cells are so last year. Take your time, I'm not going anywhere.

> As for being ashamed mister, you have nothing to be ashamed of, it happens. In fact it happens to a lot more people than you could imagine, people find different ways of coping with it. I just talk, lots! Helps keep my mind off it.
>
> Anyways, that's enough of my rambling.
>
> A ever so not freaked out, and not running in the opposite direction.
>
> me x

"You say you killed your best mate."

"He was at my house the night before he died and I let him go. He came round on a Thursday and I was trying to persuade him not to go to school the next day and spend the day with me instead."

"You feel like it was your responsibility you mean?"

"I'm not stupid. I know that the world is made up of endless possibilities and events fuse, and things happen. I'm not a great believer in fate, although I do believe that our lives are pre ordained. It's just so lame. Normally, I would pester the kid to stay with me and provide him with another bong and we'd drink together and everything would get hazy. It's just that day, I thought it was best to give in, a nagging doubt that I was pressuring the guy and that he really needed to go into school on Friday stopped me."

Silence.

"Tom didn't invite him for a fag at lunchtime because they had had an argument. If Tom would have called for him, he would still be alive. And so on and so on. It just feels like a massive set of events that all conspired into killing him. But that's just how I feel, and I know that it's not true."

I've been seeing Bruce for six months. When I first entered his house, and stated that I had never really been good with introductions, that it is a failing - I was a nervous wreck. The end result of years of pulling myself in the wrong direction and analysing brought me to what felt like my last chance saloon. Cath sent me another email after her swift reply, suggesting that I look into *Cognitive Behavioural Therapy.* I did some research about it and it seemed like a good idea. I had no cynicism about the therapy; the way in which it was described to me made me feel intensely hopeful and logical.

You have a fear of something; you have files in your head that prove that you need to be afraid of these things because past experiences have told you this. The brain needs to be rewired by creating new memories and experiences that change this cycle so as to prove to yourself that this thing should not be feared. And in between all of that, you talk your little heart out and follow the flow of wherever the conversation takes you. That's not to say though that this is an easy process. I come to this house every Thursday. It costs me a substantial amount of cash but in the grand scheme of things, it isn't that much when I consider that it's my life that I am investing in. I suppose I better give *you* some proof on CBT, so *your* brain can be happy....

It's a form of psychotherapy that emphasises the important role of thinking in how we feel and what we do. When our brains are healthy, it's our thinking that causes us to feel and act the way we do. Therefore, if we are experiencing unwanted feelings and behaviours, it is important to identify the thinking that is causing these, and to learn how to replace this thinking with thoughts that lead to more desirable reactions. As soon as this was explained to me, my heart melted at its simplicity and potential.

It's based on the Cognitive Model of Emotional Response; on the scientific fact that our *thoughts* cause our feelings and behaviours, not external things, like people, situations, and events. The benefit of this fact is that we can change the way we think to feel better even if the situation does not change. The therapy is considered amongst the fastest in terms of results obtained. The average number of sessions clients receive is only sixteen. I felt the benefits after four. Other forms of therapy, like psychoanalysis, can take years. What enables the process to be briefer is its highly instructional nature and the fact that it makes use of homework assignments. Goal achievement could take a very long time if a person were only to think about the techniques and topics taught for one hour per week. That's why therapists assign reading assignments and encourage their clients to practice the techniques learned. Some people assume that the main reason people get better in therapy is because of the positive relationship between the therapist and client. Cognitive-behavioural therapists believe it is important to have a good, trusting relationship, but that is not enough. They believe that the clients change when they learn to think differently; therefore, therapists focus on teaching rational self-counselling skills. It is a collaborative effort between the therapist and the client; therapists seek to learn what their clients want out of life and then help their clients achieve those goals. The therapist's role is to listen, teach, and encourage, while the client's roles is to express concerns, learn, and implement that learning.

It's based on stoic philosophy; it does not tell people how they should feel. However, most people seeking therapy do not want to feel the way they do. It teaches the benefits of feeling, at worst, *calm* when confronted with undesirable situations. It also emphasises the fact that we have our undesirable situations whether we are upset about them or not. If we are upset about our problems, we have two problems -- the problem, and our upset about it. Most sane people want to have the fewest number of problems possible. Therapists want to gain a good understanding of the concerns of their clients. That's why they often ask questions. They also encourage their clients to ask questions of themselves, like, "How do I really know that those people are laughing at me?" "Could they be laughing about something else?" It is structured and directive; therapists have a specific agenda for each session. Specific techniques and concepts are taught during each session. It focuses on helping the client achieve the goals they have set. However, CBT therapists do not tell their clients *what* to do -- rather, they teach their clients *how* to do.

Most emotional and behavioural reactions are learned. Therefore, the goal is to help clients *unlearn* their unwanted reactions and to learn a new way of reacting. CBT has nothing to do with just talking; people can "just talk" with anyone. The educational emphasis has an additional benefit - it leads to long-term results. When people understand how and why they are doing well, they can continue doing what they are doing to make themselves well. A central aspect of *rational* thinking is that it is based on *fact,* not simply our assumptions made. Often, we upset ourselves about things when, in fact, the situation isn't like we think it is. If we knew that, we would not waste our time upsetting ourselves. We are encouraged to look at our thoughts as being hypotheses that can be questioned and tested. If we find that our hypotheses are incorrect (because we have new information), then we can change our thinking to be in line with how the situation really is.

The homework is different for everyone as you are learning about your own life and getting to know yourself better. We spend so much time trying to get to know other people, we sometimes lose touch with ourselves. I don't mean the inner child and all that bollocks. I mean just knowing who you are and what you want out of things. It comes with age, it doesn't come with intelligence. In fact those people with increased intelligence often have difficulty with moulding their self-awareness in the formative years. The therapy acts as a catalyst, and it's a tool that I can heartily recommend to one and all. In fact, I kinda think it should be taught at school. I've certainly learnt more doing this than I did in Geography or History lessons when I was younger. I *do* know all about tributaries and a little about isobars though so maybe I am barking up the wrong tree here.

Rely on your own resources.

Chemical imbalances are a hypothesis.

I didn't know when the sessions would end and was beginning to count my pennies toward the end. I'm not made of money. My homework began with what I deemed to be pointless exercises. The phone exercise was effective though. I mean look at me now, I answer the fucking phone. I didn't think that would ever happen. One thing I got bogged down on during the sessions was whether it was necessary to always push yourself. Surely some things that you don't want to do are because you have no interest in doing so, or because it's not something appropriate. I don't want to go travelling, so should I fight this and go, slowly becoming more accustomed to it? What a waste of a life that would be; constantly attempting to change the person you are. Surely becoming what you are is the most important thing any person can achieve. How do you know what you are meant to become? I don't think I have fully realised an answer for this yet. But I am still young. I am looking forward to getting old with a greater awareness and I predict a happy time ahead.

The first piece of practical homework that I did was to take some clothes back. We loosely came to this together and I formulated my plan after coming back from his study one Thursday. I hate taking clothes back to a store – I hate taking anything back to a store. I feel the need to develop a water tight reason for why I do not require the product and the more honest the reason actually is, the more of a fraud I feel and the more panic I exert. I had bought some clothes from a retailer a month before and didn't try them on at the shop. I had no clothes to return and I did not want to buy some simply to take them back as I felt that would be forcing the issue. I decided to go to my retailer of choice and try some clothes on that I wouldn't normally even look at. I felt that this would achieve two things. Firstly, it would ease me out of my comfort zone as I would be trying new things (some of them may even look good – I doubt it though), but most importantly, it would enable me to tell the lady in the store that I didn't want these goods, and not feel the need to give a long convoluted mumbled reason as to why they weren't suitable.

    I spent thirty minutes in the store, looking, trying on and discarding. It soon came to the point that I had to take the unwanted items to the girl at the checkout, and leave. I started to sweat a little as I feared her reaction to my new way of expressing my dislike for items. The two shirts were too long, and I yearn to tell her this, but I mustn't. I mustn't if I am to pass this crucial test.

And so with all my restraint I pass her the clothes and say, "No, I won't be taking any of these."

I don't apologise and I look her straight in the eye. It feels awkward and alien and I wait for her disapproval with malicious intent.

She smiles, takes the clothes and says "Okay, No problem, bye."

I leave the store without saying goodbye as I have forgotten that bit. I get to my car and feel great. Really rather good. I can barely wait until next Thursday when I will be able to tell someone about this who will be as equally impressed as I am. I don't even toy with the idea of telling anybody else, because at the moment, this is my thing and no one can fucking take that way from me. I'd die trying to stop them.

Other People Do Not Have The Upper Hand

(Rule One)

That's a rule. I have a rule. I can see an ethos being melded. I am excited. I curb my enthusiasm and get back to work. I find myself getting over excited sometimes. As the sessions progress and I tap into the skills that I wasn't aware I had, euphoria threatens to usurp the balance I am attempting to attain. I tell my therapist about the success of the homework and he is pleased. Before I see him, I put the rule to another test as I walk across the road to get to his house. Usually if I spy a zebra crossing, I will wait until the road is clear before I close in, or I will walk twenty seconds or so up the road and cross there. Because no one wants to be stopped at a zebra crossing. I don't mind stopping for other people, I mean it's their right, and as I am driving and see people hovering on the periphery of the lines, I slow down because they are telling me to stop. I must stop. Being a pedestrian though is unfortunate. There are people wanting to get to wherever it is that they are aiming for, and I am actively impeding their progress with an arrogant walk across the road. I think of all the ways in which I could approach this crossing and all of the possible outcomes and thoughts the person who has stopped will have to endure. It drives me crazy, or at least it used to. For today, with the knowledge that the fact is there; nobody has the upper hand - I briskly walk across the road, forcing cars to pull up and stop. I don't thank them, for this is what a zebra crossing is for. I remember how I feel myself, when somebody thanks me at a zebra crossing, and it's annoyance. They shouldn't be thanking me. If I let them cross the road somewhere where there wasn't a crossing, then fair enough, but there should be no thanking here. Just a slight raise of the head to make sure that this car is not going to kill you, and move on. Fucking move on. And so I do, and I have.

As my time with this guy becomes validated, I find myself conjuring two more rules. I will not talk about how I got to these rules, because they are private. However, they are as important, perhaps more significant even than the first.

Make the Best Out Of Your Current Situation
(Rule Two)

Do the Very Next Thing To Get To Where You Want To Be
(The Final Rule)

I think that maybe these two are interchangeable. They are certainly connected. People talk of pipe dreams and flashes of inspiration. People like to have grand ideas yet never follow through and it is often not through laziness. The sheer weight of work that needs to be done to get from the point in which they find themselves in, to the point that they aspire to - crashes down, crushing any plans that are evolving. If you want to be something, get on the road. It's a horrible saying (it isn't really); every journey begins with a first step, but I reluctantly accept that it is true. If I can do something now that gets me a little bit nearer to what I want, but the end result isn't perfect, or anywhere near how I'd imagined, I will still go ahead and do it and it is still progression. I think out of all the sayings, onwards and upwards in my favourite. It's Paul Weller's favourite too. Well, it was an answer he gave years ago in a magazine article. I'd like to think it was his favourite, but it probably isn't.

So where am I now? Who have I been talking to and what has become of my friends and family? Is this a memory, and who are you? Well it doesn't really matter anymore. I'm good, I still behave in ways that continue to astound and disgust me, and my shutters are down most of the time, but it's okay.

"Are you ready then?"

"Yep, I think so." I reply.

I look into the eyes of the person standing next to me and feel warm and content. I hadn't imagined that this is the person I would be doing this with, or that I would be doing this at all.

We walk up the stairwell and pass a young family on the way. I look at the young girl who is carrying no baggage and is clutching the coat of her father. She sees me looking and stares at me confused and with naive charm. I give her a nod.

Thank You.

Clare Young
David Noel
Gregory Robert McKay
Daniel Ripley
Tracy Thompson
Tom Daish
Alex Herodotou
James Guthrie
Dan Graham
Katie Baker
Tony Harwood
Mike Curtis
Christine Hendy
Alison Sperry
Louise Guthrie
Barry Hendy
Jon Prout
Chris Hero
Peter Matthews
Robbie McWilliams
Marianne Jones
Chris Evans
Ann Hendy
Rick Evans
Tupon Bhowmik
John Always